MIDSUMMER MOON

No one could ignore the electricity that crackled between them. Matt caught her hand. "June."

The raspy voice tore at June's senses as the feel of his rugged hand in hers sent her equilibrium into a tailspin. If a train were bearing down on them, she could not have moved fast enough to escape certain death, just as she couldn't escape his lips merely an inch away from hers. "Matt," she murmured.

Spurred by his long-denied desire, Matt clasped her tightly against his body and kissed her lips hungrily. Encouraged by her response and his need to touch her again, he slid his fingers down her bare arm and winced from the exquisite warmth filling his belly.

Flustered and confused, June stepped back.

"Was this a mistake?" he asked.

"Mistake?" June whispered. "How could something like this be a mistake?"

"Then you felt it too?" he said in a tight voice.

"I've got warm blood, Matt."

He smiled. "You wouldn't kid a brother, would you?"

BOOK YOUR PLACE ON OUR WEBSITE AND MAKE THE ARABESQUE ROMANCE CONNECTION!

We've created a customized website just for our very special Arabesque readers, where you can get the inside scoop on everything that's going on with Arabesque romance novels.

When you come online, you'll have the exciting opportunity to:

- View covers of upcoming books

- Learn about our future publishing schedule (listed by publication month and author)

- Find out when your favorite authors will be visiting a city near you

- Search for and order backlist books

- Check out author bios and background information

- Send e-mail to your favorite authors

- Join us in weekly chats with authors, readers and other guests

- Get writing guidelines

- AND MUCH MORE!

Visit our website at
http://www.arabesquebooks.com

MIDSUMMER MOON

Doris Johnson

ARABESQUE

BET BOOKS

BET Publications, LLC
http://www.bet.com

ARABESQUE BOOKS are published by

BET Publications, LLC
c/o BET BOOKS
One BET Plaza
1900 W Place NE
Washington, DC 20018-1211

All Kensington Titles, Imprints, and Distributed Lines are available at special quantity discounts for bulk purchases for sales promotions, premiums, fund-raising, and educational or institutional use. Special book excerpts or customized printings can also be created to fit specific needs. For details, write or phone the office of the Kensington special sales manager: Kensington Publishing Corp., 850 Third Avenue, New York, NY 10022, attn: Special Sales Department, Phone: 1-800-221-2647.

BET Books is a trademark of Black Entertainment Television, Inc. ARABESQUE, the ARABESQUE logo, and the BET BOOKS logo are trademarks and registered trademarks.

First Printing: November 2001
10 9 8 7 6 5 4 3 2 1

Printed in the United States of America

To our beautiful granddaughter,
Paige Kiara Johnson

ACKNOWLEDGMENTS

Rebecca James, Lorraine James, Jennette James, Stanley Brooks, Joyce Brooks, the James family, and friends—thanks to you all for that special day I spent with you in beautiful Oyster Bay. The interesting childhood stories and the tour with Lorraine all over town to the hundred-year-old house on Tooker Avenue and the hundred-year-old Hood church helped my characters come alive. I hope June and Matt turned out to be like two people you know living right next door. Stan, the map was great. Thanks again and hope to see you all next year.

Prologue

The tinkle of crystal against crystal was heard above the soft laughter of the two women as they touched glasses and then tasted the champagne.

June Saxon smiled and stared happily into the pretty, heart-shaped face of her friend, Carlotta Graham. Almost instantly, the smile faded and a wary look settled in her round, dark brown eyes.

Carlotta saw the sudden change in moods and laughed.

"What now, Ms. Worrywart? Too late to have second thoughts, honey." She lifted her glass and sipped. "Especially not after treating ourselves to this fine wine." She winked. "It's time for celebration, not worriation." Her melodic laugh sounded softly at their corner table in Akwaaba, a popular Brooklyn restaurant. The dinner hour was just beginning and the place was fast filling up even on a cold Tuesday night in January.

June sighed and sipped. "You're right about that," she said and then shrugged, the smile returning to her eyes.

"You know me, girl, can't help myself." She tapped the manila envelope that rested on the table between them. "It's hard to believe that we've finally done it. Entrepreneurs!" Liking the sound of the word, she repeated it and her friend joined her in a companionable laugh. They ate in silence for a moment, each reflecting upon their new venture. Quietly, June spoke.

"I know it's after the fact since you've already started your leave of absence, but I have to ask again. Are you sure you're all right with this? Three months is a long time to be away from a job, especially with what's going on with these airlines."

Carlotta sat back eying her friend. She raised one perfectly arched eyebrow and lifted a shoulder. "What's to do about it? One day you're a flight attendant and the next you show up, ready to fly, and you find that the doors are locked and you're waiting outside the terminal with all the angry passengers. Like everything else, honey, we just have to deal with it." She nodded at the envelope, filled with bank papers and contracts from the building contractor, which they'd received hours before. "Isn't that our insurance against our being left with nothing? We own our own business now!"

"At least the bank does, for a few years anyway," June, added, beginning to brighten up.

"That's more like it," Carlotta said, pouring more wine. "We're going to be fine, and to answer your question *again*," she emphasized with an exaggerated sigh, "yes, I'm okay about being the one to watch the business from the giddyap. I have more seniority with my airline than you do with yours and besides I'm not as soft a touch as you are. You'll probably have us in the red for months with your *expert* business sense." She clucked her tongue. "Girl, how in the world did you ever pass high school math?"

"Very humbly and delicately, and lots of repeats," June answered.

"I hear that," Carlotta said, fluffing her auburn curls as she looked about.

"What?" June said, noticing the sudden dreamy look.

"Mm, nothing. Just wondering. Did you notice the contractor? Kinda cute, huh?"

June groaned. "Girl, stop. Don't go there. He'll only be in our lives for a minute. It'll take him just that long to build our Laundromat for us. Then he's off to wherever and what will you have gotten out of it? A few dates and a thank you, ma'am, I'm going home to the wife and kids."

"Maybe, maybe not," Carlotta answered. "One has to look at opportunity from all angles, honey. Grass is growing under my feet like I stepped in a pile of Miracle Grow, and at thirty-four I'd better watch my step or that marriage ship will pass me by. I think it's already left the dock."

"What makes you think he's your type? He gets dirt under his fingernails."

"Uh-uh, not with *that* manicure. *He* gives the fetch and carry orders."

"You would have noticed," June said dryly.

"Can't afford not to, honey; otherwise—"

"I know, you might miss that ship," June cut in. She wrinkled her nose. Carlotta was always on the lookout for a man who even remotely smelled of money, and always sized him up as her potential rescuer. She dreaded never living a luxurious life and feared that she would spend her years eagerly awaiting a pension check. It was with that thought in mind that she changed from a domestic to an international airline, early in her career, in hopes for better opportunities. But, she'd never met King Midas.

June signaled for the check. It was her treat, she'd told Carlotta, and probably the last of her splurges for a long while. As the two women parted, June promised to call when

she returned from her flight run. She jokingly reminded
Carlotta to take care of their business and smiled as Carlotta
gave her the thumbs-up sign as they scurried to their cars.

On the long drive from Brooklyn's Bedford Stuyvesant
section to her home in Oyster Bay, Long Island, June's brow
furrowed, but only for a moment. Now was not the time to
doubt her decision. Both women knew that had it not been
for June putting up the bulk of the money for their business,
there would be no such enterprise. That's why it had to
work, June thought. Otherwise, she would be on the way to
the poorhouse.

June was perplexed. She hadn't heard from Carlotta in
three weeks. It was the end of April and the grand opening
for the business was only a week away. June had taken care
of the invitations and the catering in preparation for the open
house party. She was disturbed and annoyed that Carlotta
hadn't kept in touch. It wasn't like her. For the last two
months she had received updated reports like clockwork.
Something must have been wrong, she thought. On the verge
of driving to Brooklyn where her friend lived in Kensington,
she was stopped by the phone bell as she was about to get
a jacket. It was her childhood friend, Beverly Lancaster.

"You put the wrong address on those invitations, my
friend," Beverly said, in a teasing tone.

"What are you talking about?" June's mouth went dry.

"I mean, all I see when I go to 2222 Remsen Street is a
rusting steel hulk that's a blight to my neighborhood, girl.
And here I was, looking forward to sudsing my duds in your
brand-new exclusive establishment."

"That *is* the right address, Beverly." June's head started
to throb.

The silence was too loud as both women pondered their
words, refusing to voice their thoughts.

"I'm coming to Brooklyn," June said in a voice that was not her own.

"I'll meet you there."

Almost two hours later, June stood in front of 2222 Remsen Street, the site of her new business. With tears in her eyes, she backed away until she felt the fender of a car on her backside and she gratefully sagged against the cold, hard metal.

Beverly looked in horror, then disbelief, from the steel frame to her friend. "What's going on?" she finally managed.

"I've been robbed." The words burned June's throat as they escaped in a hoarse whisper.

Chapter One

One year later

June Saxon heard her friend and neighbor Caleb Lancaster before she saw him. For years, the familiar whistle had sounded between the two large Victorian-style houses on Long Island, which had been home since they were youngsters. She didn't move from the comfortable lounge chair but lazily turned her head as Caleb rounded the corner of the wood deck from the back of the house.

"Hey."

"Hey yourself, Junie Bug." The stocky man with the deep tan skin and rugged complexion cocked his head and looked down at his friend with a quizzical eye. He squatted beside her and stared unblinkingly into her eyes. After his intense examination, he made noises sounding very much like the mysterious doctor who doesn't want to admit to the patient that something is seriously wrong. "Uh-huh," he grunted and sat down with his bare legs stretched out and his back against the white wood railing.

June frowned. "Uh-huh what?" she said, annoyed at being disturbed. It was Friday, just past noon, and the sun was as hot as if they were already in the muggy dog days of August.

"We were right," Caleb said, still squinting at her out of one eye.

"By 'we' I take it you mean you and your sister Beverly," June said disinterestedly.

"Something's working up there, after all," Caleb said, tapping his forehead. "Told Bev, that." He grinned broadly and when he did a hole appeared in the right side of his cheek so big that one could lose the tip of a finger inside of it.

June turned away and closed her eyes. "Go home, Caleb. I want to finish my nap." But her curiosity was piqued. She murmured, "Right about what?"

Caleb, the grin gone, got up and lay down beside her in a matching lounge. His tone was no longer teasing. "That you're still moping after a year and it's long past time to put an end to it." He swatted at a fly that crawled from his khaki shorts to his bare thigh.

One year? June moaned inwardly. *Has so much time gone by already? What have I done in all these months?* she wondered. It was just yesterday, wasn't it, that she had stood in front of that steel frame in Brooklyn, staring in disbelief at her stolen dream?

Caleb watched the anguished shadow cross his friend's face. In the last year, instead of seeing her normally pleasant face, he and everyone else were met with constant frowns and wrinkles, and her genial smiles were rare. Her jet-black hair, worn in a curly cap, was mixed with a smattering of premature gray. That family trait only enhanced her attractive features. But he could swear that it was grayer now than it had been a month ago.

"So," Caleb said, casually, "we have a plan."

June's eyes flew open and she turned to stare warily at him. "What, this time?" She remembered a few occasions that were best left unmentioned. "I refuse to go anywhere with either of you," she said firmly.

Caleb smiled smugly. "This time instead of taking you out into the world, we're bringing it to you."

"What?" June adjusted the chair until she was sitting upright.

"Yeah, we decided something had to be done, especially with the big three-oh just a few weeks away. We didn't want you to go catatonic on us when the great day came, so we're throwing you a party." Caleb looked pleased with himself as he stared at her with twinkling eyes.

"Three-oh!" June sputtered. "I won't be thirty until next year!" she exclaimed.

Caleb laughed. "Thought that would get a rise. You're alive after all."

"You know very well that Beverly and I are twenty-eight!"

"So you are," Caleb answered as if just enlightened.

June continued to look at him with wary eyes.

"Don't give me that look, it's happening already. Bev mailed the invitations last night."

This time June did groan aloud. "Oh, Caleb, y'all know I'm not in the mood for that nonsense. My birthday can pass just as quietly as all the rest."

"Not this year, Junie Bug," Caleb answered. His mood and his voice had grown somber. He sat up and watched her. "It's time to stop beating up on yourself and hating the rest of the world because of a scheming witch."

June's eyes darkened. "You have my permission to use the 'B' word this once."

"You call it," Caleb said easily. "But you let that woman break your spirit and chase all the spunk out of you. We want you back."

"Been that bad, huh?"

"You got it." Caleb gestured toward the interior of the house. "Have you gotten rid of that letter she sent you? Reading that thing over and over sure didn't do much for your psyche. I should have taken it and burned it myself."

June sat back and stared at the white heat waves that rippled across the grass. "No," she finally answered. "I keep it to remind myself of the fool I was. Won't happen again," she muttered. "Not in this lifetime."

"And she never sent any more money?" Caleb already knew the answer but he hoped by talking about it June would let out some more of her anger.

"Just that five thousand dollars in traveler's checks," June responded. "No more letters, no more checks."

Caleb shook his head. "Do you think she's still living in Paris?"

"For her sake, I hope she is."

At that, Caleb smiled.

"What's so funny?"

"Sounds like you wanna get down with that fine Ms. Carlotta Graham." His grin widened. "The last time I saw you rolling around in the grass was with Beverly when you guys were eleven years old. What was that catfight about anyway?" he asked.

June grinned at the memory. "A boy, of course. What else? Wilton Maitland, to be specific."

"Hmm, well, I hope both you young ladies will be real cool with your bad selves in a few weeks," Caleb said.

"What's that supposed to mean?"

"Mr. Wilton Maitland was mailed an invite to your party. Sure he can't wait to see you ladies."

"You can't be serious," June exclaimed. "You mean

you and Beverly dredged up our old high school crowd? I haven't seen Wilton or the rest of those people since we graduated!''

"Well, it's about time, don't you think?" Caleb stood up. "Maybe somebody in that group will have better luck than me and Bev in knocking some sense back into you."

"Wilton Maitland," June said and then chuckled. "I always did hate that name. Who in the world saddles a little baby with the name of Wilton?"

Caleb was amused and tickled that he had succeeded in making her laugh. A very rare sound these days. "I'd better get going. Gotta finish up a few things before calling it quits for the weekend."

June stood up and walked him around the side of the house. Caleb was a financial adviser and worked a lot from his home. A few times a week he took the Long Island Railroad into Manhattan to the firm that employed him. He was a hard worker and she was glad that he wasn't spending another beautiful summer weekend working. She gave him a sideways glance, curious to know if he was still having heart pangs.

Caleb, without looking at June, said, "No need to check me out. I'm okay and no, I haven't gotten used to being jilted but I'll survive." He was standing on the grass, one foot on the bottom step, as he looked up at her. "I'm not the first and I won't be the last guy who thought he found Ms. Right, only for her to say it isn't so." He shrugged. "Better for all concerned to have caught the mistake before kids came into the picture." A faraway look came into his eyes, but it soon disappeared. "Hey, I came over here to invite you to your party, not rehash my sad story." He pushed himself off the step and winked. "Now you can call Bev and chew her out. See you later." He walked across the wide expanse of grass that separated the two houses, and entered the house through the back door.

June watched him disappear and then went inside. Caleb's visit had stirred pleasant memories and she was beginning to like the idea that he and Beverly had cooked up. Seeing old friends might be just the boost she needed to jolt herself into doing something. Anything!

She was sitting at the kitchen table drinking a cold Pepsi and staring at the calendar. Four months! June couldn't believe that she had been home for four months now. But the calendar didn't lie. It was in February that she'd been injured.

"Where'd the time go?" she said aloud. Restless, she stretched her limbs and flexed the muscles in her shoulders and back. Only once in a while did she feel the slightest twinge in her neck and back. She hadn't had a dizzy spell in over a month. At least that was the last time that she'd remembered, clutching at the bathroom sink while she was brushing her teeth. But she felt fine now and the reason for her disability was getting to be a hazy memory.

While she was working a flight from JFK airport to Reno, Nevada, the pilot was doing his best to avoid the terrifying pockets of turbulence. June was in her jump seat more than not. She'd called a young boy and his parents everything but children of God when she spotted him playing in the aisle as the plane dipped and dived. Running down the aisle to slap him into his seat, she was on the way back to fasten herself in when the plane dived.

Unprepared, June was propelled into the air, her head hitting the ceiling with a sickening thud. All she remembered was her scream, biting her tongue, and the thought that she'd broken her neck. She stayed in a Reno hospital for two days before flying back home. The back and neck pain and the dizziness prevented her from returning to work. After three months of physical therapy and several visits to her doctor who only a month ago had approved her for light duty, the airline's medical personnel refused to give the okay.

June's thoughts turned sour again as a new wave of self-pity washed over her. Her troubles hadn't started four months ago with the accident but over a year ago when she had been duped by Carlotta Graham. Bitter memories still plagued her.

She never knew how she'd driven back to Long Island that night after she'd left Beverly. The thought that she had lost her inheritance numbed her brain. Forty-eight thousand dollars! Gone. Stolen by her former friend and business partner-to-be.

Hindsight is a sobering clarifier, Caleb had told her, but that did nothing to soothe her wounds. And nothing to hide the fact that she'd been so fired up to become an entrepreneur that she'd gambled away her inheritance. The big joke was that she hadn't even seen it coming. But how could she have? She had known Carlotta for eight years. For six of them, they were considered friends; people who could trust in each other.

It wasn't long into their friendship that they learned they had a common goal, to become independent and own a business. Neither had the slightest inkling what that would be but they opened a joint bank account and funneled money into it like crazy. For six years, give or take an emergency or two, they saved. When the time came, they decided on buying a franchise.

June laughed at the memory. She recalled the disdain on Carlotta's face when June remained adamant about settling on the Laundromat franchise. It was not the glamorous business that Carlotta desired, but it was the most stable and lucrative, and was the best chance of getting money from a bank. The new concept took the drudgery out of washing dirty clothes. Even Carlotta looked impressed while watching the video at the franchise seminar. Laundromats were now brightly lit, half-block-long showplaces with at least forty washers and as many dryers. Services were provided and there was a room for children and strollers. But when they had come up short even with the bank loan, June decided to use the money her grandparents had left her. It was a gamble but she trusted that the two of them, with diligent effort, could make it work. Even though June would keep her job and Carlotta's three months' leave would end, they were confident in their ability to make the business a success.

Confident? June thought. The ringing of the telephone prevented her from sinking deeper into the doldrums.

"Hey, girl. So you know, huh? Gotcha." Beverly laughed.

"Yeah, y'all did," June answered.

Beverly frowned. "Hey, I thought you'd be sounding happier than that. Unless Caleb just lied to me."

"No, he didn't. I think the idea is great. Looking forward to it."

"Then what's making me think you're thinking otherwise?"

June hesitated. "No, I'm fine with the party, it's just that you caught me coming out of a 'CG' moment."

"Umm, thought that's what it was," replied Beverly. "You know, I'm like Caleb. I should have burned that letter for you myself. If I wasn't living here in Brooklyn instead of across the way it would've been done!" She paused. "Don't tell me it's still plastered on your refrigerator door." Silence gave her the answer. "Listen, when I come out there next weekend, don't be surprised to find that space empty after I've gone. Catch you later, hon, duty calls." Before she hung up, Beverly asked, "What you got going on for the weekend?"

"Nothing much. Just planned to finish up painting the spare room. I was taking a break when Caleb came over."

Beverly held her tongue. Another lecture was not what her friend needed just now and she understood very well the cash flow situation at the Saxon home.

"Okay, don't overdo it. Give yourself a two-day break. I'll talk to you later."

June stared at the piece of paper on the door of the fridge. The grease-splattered thin sheet was held in place by magnets and the edges were beginning to curl. She didn't have to read the words to know what was in the letter. She could read it verbatim if she had to. Sliding it from beneath the magnets and smoothing the edges, June sat down at the kitchen table and stared at the hasty scrawl. The letter was dated three months after Carlotta left without a word.

Dear June,

By now, you've probably heard through our extremely reliable pipeline that I'm married and living in Paris, France. Even so, I doubt that your sources know who my husband is or his name. For the obvious reasons I elect anonymity for both of us because I'm sure you've guessed that I married a wealthy man. He proposed and I accepted without giving the rest of the world another thought. At last, the opportunity to live my dream was being handed to me! How could I walk away from that to run a laundry? Don't deny that you would have done the same thing! A woman would have to have ice water in her veins to pass up being wooed and loved by such a hot-blooded sexy hunk of black male pulchritude! Anyway, honey, this bit of money is simply the first installment. I promise you will have it all very soon. I know that you are finding it hard to forgive me but one day, you'll understand. Putting yourself in my place, you wouldn't have gone to your man with yards of bills for him to pay and a few rags on your back.

Looking in disgust at the last words, *Warm embraces, Carlotta*, she stood and returned the page to its place on the door and left the room. Mimicking her former friend's voice, June said, "*I promise you will have it all very soon.*"

Surveying her amateur painting with a critical eye, June was happy to be nearly finished. The walls and most of the trim were done, leaving one window frame and the baseboards to complete. Dipping the small bristles in the can of celery-green paint, she smoothed the pretty pastel color on the window frame. The quick, even strokes soothed June as she worked. Pushing all bitter thoughts from her mind, she concentrated on how much she'd appreciate her worthwhile efforts. Although visitors were rare, the room would be used for guests as well as a getaway place for herself. Since her accident and loss of steady income except for her disability insurance payments, money was scarce. She had closed off the upstairs rooms to conserve on utilities and had turned the large first-floor family room into her bedroom.

For years, after her grandfather's death, June and her grandmother had used this smaller room for storage. Even after Belle Saxon's death, June had continued to use the room to toss things in that were waiting for a permanent place in the big house. But a year ago, when June had been left with almost nothing, she had had to find a way to cut costs. The repairs that were needed in the house were many; appliances were old and needed replacing, and the outside paint was badly weathered. She had refused a loan from Caleb and Beverly. She was a firm believer that large sums of loaned money between friends were akin to a death knell for the friendship. Her own folly only confirmed her belief. So she'd struggled on her own, making the repairs that she was capable of and buying only necessities.

When the five thousand dollars had arrived, June was torn between seeking an attorney who could help her get her money back, or buying needed appliances. In the end she opted to replace the refrigerator, buy a new water heater, and install a couple of new air conditioners. She'd decided that a lawyer would tell her the same thing that the bank officer had told her. There was no act of theft or fraud. Their joint bank account had given Carlotta every right to withdraw funds without the need for another signature.

June finished applying the ivory paint to the baseboards and stood back admiring her handiwork. The pastel room with furnishings in pale yellows, greens, and shades of white would be a welcome refuge.

After June had finished cleaning up, showering, and eating a light supper, her sour mood of a few hours ago was replaced with a feeling of satisfaction and accomplishment as she watched the onset of evening from the comfort of the porch. She often sat here. Only a residential street separated the homes from the beach so there was little traffic. The sound of the wind over rippling waves was soothing and often lulled June into a peaceful rest.

The house had belonged to her paternal grandparents, William and Belle Saxon, and when Belle died the property had been left to June. Her father, Jonathan Saxon, was raised here. His best friend was Tanner Lancaster, Caleb's and Beverly's father. The two men were best friends and when they married the group became an inseparable foursome. When June and Beverly were eight years old and Caleb was fourteen, their parents were killed in a plane crash while starting a Caribbean vacation. June had come to live with her grandparents and had been there ever since. Their paternal grandparents who were now dead had raised Beverly and Caleb. Like their parents before them, the Saxons and the Lancasters remained close, steadfast friends.

June wriggled comfortably in the lounge. She realized that she hadn't felt so peaceful in months. Nor had she felt so healthy. It occurred to her that she could be back on her job, instead of malingering here in this big house all alone.

"What does that doctor know?" she muttered. "Bet he can't show me one person who doesn't complain of an occasional ache." After a second of brooding, a decisive look settled on her face. Monday she was going to make some calls and if she had anything to say about it she would be back to work before another week passed.

The cotton cardigan was not enough to ward off the cool and damp air, and June stood. "Time to call it a night," she said. As she bent over to gather her snack plates she felt a sharp pain in her head.

"Ow," June cried. Before she straightened the pain was gone. She stood for a second, waiting, holding her breath. When nothing happened, she shrugged. "What was that?" she said and picked up her dishes and walked around to the back of the house to lock up.

June was reaching for the doorknob when suddenly a dizzying wave swept over her and the pain in her head returned with double the force. She swayed. In her effort to keep from falling she dropped the dishes and they fell to the deck in a clatter.

"Oh my God!" June slumped to the floor.

Caleb was in his kitchen, rinsing dishes, and using one shoulder to prop up the phone while he talked. He could see June on the deck, preparing to lock up, as was her ritual. The instant he saw her wobble, he ended his call and was out the back door. Before he could reach her she had fallen. Her cry stung his ears.

"June? God, Junie, what the hell happened?" Caleb turned ashen. She was as still as death.

The volunteer ambulance arrived in less than ten minutes. No sooner had Caleb climbed in after the stretcher than it sped off.

Neither June before she'd fallen nor Caleb when he'd run to her had seen the man on the beach. In the quiet of the night he had heard her first cry. He'd watched as she walked around the deck. When he heard the second cry and watched her fall, he'd started across the road but stopped when he saw a man racing across the grass to get to her. He watched.

After the night was silent once again, the man whistled and turned on his heel. As he walked away, a small dog appeared and scampered around his legs. He stopped and turned once more to stare at the deserted house. Minutes passed. As if a decision had been made, he nodded his head and once again walked along the deserted beach, lost in thought.

Chapter Two

The two weeks that had passed since June's release from the hospital seemed to have flown by like the stiff breeze that now slapped her face. Usually a Sunday afternoon would find the beach crowded with walkers and bathers, but today with the absence of the sun, few people braved the unseasonably chilly winds. The sounds and the good smells drew June from the porch and inside the house. Her nose propelled her to the kitchen.

"Mm, smells good," June said to her friend Beverly as she lifted pot covers. Golden brown muffins sat cooling on the counter and June took one and bit into it. "Mmm, cinnamon and raisin. What else you got in the oven?" she asked, smearing butter on the muffin.

Beverly Lancaster opened the oven door, removed a roasting pan, and spooned drippings over the stuffed, honey-colored bird. "Chicken, of course. Ain't today Sunday?" She raised a slim brow. "You ready to eat now? Hope that's not spoiling your appetite. Especially after I've done all this.''

"No fear of that. I'm more than ready," June said as she got a plate and filled it with some of everything Beverly cooked. "Don't know why I'm so starved."

"No joke? I'd be willing to bet that's how people usually feel when they don't eat." Beverly followed suit and when her plate was filled she sat across from June and waited as her friend blessed the food and the hands that made it.

"Amen," said Beverly. "You're more than welcome. Just glad I could come out this weekend to do it." She watched her friend carefully. Satisfied that her golden scalloped potatoes and tender spinach had helped bring back June's appetite, she relaxed and began to enjoy her food.

June was aware of the close scrutiny but she didn't mind. The last two weeks brother and sister had been there for her when she needed them. The first week she'd been home, Beverly had stayed with her, commuting by railroad to her Manhattan job where she worked as an administrative assistant in a law firm. This past week, Caleb had been over every night cooking and trying to get some food into her. He must have sent an SOS to his sister because she arrived on Friday night.

A lump tightened in June's throat. "Don't know what I would do without you guys."

"Told you, no thanks necessary. You'd do the same for us." Beverly noticed the nearly empty plate and grinned.

June smiled at Beverly. Like her brother she had a dimple in her cheek, but it wasn't nearly as deep as his. Her skin was close in color to his, but the sun had darkened it to a pecan brown, nearly the same color as June's smooth complexion. Her eyes were big and dark and her brown hair was worn long and straight with a part in the middle. Her big bright smile made her look twenty instead of the twenty-eight that she was.

The two women pushed away from the table and they shared a laugh as they did so. Many times they found themselves doing the identical thing simultaneously. Over the years they had gotten used to exchanging Christmas gifts only to find that they had duplicated their gifts to each other.

Beverly cleared her throat but was stopped by June's voice.

"I know what you're going to ask. No, I haven't had any more pain or blackouts," June said. She did not sound bitter, only accepting of her condition, whatever that was. Until further test results came back, no one knew exactly what was wrong with her. The last visit to the neurologist garnered nothing but his speculation that her flying days might be over. It was unlikely that any medical doctor would give her an A-OK to work up in the sky.

"So is it okay for you to be driving yourself around? You have an appointment with the doctor on Tuesday, don't you?"

"Yes." That worried June. What if she was grounded from that too? How would she get around to do things for herself? She'd always been independent. And what if she blacked out behind the wheel? The thought brought a shiver. She raised fearful eyes to Beverly.

"Why don't you let Caleb take you? He won't mind. Then see what the doctor says about it."

"I can't keep asking him to chauffer me about."

Beverly didn't answer, just gave her a look.

June sighed. "I guess this time will be okay. Maybe I'll be cleared to do that at least."

"Good. Those test results will probably be good news and you can get back down to business."

"What business?"

"Not flying but some other job with the airline. I'm sure you can transfer to another position."

June shook her head. "No, there's nothing else I want to do there. Ground positions aren't for me."

"Then what about going back to teaching? Surely you can still do that?"

"I left the classroom years ago to satisfy my craving for travel and adventure. Picture all the adventure I'll have with five-year-olds as rusty as I am! I wouldn't last a week."

"Um, they can be adventurous," answered Beverly. She could see that the conversation was getting to June so she changed it. "I sure like what you did with the place. Your guest room is fabulous. Makes me miss being out here with you guys."

"Yeah, it is cozy, isn't it?" June said proudly. "That was the last project I worked on before . . ."

"Sorry I reminded you," said Beverly. She got up and began to clear the table. "Come on. Let's clean up so we can watch a tape before I hit the road. I like leaving later rather than earlier, hopefully to beat the traffic."

"Sure, that'll be great," answered June. "I'll fix the banana splits just the way you like them. Gooey."

"Okay, but hold the whipped cream, the wet walnuts, and the chocolate syrup," Beverly said.

June laughed. "That's nothing but a banana with ice cream thrown on top."

"Better for my waistline at this point," Beverly said with a wink.

June rolled her eyes and shook her head. She'd never understand why the perfect-figured woman worried about gaining weight.

The movie was over and June reached for the remote to rewind the tape. An envelope fell to the floor and she picked it up and tossed it back on the table. It was unopened.

Beverly had noticed the letter when she arrived on Friday. "Something you don't want to know about?" she said easily.

June waved a hand. "It's from an attorney I never heard of. Probably just another collection agency."

"Attorney?" Beverly clapped her hand to her head. "Oh, goodness. You had a call from a lawyer while you were sleeping, but I didn't want to wake you."

"On a Sunday afternoon?" June said. "Getting pretty desperate, aren't they?"

Beverly picked up the envelope. "This is the guy who called. Paul Denton."

"Never heard of him."

"He said he'd called because he hadn't heard from you since he'd mailed you a letter. He was wondering if he had the right address." Beverly handed the envelope to June. "This might be important. Open it while I'm still here."

"Just in case, huh?" June said with a smile.

"Something like that." But Beverly wasn't smiling.

"Oh, all right," June said, pulling the flap open. "Let's see who wants money that I don't have."

Beverly watched her friend anxiously, praying that it wasn't more bad news. When June dropped the letter back on the table with a shrug, Beverly said, "What?"

"Beats me," answered June. "There's some urgent matter he needs to discuss with me in person. I should call and set up an appointment."

Beverly read the letter. "It is strange," she said. "What are you going to do?"

"Nothing. Whatever it is will go away sooner or later."

"Ignoring it?" Beverly asked.

"Like the others," June replied. "When I'm in a position to do something about overdue bills, I will. Right now, I'm doing the best that I can."

Beverly didn't miss the frightened tone or the worried look in her eyes. They were still sitting on the sofa, and Beverly reached over and squeezed June's hand. "Look, things will get better, as soon as you begin working again.

On Tuesday, I'm sure the doctor is going to give you the okay to get back to work.''

"Yeah, doing what? I don't have a job to get back to!'' The words, said aloud, scared June. Strange how not until now did she feel frightened. She'd always thought that one day she would be going back to the work she'd made her career. Now? Her future was one big question mark. She turned to Beverly.

"What am I going to say at the party next weekend?'' June's voice was full of disdain.

"How'd we get from your job to your party?'' Beverly was perplexed.

"We'll be seeing people we haven't talked to in years,'' June said. "You know as well as I do that the question we'll hear over and over will be 'So what are you into?' ''

"And?''

"So what am I going to say? That I'm in between jobs right now and there's absolutely nothing waiting on the horizon? 'If you hear of anything, let me know' ?'' June frowned. "Be a little realistic with me, old friend.''

Beverly stood up. "I'm not even going to entertain that thought with you, old friend. You don't even have the final word on your health and you're calling it quits. When you have something concrete from your medical man, let me know and then we'll discuss your future. Until then, we ain't talking nothing but party, party.'' Beverly walked to the front door and picked up her overnight satchel and slung it over her shoulder. "And don't think because it's your day, you're going to play Queen on me and Caleb. You're being assigned the potato salad duty.''

June grinned. "As if I didn't guess. Okay, you got it.'' She threw her friend a knowing look. "And cleanup duty as well?'' They both knew that Caleb wasn't a neat freak.

"I hear you,'' Beverly said with a chuckle. "But my brother surprised me. The place is picked up and together.

He had a service go over the place a week ago and he'll do the same in a few days. So we're getting a break in that department, thank God.''

"Amen," answered June.

After the bright red Mazda pulled off, June stayed on the porch for a while listening to the beat of the waves against the beach and the slow ebbing as they slid back into the bay. It was dark and past nine and not surprisingly, the beach was deserted. She was about to leave the porch when she was startled by a figure on the beach. In the distance it was just a dark shadow, but it was definitely that of a man.

June frowned. She was certain that in the
she'd caught a glimpse of a lone figure
Once she'd thought he was looking
turned and walked away wi
heels. Strange, she tho
cooling walk on a bea
house and entered t
She locked up a

Early the nex
sleep. Surpris
thoughts befo
on the dis

"M
fort

scrambled eggs and then sat across from her. He filled his plate and began to eat heartily.

June had an appetite and ate hungrily. She drank the deliciously brewed coffee, enjoying every drop. "What got into you so early in the morning?" She smiled. "Whatever it was, I'm grateful," she added.

"Beverly called me last night after she got home," Caleb said, eyeing June thoughtfully.

June took another sip before speaking. "And?"

"She ran the job thing by me and the possibility of you not going back to the airline." Caleb saw the defensive look ___ eyes. "Listen to what I have to say before you ___ ling in your business. All right?"

___ atched him with a wary eye.

___ thought of even before last ___ 'But I didn't think you'd ___ June's eyes flickered.

___ ear the excitement ___ came into his

___ who's in town ___ flew home. ___ ked you

___ hat
___ "

"My friend, well, let's just say that he has a unique personality."

June cocked her head. "I like this already."

"For months, he's been looking for someone, preferably a woman, whose personality is compatible with his. In the last year he's gone through four business associates because of irreconcilable differences." Caleb saw that he had June's full attention. He hurried on. "The man is a confirmed bachelor, is a wealthy banker, and also has several businesses that need constant monitoring. He needs an honest, intelligent, competent office manager who has the ability to weed out inefficient and dishonest help."

"Hmm, sounds like someone I know very well," quipped June.

Caleb smiled. "Hold on, I'm not finished." both their coffee cups. "He pre ful, and a pleasant conversati of French and Spanish expected to travel and

June fidgeted a There was more.

"For one mo where he has as well as have a depe
"

Sounds like an adventure to me,'' he said with a teasing grin.

"Paris?" June's jaw gaped. Flabbergasted, she said, "Did he by any chance say what he's paying?" When Caleb mentioned the salary, June nearly fell out of her seat. After a minute, she stood and cleared the table, her thoughts on all that she'd heard.

Caleb helped clear but noticed her sudden silence. "What's going on up there?" he asked.

"Nothing," June answered. "Just the most unbelievable job offer I've had all day." They cleaned up and when finished, June thanked Caleb for the breakfast and ran back home.

ne, June had time to really hear herself think. Later was amazed at herself for actually toying ying for the job. What had she d the letter on the table from rrying it to the kitchen.

the gift horse that I'm to clear up all her to think about it, *well see who* he'd be in the all her other ed.

look the s-

for symptoms of some other activity. Of course, any more blacking out means further probing. As for the pain, if it's lasting, I just have to take a pain pill."

"That's it?"

June nodded. "That's it."

"What about driving and other stuff?"

"I'm free to do whatever I want. Since the blackout was only one occurrence, there's no need to restrict me. The dizzy spells are only occasional and he didn't seem to place too much importance on them."

"Then you can go back to your job?"

June shook her head. "Given the nature of my medical history, he still wouldn't approve me going back in that capacity." She gave Caleb a wry grin. "Exactly what I wanted to hear," she said. "Now call my new employer and ask him when I can start." She left the car and walked briskly to the lawyer's door, leaving her friend with an amazed look on his face.

Thirty minutes later, Caleb, who was lounging casually against the car fender, ankles crossed, straightened up and uncrossed his arms when he saw June come sailing out of the lawyer's office. If there hadn't been a swing mechanism on the door to prevent it from slamming shut, he was certain that the glass would have shattered the way June flung the door open and marched down the redbrick walk. He lost no time in opening the door for her and she slid inside, fastening her seat belt with a vengeance. He walked around and slid in the driver's seat of the dark gray Jeep SUV.

"Back home?" Caleb said as he started the engine.

"Yes," June snapped.

Minutes into the drive, Caleb heard her breathing ease and felt her relax against the seat. He knew that she was calm enough for civil talk.

"What happened back there?" Caleb asked in a low voice.

He glanced at the white envelope she was still clutching in her hand.

June's left eye no longer twitched and her hands had stopped shaking. She looked at Caleb. "Sorry for that," she said. "I had to get out of there before I blew up."

"Something tells me that you already did," Caleb said in a solemn voice. "Feeling better?"

A wry smile touched June's lips. "I guess I will be." She lifted the envelope flap and took out a check and held it up so that Caleb could get a glimpse. "Can you see it?"

Caleb saw the figure with all the zeros. He whistled. "Where'd that come from?"

June recalled the last half hour, and her voice shook with renewed anger as she stuffed the envelope in her bag. "Carlotta Graham Gardiner's husband."

Chapter Three

Matt Gardiner arrived at his attorney Paul Denton's office, unperturbed that he was running a little late. It was probably just as well if this planned, face-to-face meeting with the Saxon woman failed. She would probably rant and rave like a wild person and he didn't have the stomach or the time for female hysterics. Since there was other business he wanted to discuss with June Saxon he thought it a good idea to be formally introduced instead of showing up at her home unannounced. He didn't intend to spend a whole lot of time laying out his proposition to her and expected that before they left the office Paul would begin drawing up the necessary papers. He didn't anticipate any problem or objections, given her state of affairs. Determined, and like a man who'd already scratched a bothersome itch, he entered the office and was surprised to find the waiting area empty. The secretary greeted him and asked him to have a seat. Paul was with a client.

Five minutes later, the door opened and June Saxon

walked in, not looking the least bit flustered that she was late for her appointment. Matt heard the exchange between her and the secretary and watched as she sat in a chair, opposite him.

Surprised that she wasn't the client that was with Paul, as he'd thought, Matt raised his eyes from the magazine that he was idly flipping through, and looked at her with annoyance. Her quick glances to her watch were just like a woman, he thought. *Show up late and act the aggrieved one for being made to wait.*

When her dark eyes met his probing stare, Matt, taken aback, drew in a ragged breath, hoping that the sound hadn't gone beyond his own ears. This woman that he'd watched from a distance for weeks and whom he'd prejudged, had knocked him in his solar plexus with one up-close glance. She was not the woman he'd presumed to be meeting. He hadn't expected to see a woman with a sadness buried so deep within her round, dark eyes that it pushed its way to her consciousness, affecting the smooth contours of her oval face. Her look was strained. June Saxon was hurting.

Matt was almost never wrong in his judgment of people. In his business, he couldn't be. He was beginning to wonder if his pursuit of what he wanted should have taken a different tact. Should he have arranged a more private meeting?

The office door opened. A man came out, said a few words to the secretary, and left. The pleasant-faced woman gestured to the inner office. "Ms. Saxon. Please go in."

Matt's eyes met June Saxon's when she looked from the secretary to him with an inquiring stare as if to say that she'd wait her turn. His eyes never left her when she rose and, with head held high, shoulders erect, walked into the office and closed the door. His thoughts were deep as he began to think that this one time he might have made a mistake.

He had the oddest feeling that he never wanted to be the

one to bring more pain to this woman. Assured that that
would never happen, he relaxed. The generous offer that
was about to be presented to her would make June Saxon
a happier woman.

Matt's mouth turned to a grim line when he realized that
he might be wrong. But it was too late to alter this one
moment in time.

"He's here?" The words emanating from behind the
strong wood door were not those of a pleased client. Instead,
the door opened and an exasperated Paul Denton beckoned
to Matt.

"Come in please, Matt." The lawyer, who was inches
less than Matt's five-eleven, ushered him inside and hastily
made the introductions.

"Ms. Saxon, Matt Gardiner. Matt, this is June Saxon."
Paul Denton wearily pushed the glasses up on his nose and
gestured for his clients to have a seat.

June glared at the man whose check she held in her hand.
She waved it in disgust.

"This makes your wife's thievery all right in your eyes,
I guess." Her voice was full of disdain.

"Ms. Saxon," Matt said, observing the changed
demeanor. Replacing the quiet sadness was anger and a
strength that had been undetected. Her reaction to his check
puzzled him. He knew without a doubt that she could use
the money.

"I'm here merely because I wanted to extend my apologies in person for any inconvenience my . . ." He hesitated.
"My wife's actions have caused you." Matt gestured to the
check clutched in her hand. "I hope that your pain and
suffering is adequately compensated by that, which is over
and above what you lost."

June's round, dark eyes widened as she stood. "L—lost?"
she managed to sputter in disbelief. "You mean stolen, don't
you, Mr. Gardiner? Of all the nerve for you to bring me in

here to play lord of the manor and expect me to bow gratefully at your feet in receiving what's rightfully mine! Nerve
isn't the word for it!'' Her long-legged stride carried her
swiftly to the door. She waved the check so close to his
face that he instinctively turned his cheek. ''Compensated?
Yes, I will be if I use this to sue your wife for what you so
cavalierly call my pain and suffering!'' She opened the door
and marched out of the office and into the street.

Matt stepped aside as she whizzed by him. He followed
her and watched as the man who was waiting opened the
car door for her and the angry woman climbed inside. When
the car was out of view, Matt returned to a waiting Paul
Denton who spread his hands helplessly.

Matt closed the door but didn't sit down. ''Hold up on
those plans for a hot minute, Paul.'' Deep furrows in his
forehead marred his dark brown face. He ran a big hand
over his square jaw as if that would help smooth away his
confusion. ''I'll go by Ms. Saxon's and present the plan
myself. I didn't anticipate that there would be a problem.
I'll keep in touch.'' He opened the door but looked back
when his attorney spoke.

''Good luck.'' Paul Denton sounded anything but hopeful.

The fifteen-minute drive from the South Street business
district to Queens Lace Road was enough time for Matt to
gather his thoughts. He'd toyed with waiting a day or so
before visiting her, but decided against it. His guess was as
good as gold that anger would fill June Saxon's eyes whenever she spotted him, be it a day or a year from now.

The drive was a pleasant one, and the more that he looked
at the quiet residential area and the spacious homes, the
more he was convinced that he was right in approaching
her with his plan. Thoughts of the future and determination
set his jaw as he turned onto the street that was three blocks

long, and wended his way to the house that was the last one in the last block. As he'd seen her many times before, she was on the porch. But instead of lounging on the chaise, she was watering the flowers in the many hanging pots. The raucous display of colorful impatiens, pansies, and fiery salvia was eye-catching, and from afar he'd always admired the neatly landscaped garden that was an artist's palette of color.

June looked up at the sound of the approaching car, her long-held anger giving way to curiosity. Because she was at the end of the dead-end street, anyone coming this far was usually visiting her. She didn't recognize the black Mercedes. When the man emerged, her anger was renewed. Matt Gardiner! What was he doing here? She set her watering can down and walked to the stairs to meet him before he could put one foot on her steps. What nerve the man had!

"Mr. Gardiner," June said in controlled tones. "Was there something you missed?" She folded her arms across her chest. The involuntary feminine move showed weakness, and annoyed her. It was almost as if she were protecting herself. *From what?*

Matt stopped at the bottom step. Although sunglasses shaded her dark eyes, her pose and stance didn't fool him. She was still seething with anger. Yet, he sensed her fear. Of him?

"Yes, there was, Ms. Saxon," Matt answered, deliberately keeping his voice nonconfrontational. He didn't relish another volcanic eruption. "You left little time for further conversation."

"Conversation?" June almost smiled at the thought. "Oh, is that what you call that encounter?" she said, in saccharine tones. Tilting her head, she added, "What in the world would *we* have to converse about?" The thought did cause a tiny, but genuine, smile. She removed her sunglasses and brushed away little beads of perspiration from her forehead. At four o'clock the sun was still hot, but June, much to her chagrin, felt that it wasn't Old Sol causing the unfamiliar discomfort. Choosing to ignore the tiny warning signals, she said, "I suppose you expect me to invite you inside for a cold glass of ice tea, Mr. Gardiner?"

Matt removed his own dark glasses. He stared up at her. The one thought he had was that if he'd amused her to such an extent that he'd chased the sadness from her eyes, he'd be happy to give a repeat performance. Her smile had transformed her face. Her deep pecan skin with faint reddish hues, damp from perspiration, glowed with the looks of good health. His mouth twitched. "No," he answered. She raised a brow and he added, "Out here on the porch would be fine."

Not expecting his frank response, June's mouth formed a perfect O as she looked at the man whom she thought had lost his mind.

"You can't be serious," June finally managed.

Matt wiped his brow and squinted up at the sun. "Then I take it your offer was just empty words?"

June was speechless as she stared openmouthed at the husband of her former friend whose words stung her ears. If her Grandmother Belle could see and hear her display of rudeness! But thoughts of Carlotta were stronger than her grandmother's specter.

"If I were to invite any Gardiner into this house for tea it certainly wouldn't be the one I'm looking at," June snapped. Carlotta's perfectly made up face swam before her, and she could feel her temples throb. "Perhaps if you sent your wife over, I would be *more* than happy to offer her something iced." Another image glided by and June suppressed a giggle. She gestured into the air behind Matt's head. "Just where is your wife, Mr. Gardiner, and why does she have you doing her bidding?" She already knew the answer to that. Carlotta had never had a problem getting a man to jump through hoops for her, and her husband was obviously no exception.

Matt rubbed the back of his neck. "Do you really want an answer?"

"Of course!"

"Then do you want to come down, or do you want me to join you up there?"

June stared at him for a second. She backed away. "Come up." When he reached the porch, she sat and waved at a chair opposite her. "Have a seat," she muttered. Passing up an opportunity to meet face-to-face with Carlotta was one not to be missed.

Matt sat, looking amused.

June glowered at him, knowing exactly what he was thinking. As if her grandmother were standing by Matt staring at her granddaughter with reproachful eyes, June said under her breath, "Oh, all right." To her uninvited guest she mumbled, "Excuse me," and went inside.

In her absence Matt took the opportunity to study the house, all that he could see of it so close up. Just as he'd guessed, it appeared to be sound. The exterior was badly in need of paint, but that was cosmetic and the least of his problem. There were no visible signs of structural damage or evidence of termite infestation. He had an idea of the general layout of a Victorian, but he wanted to see inside this one. Even if he didn't get the chance, the offer would still be made.

June returned, carrying a tray with two glasses, and offered him one. "Fresh out of tea so lemonade will have to do."

"Thank you," Matt said, taking a sip. It was ice cold and he relished the cooling of his insides as the beverage slid down his throat.

June set her glass down on the small side table and stared at the quiet man who was engrossed in looking over her property. His scrutiny was making her uncomfortable. She

suddenly wanted him to disappear. "Why did your wife
send you here, Mr. Gardiner?"

Matt set his glass down. "I don't have a wife, Ms. Saxon."
His eyes hardened as the words left his mouth, turning the
air as icy as the beverage he had just drunk. He stared at
her with eyes just as cold.

"What?" June returned his stare in disbelief. His whole
demeanor had changed.

"Carlotta and I are no longer married."

"But in the lawyer's office, you said . . ."

Matt waved an impatient hand. "It was easier to say
'wife' than to go into a history of my personal life. *That*
wasn't the object of wanting an arranged meeting with you."

"Not married?" June could only stare at the man who
when he first appeared at her steps had an air of calm arrogance. His mantle of ruthlessness startled her. Shocked by
his words, she stammered, "B—but where is she?"

Matt raised cold eyes to hers. "Now, why would I know
or even care? It's been a year since I've seen her."

"A year?" June felt dazed.

"I see you are upset at the idea of not seeing my ex-wife,
Ms. Saxon. If you're that bent on finding her, I can give
you the last Paris address that I had."

The hint of sarcasm in his voice was like a dash of cold
water in her face. June drew herself up and she sat on the
edge of her seat. Her eyes glinted dangerously. How dared
this man sit there as if he had every right? Lying about his
wife's whereabouts so she would listen to him. Suddenly,
June froze. What did he want from her?

"Why are you here?" Her voice was sharp and clear.

Matt saw the anger fill her eyes. "I want to buy this
property."

June knew she'd heard right. Somehow his words didn't
compute, and the drumming that started slowly in her head
as a soft tap now slammed her as if she'd been caught on

the side of the head with a horse's hoof. Her hands were clenched in her lap.

"What are you talking about?" she whispered.

Matt got up and walked from one end of the porch to the other, peering around the sides of the wraparound porch, looking up at the eaves, and then walked back. "This house would suit my business needs perfectly. I've looked into the situation and there would be no zoning restriction." He was sitting with one hip resting on the sturdy railing. "My offer is generous and I understand that it would come in handy." He paused. "Perhaps you might want to reconsider that little business venture that you and my . . . Carlotta were about to get into." His stare was hard and unwavering.

He's mocking me, June thought. *Little venture?* She was shaking when she rose and stood by the steps.

"Buy my property?" June let out a small laugh that was borderline hysterical. "Your wife stole my inheritance. She ruined me and killed the desire in me to *ever* start another *little venture!* And you come over here, cool as ice and casually tell me that you want to take the roof from over my head? That it suits your business needs? You Gardiners! I hope the mold you both came from has been smashed to smithereens. Your kind will hardly be missed." She could feel the sting of tears behind her eyelids, but she refused to let this man see her cry. "Well, I don't think so, Mr. Gardiner. Not today, not tomorrow, and not next year! Now, do me a favor and get off my porch and don't even think about coming back here to repeat your asinine proposition." She moved aside so she wouldn't have to catch his scent as he passed by. When he walked down the steps, she stepped back to the screen door and opened it. "Forgive me, if I don't wave good-bye like a good hostess. I'm sure you can find your way." She went inside and closed the door.

June listened to the soft purr of his car engine that soon faded in the distance. She went down the hall to her calming, pastel sanctuary and sat on the prettily covered day bed. There, she let the tears fall.

The quiet must have awakened June because the phone wasn't ringing and there was no one knocking on the door. It was hours ago that she'd lain down, weepy and frustrated. Apparently, before she'd drifted off, she'd gotten the check off the kitchen table and carried it to bed with her because the thin piece of paper was caught beneath her foot. She reached for it and as she settled back down on the pillows, she held it up and stared at the figure. Sixty thousand dollars, seventeen more than Carlotta owed her.

June rubbed her eyes, letting the check flutter to the bed. Her head began to ache, and fearful that she was about to have another episode, she willed herself quiet. She couldn't run for a pill every time she had a common headache. Every day millions of people experienced a headache, but it didn't mean that they suffered from some deep, dark malady. Refusing to read anything more into the pain, she calmly rehashed the day's events in her mind.

Why would Matt Gardiner pay his ex-wife's debt? And include the five thousand that Carlotta had already paid her? Correction. That Carlotta had paid her from his account! What was behind his generosity? she wondered. Was he that wealthy he could give money away like that? The thought that she would be written off as a charitable contribution brought a smile to her face. The June Saxon Charity Fund. And he wanted to buy this house uninspected? *Whatever business you're in, Matt Gardiner, maybe I should be looking into it,* June thought.

Suddenly, old feelings of inadequacy returned, filling her up like kneaded dough that had been left to rise. *Where am I going? What am I doing with my life?* These same questions had tortured her during the last year and she still had no answer and nothing to show for the past months. Almost wildly, her gaze encompassed the room, which still smelled of fresh paint and brand-new fabric. Colorful hydrangeas and daisies spilled from a clear bowl on her dresser. "Except this," she whispered. She reached over and turned on the bedside lamp. It was eight o'clock and dusk had long since settled over the island and was already sliding into the dark of night.

June slid off the bed and, barefoot, walked through the dusky house, closing windows and pulling shades. The back door was already locked. Through the sheer curtain she looked across the lawn. Caleb's kitchen was dark and so was the rest of the first floor of the big house. His car was there so he must be on the other side of the house in his den. He was working late. June walked to the kitchen and idly searched the refrigerator. She was hungry but didn't see a thing that tempted her enough to bother nuking and then eating it. She settled for apple juice, cheese, and Ritz crackers, turned out the light, and went to her bedroom.

As she lay in bed, June wondered at the feelings that continued to plague her. She hadn't dwelled on the memory of her parents in years. Or her grandparents. June shucked it off as just the last vestiges of the image of her reproving Grandmother Belle this afternoon, when she had envisioned her standing over Matt Gardiner's shoulder.

She turned off the lamp and slid beneath the sheet, kicking the summer-weight blanket to the foot of the bed. Her bedroom faced the side of the house where the road ended and there was nothing but dense woods, and beyond, a sloping stretch down to the sandy beach. Though the light of the moon shone over the house, little light filtered through the sheer curtains. The trees, short and tall, looming in the dark, the leaves swaying ever so slightly, danced and played as if this were their time to frolic: when all earthly creatures ceased to exist.

June lay watching the dancing shadows, as she loved to do. Night and darkness had never frightened her and she'd never given any thought to remaining alone in the big house after her grandmother died. Only today did she think about it. Not being alone, but being lonely. The thought had hit her only after her visitor had gone. As intrusive as a Peeping Tom, the thought had inveigled its way into her mind even as she flung herself on the day bed and drifted off to sleep. Matt Gardiner had made her feel lonely.

In her dream she had seen his face and its different expressions. The puzzled concern in Denton's office, and later the calm arrogance, and later still the cold, hard mask.

What complexities, she thought. But the worst feeling she'd had was the inexplicable flame that fanned her torso when he had emerged from his Mercedes. Though he was the last person she'd expected to see, she couldn't help but wonder at the fleeting flicker of joy that had tickled her chest. *Joy?* There was no other way to describe it. The feeling evaporated just as quickly. The man had been her enemy's lover. Husband. How could she entertain thoughts of him in a lustful way?

June knew that there must be something seriously wrong with her. Not in the head department but in matters of the heart. There had to be if she was having romantic notions about a stranger who was ready to pull the rug out from her feet, or more aptly, the floor upon which her bed sat. Not that she never wanted the love of a good man, if that was to be her fortune, but, she wasn't man-starved. Not like her former friend. But, her and Matt Gardiner?

June smiled and closed her eyes, turning over on her side, rather hoping that Wilton Maitland showed up at her birthday party. He *had* to be a better bet for romance than a man who would even think himself to be in love with a Bwitch named Carlotta. Divorced or not, his taste in women was too crass, and she'd take it as an insult if he ever put the moves on her.

Moments later, June's smile was replaced by a tiny frown. She shook her head as if that would erase the image of Matt's face.

In the morning June was at the bank when it opened. After taking care of her business she left, had a leisurely breakfast, dawdling until the department stores opened. She was going shopping.

By three o'clock, June was back home, hanging up the dress she'd bought. The moment she'd seen the lemon-yellow dress on the mannequin, she knew it was hers. Simply made, sleeveless, with a V-neck, the soft, clingy fabric ended in swirls a few inches above her knees. The color was a great pick-me-up shade, daring its wearer to feel blue.

After her restless night, June had awakened, determined to shake the melancholia of the day before. With a pocket full of money she had options now. Maliciously, she'd thought about buying new duds and flying off to Paris, wondering exactly where the ex-Mrs. Gardiner was living. Had she stayed on in Paris to snare another Mr. Rich Guy? Or was she living in New York, afraid to confront her former friend?

There was nothing like having a few dollars to make a body get off the pot. By the time June got back home, she'd made up her mind. Whereas she'd halfheartedly toyed with the idea a few days ago, now determination burned inside of her like a bad case of heartburn. She had spied Caleb's car and now she ran across the grass and knocked on the back door.

"Hey, what's up?" Caleb said. He cocked his head as June sailed by him and plopped down in a kitchen chair. He hadn't seen her smile like that in nearly a year. He sat across from her. "Oh, I get it," he said knowingly. "This all has to do with that little piece of paper, huh?"

"Umm, in a way," June answered. Unable to contain herself, she said, "Have you heard anything yet?"

"About?" Caleb was curious.

"My résumé. Has your friend gotten back to you?"

Caleb hesitated but answered with a shake of his head. "I faxed it to him the night you gave it to me, but he hasn't responded. At least not about that."

"You've spoken to him, though?"

"Yes."

June looked crestfallen. "Then I suppose he's not interested in me."

"I didn't say that. The man carries a heavy load. Even so, he's desperate to hire someone and I'm sure he's looking the prospects over very carefully, this time."

June sighed. "Yeah, I guess you're right." She looked at him hopefully. "I want that job. I *need* that job, Caleb. Getting away for a while, doing something totally different and challenging will be good for me. Maybe when I return, I'll have my head back on straight."

Caleb took his time in answering after giving her a thoughtful stare. "Stop selling yourself short, June. You've always been focused. It's just that when you got burned it rattled you for a while. It happens. I'm confident that when you set your mind to it you'll knock the world dead."

"Oh, you are, are you?" June teased.

"As sure as I'm sitting here," Caleb said quietly.

She was hardly used to the serious big brother tone he used. She hadn't heard it in years, especially not since he'd used it when he was getting on her and Beverly for some teenage foolishness.

"Thanks," she answered. "Appreciate your confidence." She stood. "You'll let me know as soon as you hear anything?" Her voice was anxious.

Caleb stood and followed her outside. "Sure thing. Soon as I hear."

"Okay, don't make me wait."

Caleb watched June. If anybody needed a break, he was looking at a woman who was desperate for one. He turned and went inside. If it was in his power he was sure going to try to make something happen for her. He returned to his den, and minutes later the soft whir of the fax machine was humming in his ear.

Chapter Four

After leaving the Saxon property, Matt drove slowly to his home, which was fifteen minutes away. He required the quiet time to sort out his feelings before running into anyone. That meant no dogs and no people. He made a wry face. As if that were possible on his property. As a rare-dog breeder, he was surrounded by both. His caretaker, Andre Heath, and his wife Diane, were always about. They were good handlers and Matt trusted them without question when it came to his animals. He conferred with them daily about the animals and usually saw more of Diane because she was also his housekeeper. When Andre was not in the kennels with the dogs, he pretty much stayed in their cottage. A few part-time workers were usually gone by four o'clock.

Although he kept some German shepherds for stud purposes, the basenji was Matt's forte. A special dog, the African basenji, with its distinct personality, needed certain training. Not everyone had the temperament to work with them, and Matt blessed the day that he'd found the Heaths.

As he pulled into the street leading to his home, Matt was relaxed enough to think about his reaction to June Saxon and *her* reaction to his offer. Why had she been so turned off? And angry with him? He couldn't believe that Carlotta had been on her mind for the past year and that she would be *more* than happy to see her, as she put it. *To do what?* he wondered. He rolled his eyes when he thought June Saxon had gotten a glint in her eyes about the possibility of meeting Carlotta again. The past was history and she should get over it. A visit from Carlotta wasn't going to change a thing. Or would it?

Matt hugged the wheel. He was a firm believer in letting life's upsets be done and over with. Dwelling on a hurt did no one any good and only thwarted whatever creativity one had. When he'd learned that his marriage was a mistake he'd done just that, put it behind him. *Oh, you did?*

Matt pulled into his driveway and got out of the car, shrugging off the little voice in his head. He wasn't going there. Not tonight. *So, if you are a master at handling hurts, why did you hide out overseas for damn near a year, licking your wounds?*

"Oh, keep quiet," Matt muttered, while unlocking the front door. He tossed his keys on the foyer table, listening for sounds of Diane as he walked to the kitchen. She was gone but she'd prepared his dinner. The spicy smell of her special spaghetti sauce filled the room.

Matt's appetite wasn't what it should have been. Usually he couldn't resist diving into anything Diane prepared. He decided that he was probably still feeling uptight after his visit with that strangely disturbing woman. He took a beer from the fridge and carried it to his den, ignoring the sounds of Kagi, his pet dog who had the run of a small room off the kitchen. Basenjis were notorious for temperament, and if left alone for hours, showed their disfavor with their owners. He'd learned early on that he wasn't about to be redecorating every few months. Matt knew the dog had heard him come in, but he wanted time to think before letting the animal out to play.

Matt's den was a place where he spent a lot of time and he'd decorated to suit his tastes. He liked big, comfortable furniture that allowed reclining and slouching. When he'd had the house built, on two acres, he'd made allowances. The den accommodated a large, dark walnut desk, a six-foot-long brown leather sofa with wide cushions, and a man-size chaise longue in a sturdy brown and white plaid fabric. Many times he'd fallen asleep on the chaise after spending long hours at his desk. He'd often wake up and take his dog for a long walk on the beach where it was quiet and peaceful.

Since returning home from Paris after terminating his marriage, he'd begun walking more frequently on the beach. Day and night. He told himself that he was just continuing his normal habits, but deep down he knew that wasn't true. When he'd learned from Carlotta where June Saxon lived, he couldn't believe it. She was practically his neighbor. Although it was a fifteen-minute drive on the winding, hilly streets, walking along the beach for almost a mile brought him right to her door. That is, if he wanted to run across a divided four-lane street to ring her front doorbell.

Matt wanted to know more about the woman who had allowed herself to be used and abused by his ex-wife. A person had to be just this side of stupid to have been duped so grandly.

Yeah, just like you. Matt sucked his teeth, wishing the voice in his head would put a clip on it. But he had to admit that it spoke the truth. He'd fallen under the spell of the glamorous Carlotta Graham. It never ceased to amaze him how bedazzled he'd been. Or had it just been loneliness that had made him court her for a whirlwind week that ended in a marriage ceremony in Paris?

Matt got another beer and returned to the chaise. He'd

worked long years to build his dog-breeding business, often being the butt of family jokes from his father and four brothers, who'd thought that he was going through a rebellious phase. He'd proved that he could make it on his own, instead of becoming an executive in the family business, Mabel Foods, which had fed families of America for the past forty years.

At the age of thirty-five, Matt awoke one morning wondering how he'd come so far so alone with no one sharing his life and his good fortune. He'd always wanted to marry and have kids but never actively sought a wife. He'd met Carlotta on his trips to Paris and they'd dated a few times. When they were apart, he missed her. Several months passed without their meeting and he'd tried without success to reach her.

What they say about absence making the heart grow fonder must be true, he thought, because she was constantly on his mind. Then one day he'd had the good fortune to bump into her in New York City, and he wouldn't let her out of his sight. He convinced her to fly with him to Paris and she'd accepted. Who knew that they would be married after only seven days together?

After living in Paris for two months, Matt had seen some things in his wife that'd made him wonder about the kind of woman he'd married. Selfish and vain were her middle names. When he discovered the large amount of money she'd sent to a stranger, he'd confronted her. The tale she told made his stomach turn. He knew without a doubt that he'd made a mistake. At last, he listened to the little warnings and alarms that had plagued his private thoughts since his marriage. This woman was not who he thought she was and he couldn't see living with his mistake for the rest of his life. The thought of having someone like her bear his kids was repulsive. Any love that he'd thought he had for her dissipated into thin air. He moved out of their rented villa and immediately started annulment proceedings.

Matt was restless. He got up, rifled through some papers on his desk, walked to the window to stare at the magnificent green grounds, then sank heavily onto the leather sofa with his head resting on his clasped hands. He closed his eyes, then opened them when all he saw was a pair of big, soulful brown eyes staring in anger at him. He was impatient with himself for letting his thoughts stray. June Saxon was nothing but a business deal to him. When he'd first seen that big house his mind had filled with possibilities.

Matt's customers, the potential buyers for his special breed of dog, came from all over the country to see the animals. Often they had to stay in motels that were not conveniently located to the Gardiner property. Because of its peculiar traits, Matt refused to sell the basenji to the casual man. He had to be satisfied that the dog and its potential owner went through a bonding process. Most times it was the animal that made the final choice. Many times, he would allow the visitors to stay in his home for the entire bonding period, which took place over several meetings between the dog and the buyer. Because Matt found some of his visitors overbearing, he wanted to discontinue the practice. But he'd already established a fine reputation and at his most successful peak he didn't want to jeopardize his business where word-of-mouth played a key part in attracting serious clients.

The Saxon property was near enough between the two homes and Matt thought that a bed-and-breakfast setup so close by would be perfect. He could house at least three different buyers and their families for several days. The more he thought about it the more he was determined to buy that house. And Matt never gave up anything he set his mind on without first giving it his best.

Matt was interrupted by the peal of the back doorbell, and he went to answer it. Although Andre and his wife had keys to the house, when they knew he was home they never let themselves in without ringing. He had to go through Kagi's room to answer the bell and when he did, the animal, delighted to see his owner, playfully jumped all over him, and at the same time let Matt know that he didn't like to be kept waiting.

"Yeah, I hear you, dog," Matt said, bending to scratch his pet behind his ears. "You're not the boss around here, I am," he added. "Yeah, you heard right." Matt grinned and shook his head at the comical look on the dog's face. As if he were smiling to beat the band at the silly human.

"Hey, Andre, what's up?" Matt said, surprised to see the older man. "Older" was only four years. With forty years to Matt's thirty-six, Andre's face bore the ravages of a wild, unhealthful lifestyle.

Matt stepped aside. Five was usually the dinner hour at the Heath house. The serious look prompted Matt to ask, "Problems?" He sat down at the kitchen table and his visitor followed suit.

"Bron is back."

Andre was a man of few words, always was, but his flat statement brought Matt's head up sharp.

"What?" Matt's eyes darkened. He was almost certain he wasn't going to like what was coming. "When?"

"A few hours ago. After Mr. Sellers dropped him off, I couldn't wait for you so I took him to Doc Faselli. Just got back."

"The vet? What the hell's wrong with the dog?" Matt saw anger redden the light beige skin of the other man's face and knew the news was bad. "Why didn't you beep me?" The instant Matt said the words he wished for instant recall. There was no need for Andre to call him in an emergency. Matt trusted the man to run the business, to call the shots as he saw fit when he was away. That meant whether he was as close as town or as far away as Zaire.

"You were handling other business. I didn't want to call you away from that."

June Saxon and her house. Matt shook his head. "Thanks. I know there was no need. Forget I said that."

Andre nodded, his hazel eyes filling with understanding. A response wasn't necessary. More concerned with the sick animal, he swatted the air with his thick hand. "He's in a bad way. Doc said it doesn't look good," he said in a gruff voice that was filled with disgust. "Can't imagine what that man did to that dog in six months."

"Did Doc say what's wrong?" Matt was angry. For once his judgment of people had failed him. No, failed Bron, who had been one of his prized studs. He'd sold him to Sellers, another breeder from Ohio. After the man and his assistant left, Matt had had second thoughts about the whole transaction. There was something about the man's jocularity toward Andre and the rest of the kennel helpers that just didn't ring true. The rumor that the breeder was bad news had trickled down to Matt in the past but there was nothing that he could substantiate. The man's long-standing record of successfully breeding show dogs was well known. There was no good reason for Matt to refuse to sell to the man. Now he knew he should have listened to his inner voice.

"I could tell right away that he was malnourished," Andre said. " 'Bout an hour after Sellers left, Bron started to vomit. Wouldn't come to me, just laid there looking at me as if I'd done something wrong. Doc said he was anemic and likely he's got the syndrome. He won't know for sure until after the exam, but he'd bet on it."

Fanconi syndrome was a kidney disease sometimes inherent in the breed. Though Bron had been treated badly, there was no one to blame for that illness. Matt swore and could have kicked himself for mistakenly selling his animal. If Matt had had the slightest inkling of the onset of the disease,

Bron could have stayed in his home, surrounded by familiar people who cared.

"I'll get over there tomorrow," Matt said, already resigned to the dog's fate. Doc Faselli knew his business and didn't make rash statements. If the dog was suffering, it was cruel to keep him drugged day and night.

"If Bron was so sick, why did Sellers bring him back here?"

Andre's rugged face split with a half smile. "He claims we sold him a sick dog. Said get ready to meet him in court."

Matt looked at Andre in disbelief. "He what?"

After Andre left, Matt ate the delicious dinner Diane had prepared, but with little appetite. His thoughts were on Mr. Sellers and his threat to sue Gardiner Kennels.

During his eight years in business, Matt had never been in a position to have to defend his reputation or his practices in breeding dogs. There had been some instances where a dog was returned, only because the family didn't realize the care and patience that were needed to provide a good home for the basenji. But he was determined that one man, thought to be unscrupulous, was not going to ruin his reputation. He would nip this thing, whatever it was going to turn into, in the bud. In the morning, right after a visit to Doc Faselli's, he'd pay Paul Denton a visit.

Matt fed his dog, and as was his habit, he took the animal for a long walk on the beach. He already knew in which direction they would walk.

The day after she'd rudely invited Matt Gardiner off her steps, June turned twenty-nine. It was the day of the summer solstice, which marked the beginning of summer. June was glad it was midweek and that the party her friends were throwing for her was not until Saturday evening. Except for calls from Beverly and Caleb earlier, June had spent the day in relative quiet, as she'd always liked to do.

Her mother had called her a strange little girl for not liking the hoopla that came with birthday parties. Her friends had had such auspicious celebrations with the expensive clowns and other daylong entertainment. June had always found herself sitting on the outside of the action watching the antics of her little friends. The few times she'd been made to interact with the paid actors, she'd acquiesced. It wasn't long before her mother realized that her daughter was perfectly happy doing her own quiet thing. She was happy and contented being with herself and didn't crave the attention that came with being the star of the day. Her parents singing happy birthday to her in the quiet of their home around a big, dark chocolate cake brightly lit with pink candles was heaven. The presence of her grandparents made the party even better. Before her parents' death, June had already formed a bond with her paternal grandparents. She didn't get to see her mother's parents much since they lived in California. She hardly remembered them since her grandfather had died when she was three years old and his wife died only months later. Uncannily, both had been stricken with cancer within months of each other.

Growing up so near the bay, June had come to love the sound of the water. For years on her birthday, she had walked on the beach at night. The day was long, and at the end of it she had always wanted to see the bright new summer moon that made the sand appear as snow. When they were young, sometimes Caleb and Beverly would sneak out to join her and it would be midnight before they all crept back into their homes.

Earlier, June had fixed a light meal, and for dessert, had treated herself to champagne and chocolate cake. Now it was after ten o'clock and as far as she could see across the street, the beach was deserted.

"Perfect," she murmured, locking the door and skipping down the stairs. Caleb was not home and she wondered if, when he returned, guessing where she'd be, he'd come looking for her. She carried a lightweight blanket because she knew she'd be staying for a while, at least until the chill and the mosquitoes chased her inside. She spread her blanket and anchored it with her sandals.

June sat with her arms wrapped around her hunched-up knees as she stared out at the dark water, wiggling her toes in the sand. There were a few boats out on the water and their lights formed long, thin squiggles that stretched and shivered like lighted eels on the dark water, disappearing into the wet, sandy shore. In the distance along the water's edge, June made out the figure of a couple walking in a close embrace, kicking the water as they sloshed along oblivious to all. She lay down and stared up at the sky.

Though the last few days had brought some stress, June had quieted down. At least long enough to assess her situation. She realized that since the visit to the attorney's office she was in a much better position than she had been in for over a year. Not too much thought went into making the decision to have the house exterior painted. It only took a phone call and within hours the house had been inspected, the colors selected, and an estimate given. She was using Caleb's guy who'd painted the Lancaster house the year before so she didn't need to make a hundred calls trying to get an honest deal. Besides, she wouldn't know a bona fide estimate from a lousy one. Trusting Caleb's levelheaded judgment, she went with his man. If she could have she would have begun the work yesterday, but the scheduled date was five days away. It wouldn't be too soon for her because she was determined that nothing would keep her from taking that job in Paris if it was offered to her. She was ready to make some changes in her life.

June got up and began to walk. The night was peaceful

and she breathed in deeply the air that was indigenous to the shore.

Self-absorbed, June stopped when she heard a strange sound. She saw no one and continued to walk when she heard it again. The sound was like that of a muffled cry from an infant. June stared down the beach looking for the couple she'd seen, while burying thoughts of horror stories about abandoned babies. They were nowhere in sight.

The sound was very close to her. June felt something rubbing against her leg, and startled, she looked down to see a small dog. In the dark she couldn't make out his color but she could see the white throat and the pointed ears. The strange sound came from the dog's throat, and cautious, June backed away. The dog couldn't bark. Concerned, June wondered if he was wounded. "Are you hurt, little puppy?" she murmured.

After eyeing him cautiously, she realized that he didn't appear to be hurt and almost seemed playful as he continued to sniff her. When she tentatively reached out to rub its back, she smiled at his playful nudge against her leg. The cooing sound coming from his throat was nonthreatening, and June relaxed as she began talking to the animal. He was jumping up and running away and coming back to her as if inviting her to play.

"Where'd you come from, little fella?" June looked around. She saw the dark shape of a man coming toward her and then heard him whistle. He called an unusual name. The dog answered in his strange way and June watched as he scampered toward the sound of the voice. She was amazed at what sounded like a yodel.

Curious about the animal, June could hardly wait to ask about it. She was disappointed when she saw the man turn and walk in the opposite direction. She walked back to her blanket and sat down. Before she realized it, the small dog was back, playfully jumping on her lap.

June laughed and caught him in her arms, almost falling backward with his weight on her chest. He was small but powerful. "So, not ready to call it a night, huh? Me either."

"Kagi! Heel!"

"Uh-oh. You're in trouble," June said to the squirming animal that immediately jumped from her arms and went to sit at the man's feet. When she looked up the smile died on her lips. Matt Gardiner was staring down at her.

"Ms. Saxon."

Even in the dark with only the bright moon for light, June flushed at his bold appraisal of her. She felt the same attraction that she'd experienced yesterday.

June was staring at him, mesmerized. She could only think that the midsummer moon must be playing tricks with her, because she had the funny sensation that the sudden appearance of Matt Gardiner and his dog was to be remembered as the exact moment that they would change her life.

"W—what are you doing here?"

Matt gestured to the moonlit sky, then shrugged. "Enjoying the night . . . like you."

"Yes, as a matter of fact, I am. Apparently, your dog is too." June felt as though she were trying to look up and over a mountain so she got to her feet. At least, if she tilted her head she'd be able to see his eyes. All of a sudden, she felt flustered. She'd given no thought as to where he lived. Was he so close that he could take moonlit walks along the beach? Right across from her house? Something nagged her and then she remembered.

"You walk here often. You and K—k . . ."

"Kagi."

"Kagi," June repeated, letting the soft *g* roll over her tongue. The dog heard his name but didn't move. "I've seen you both several times." She looked across the street and back to Matt, who still stared at her with an impassive look.

"Is that the way you acquire all your property, Mr. Gardiner? Amble along and just point? You don't even know what the interior is like. For all you know it could be a shambles, the walls held together with chicken wire.''

Matt looked amused. ''Hardly.'' The discarded paint cans that he'd seen weeks ago were evidence of her interior decorating. One time he'd seen her taking a break on the porch, her paint-splattered shirt a pastel palette.

''Now how would you know?'' June didn't see what the joke was. ''Don't tell me that you've already been inside. Somehow, that wouldn't surprise me in the least.''

''No, I haven't. But if that's an invitation, would now be okay? It shouldn't take too long.''

''You're kidding?''

''I don't kid much, Ms. Saxon,'' said Matt. ''Sooner or later, before the closing, I'll have to inspect the interior. Tonight's as good a time as any, for me.'' He arched a brow. ''That is, unless you're pretending again.''

June was speechless and could only stare at the man. The situation suddenly seemed so funny that a chuckle started in her belly and burst through her throat. She tried to hold it in by covering her mouth but she was too overcome with mirth. Tears formed in the corner of her eyes and her stomach hurt so badly that she sat down on the blanket and let the laughter gush out. She saw the dog's ears move as he gave her a quizzical look.

With an effort, June pulled herself together. She pointed to the dog and looked up at Matt. He was staring at her as if he were wondering what in the world he was going to do with a hysterical female. ''How long are you going to make that poor animal stand at attention?'' she said.

''Kagi,'' said Matt. He gave him another command and the dog stretched out on the sand.

''I guess what they say about laughter is true,'' said Matt.

''That it's good for what ails you?'' asked June. ''I don't have the problem, Matt, you do. Is that how you became a success? Steamrolled your way? Aside from the fact that you see and buy what you want, my old friend Carlotta would never have married you if you weren't King Midas. So as wealthy as you must be, just what do you want my old house for? Surely, you can do better in a more exclusive section." June gestured to the blanket. "Why don't you sit? I'm getting a crick in my neck." She let out a sigh, muttering beneath her breath, "What a birthday!"

Kicking off his sandals, Matt sat, surprised by her softly spoken words, which weren't meant for his ears. "Some of the things you said about me are true, all except one thing. Carlotta married me with assumptions she'd made about my business." His face was blank. "I doubt she'd have looked my way if she knew."

"Really? Just what is your business?" June found it hard to believe that Carlotta had been sucker punched. She could hardly wait to hear more.

Matt inclined his head toward Kagi. "I breed basenjis."

June looked surprised. "Basenji? I've never heard of that breed."

"That's not unusual. Many people haven't."

June was puzzled. "I don't get it. Why do you want my house? To build another kennel? Here?"

Matt shook his head. "No. I think it would be very suitable for overnight guests. The proximity to my property is perfect. It would eliminate the need to play host to obnoxious strangers, roaming through my house."

"A rooming house?" June was flabbergasted.

"A bed-and-breakfast," Matt corrected. He nearly recoiled when she moved suddenly and her bare foot brushed his. The erotic feel of soft skin and gravelly sand sent chills through him. He moved away.

June merely stared, amazed.

"Why does that take your breath away?" Recovered from

that brief, sensual encounter, he was relieved to talk about the house. "You have a fantastic piece of property there."

"Not for long if you get your way," snapped June.

"A coat of paint is all it needs," said Matt, ignoring her sarcasm. "The interior probably doesn't need much, at least for another year." Matt looked curious. "Did you do all the rooms over or just the main floor?"

"W—what?" June sputtered. "How long have you been spying on me?"

"Spying? I don't think so. You're hardly hidden from view, June."

June realized that during their conversation, they'd both dropped the formal Mr. and Ms. *So easily?* she thought. Her name on his lips sounded natural and she wondered at her deep-down pleasant feelings. *Check yourself out, girl. He's the enemy.*

A slight breeze riffled the edges of the blanket, and June rubbed her arms. She rose, and then bent quickly to reach for her sandals. The sudden movement brought a sharp pain to her temples. "Oh."

Concerned at the look of pain that crossed her face and fearing that she might fall when she closed her eyes and held her head, Matt caught her arm. "What happened?"

Dazed, June waited until the pain subsided to a dull thump. "I—I don't know." Certain she would have fallen, June was grateful for his firm hold on her. Absorbed with the thought that there might be something seriously wrong, June looked up at Matt when he called her name. "I'm sorry," she murmured. "What did you say?"

"I said, let me help you to your house. You seem a little light on your feet."

"S—sure, that would be fine," June answered.

"No, I'll get that," Matt said in a firm voice as she reached down for her blanket. When he picked it up and slung it over his arm, he caught her arm again and walked with her toward her house. Whistling for Kagi, they crossed the road.

Matt saw the man waiting at the foot of the steps and recognized him as the man who'd waited for her at the attorney's office. The glasses and the bottle he held were placed on the steps as he walked toward them, and Matt wondered at his peckishness that he wasn't to be a part of the birthday celebration.

Caleb slid his arm around June's shoulders. "I saw," he said quietly. "Another one?"

June nodded. The ache was fierce. "Have to lie down," she mumbled.

Caleb looked at the stranger who was staring at them peculiarly. He held out his hand and the man shook it firmly. "Caleb Lancaster. Thanks for what you did, man."

"Matt Gardiner. Not a problem. Glad I was there." Matt looked at June. "Will she be all right?"

Raising a brow at the name, Caleb answered, "Let's hope so. She needs a bed right now. If there's something seriously wrong, I'll see she gets attention." He turned away to help June up the steps, but before disappearing inside, turned back. "Thanks again for your help."

Matt glanced down at the forgotten symbols of celebration. "Kagi, come," he said and crossed the road to the beach. Kicking up the sand on his brisk walk home, and disturbed at his thoughts, he recalled her angry words: *You want to take the roof from over my head?* Was June Saxon seriously ill? And when he bought her house, where would she go? What would become of her? Matt entered his house and uncharacteristically slammed the door. *Why should I care?* he wondered.

Chapter Five

Matt hadn't slept all night and it showed in his manner as he went about his daily activity. After he called his attorney about the Sellers matter, he went to work in the kennels but at Andre's and Diane's insistence, soon left. His funky attitude was disturbing the animals. Even Kagi made himself scarce, avoiding his master, and staying in his own space.

At noon, Matt gave in to the nagging inner voice and called the Saxon home, the only solution to what ailed him. Worrying about a stranger had cost him a restful night and was ruining a fruitful day of work. Brows knitted at getting no response, Matt sat brooding at the phone. Where was she? he wondered. Would Lancaster know? He pulled his hand back from the receiver, thinking that the other man would put him in his place for minding other people's business. Matt hadn't missed the protective way Lancaster had shielded June. The back door slammed and Matt heard voices greeting Kagi and the dog's happy response. Seconds later, Matt's three older brothers entered the study.

"Hey, brother Matt, what's up?" Sutherland Gardiner at forty-two was an imposing figure with a voice to match. He promptly propped his six-foot, four-inch big-boned frame on the sofa, barely leaving space for one of his brothers. As the oldest he was also the tallest, inheriting the Gardiner loftiness, surpassing his father by three inches. The rest of the boys took after their mother's side of the family with slender frames and varying heights topping six feet. Matt was the shortest at five-eleven.

"Hey, Matt," George Gardiner said. He was two years younger at forty and two years older than thirty-eight-year-old Reuben who sat with Sutherland while George found a chair.

Matt sat behind his desk, staring in surprise at his visitors. "Don't tell me. Dad sold the plant from under you and now y'all have to work for a living. Sorry, but I have all the help I need right now," he muttered.

Reuben's light brown eyes, forever laughing, crinkled as he grinned. "You wish, don't you, baby brother." He and George were the only two who had their mother's eyes.

"Don't call me that. As I recall there's one younger than me, making a career as a beach bum in Florida with our father's blessing," Matt said.

"David's working down there for Dad." George Gardiner spoke quietly in a firm voice as he looked at his brother.

Matt met his brother's stare. Although closer in age to Reuben, Matt had always had a special bond with George. When Matt chose not to enter the family business, it was George who believed in him and refused to let the others goad Matt in his presence.

"In Windermere? I thought Dad retired to the good life." Matt couldn't imagine his younger brother working at anything, especially in that upscale community. "Doing what?" he added.

"Dad does a little consultant work and David's assisting,"
Sutherland answered.

Matt grimaced. "Consulting on what and to whom? If it
isn't in diamonds for the latest glamour queen, I won't buy
it." He snorted. "You sure our brother's not the bait?"

The three brothers eyed Matt in silence. With his sarcasm,
all were reminded of their father's philandering and how
it'd hurt their mother for years until her death, thirteen years
ago. For as long as they could remember, they knew their
tall, handsome father to be a playboy. Even when Hank
Gardiner was struggling to build his fledgling food company
that kept him away from his family for long hours, he still
managed to find the time for extracurricular activity in the
name of beautiful, expensive women. The brothers believed
that Mabel Foods was named for their mother out of their
father's guilt.

George finally answered his brother. "Dad and David are
working with a group of young college students in Orlando,
who are venturing into entrepreneurship. Dad's agreed to
back the most promising. And for the first time, David's
enjoying work." He gestured to Sutherland and Reuben and
shrugged. "I guess we're the only three of his sons who
took to the business. With Sutherland as CEO, and Reuben
and I vice president and president, we've managed to keep
the company in the black and people employed across the
country. We enjoy what we do, Matt. You and David chose
a different path and we respect that. You just found yourself
quicker than he did."

"We kid a lot, but you know Mother was proud of what
you were doing," Sutherland said. "Too bad she didn't live
long enough to see the success you've become."

"Yeah, with your stubborn old self." Reuben chuckled,
helping to lift the gloom from the room. "Which reminds
me of why we're here," he said.

The air had become heavy and Matt was relieved to change

the subject. "And why is that? I'm curious. Did I forget a birthday or something?"

"Nope, nothing like that," Reuben answered. Hardly able to contain himself, he said, "We heard about you trying to oust a little old lady from her home. What's up with that? Ain't this enough space for you and the mutts?" Reuben was cracking up.

"What?" Matt's jaw dropped. "What are you talking about?"

"Chill, Reuben," George said. He looked at Matt, who was staring at all of them as if they'd gone mad. "Last night at a dinner party, you were the topic of conversation."

Matt looked wary but interested. "Is that so? That boring, huh?"

"The word is that you have your eye on a beachfront property, supposedly to expand your business." George paused. "If that's the case you're going to have a fight on your hands. That area is not zoned for your type of business."

"Don't you all think I know that?" Matt was amused. "Doesn't take long for gossip to circulate, does it? I'd forgotten."

"This is not Manhattan. You're not unnoticeable," Sutherland said.

"Gardiners aren't invisible. You should know that," Reuben said.

"What are you planning?" Sutherland eyed his younger brother.

"I want to renovate the property and use it as a guest house. It's been approved."

"Guests?" The three brothers spoke in unison.

George gestured. "This house is too small?"

"Something you're not telling us again?" asked Sutherland.

"Yeah, that marriage you sprung on us is still a juicy topic," Reuben said and then laughed. "I think we're the only family who's had a sister-in-law who's still a mystery lady. Not a picture, no name—nothing! Are you sure she wasn't a figment of your imagination?''

Matt was becoming irritated but said quietly, ''She was real.''

George saw Matt's change of mood and decided to end the banter before things got out of hand. ''We're not here to discuss the past. That was your decision to make,'' he said. ''But we just wanted to warn you of the scuttlebutt and to watch your back. The news has reached Windermere, and Dad wants to know what's going on. You know his fear of scandal and lawsuits against the company.''

The comment nearly made Matt laugh. If all Hank Gardiner's women weren't scandal enough he didn't know what was, but he said, ''Tell Dad he has nothing to worry about. Mabel Foods won't be tainted by anything I've done.'' Before his brothers asked, he explained his plan, knowing they wouldn't leave until he did. When he finished, he added, ''June Saxon is not a little old lady who's being put out on the street, but is young and . . . uh, young and able to take care of herself.'' *Beautiful?* Now why hadn't he wanted to share that with his brothers?

The sighs of relief were collective, all but from George, who eyed his brother. There was something that Matt wasn't saying. Instead, George said, ''So is she willing to sell?''

''Apparently I haven't offered her enough,'' answered Matt.

''Will you?''

Matt nodded. ''Yes.'' He gave George a determined look.

Sutherland unfolded his large frame and stood. ''Well, if that's all it is, I don't see any problems. I'll give Dad a call and tell him to keep his shirt on.'' He and Reuben started for the back door. ''Coming, George?'' His brother never moved.

''No. You two go on. I'll see you at work tomorrow.''

Matt watched his brothers go, then turned to George. "Hungry?"

"Sure, what's in the fridge?"

After a meal of warmed-over meatballs and spaghetti, the brothers were relaxing at the kitchen table with cold beer, enjoying the rare time together. But Matt knew George had something on his mind. "You're not worried about me, are you?" he asked.

George pushed back and crossed his knees. "No, just wondering what your plans are."

"But I told you what—"

"Not about the Saxon property," George cut in. "Your future love life."

"My what?"

"You heard me. I'm wondering if you allowed that episode in Paris to sour you on marriage." George drummed his fingers on his knee. "Look, we all know how we feel about besting our father at the female exploitation game. Sutherland, Reuben, and myself, married and thank God, we were lucky enough to marry the right women and as far as I know, nobody's looking for any outside excitement. At least I can speak for myself." He paused. "Toi and I are happy and our daughters Gina and Jade make life worthwhile."

Matt nodded. He'd always observed the way his young nieces loved and respected their parents. "I believe that," he answered.

"Since you came back after that—well, after your breakup, you've hardly visited any of us unless you get a formal invitation to dinner. You bury yourself in these kennels and don't venture out to the most informal of barbecues."

Matt shrugged. "No interest," he said.

"In your family?"

"No. Matchmakers." Matt threw his brother a look of disgust. "I'm not looking for another wife."

George had his own ideas about that, but said, "Even if the others don't, I know how much you want to marry and have kids of your own." He knew the affection Matt had for his brothers' children. "If you continue the way you are, you're going to wake up fifteen years from now realizing that you're living the life of our father. Hopping from one young thing to another."

"Never happen," Matt grumbled.

"It can, if you hold in the bitterness you feel toward women, thinking they're all like your ex-wife. It's obvious you were unlucky the first time."

"And the last," Matt said. George had been the only one that Matt had confided in, telling him the whole story of his bedazzlement with a gorgeous witch. He wasn't surprised that George hadn't betrayed his confidence to the family, not even divulging Carlotta's name.

"I'm not going to bet on that." George waved a hand. "This house can use more than just you and Kagi to make it a home."

"We're doing okay." The animal heard his name and whimpered, but stayed in his room.

Ignoring that, George said, "When's the last time you kicked back with old friends who didn't want anything from you? No networking, or business deals or ducking a guy who wants a loan?"

Matt laughed. "A lo—ng time. Don't remember doing anything like that since college. Why? You ready to go downtown and hoist a few?"

When George grinned, his light brown eyes glinted and smile lines creased his smooth face. "No, but something close to it. One of Toi's old high school classmates is giving an open house on Saturday. She doesn't remember him but her girlfriend called and said to spread the word. Sort of an informal come one, come all reunion. You know, who'd you marry and what're you doing now, kind of thing? She's anxious to go and won't go without me." He grimaced. "I could use your company."

"Toi's friends?" Matt grinned. "Won't you feel like old granddad?" Toi was six years younger than her husband. "The old nostalgia bit, huh?"

"Yeah, guess you could call it that. Wanna come?"

Matt thought about his schedule. "Saturday looks good. Where is it and what time?"

George gave an exaggerated sigh of relief. "Thanks, man. Let me know how I can return the favor. I'll have to call back with the address but the guy's name is Caleb Lancaster." George saw his brother's reaction. "Friend of yours?"

"No," Matt answered, recovering quickly. "I met him last night. He's June Saxon's neighbor."

"Last night?" George uncrossed his legs and rested his arms on the table. "June Saxon's neighbor?" He waited expectantly.

"What?" Matt glared at his brother.

Without uncrossing his arms, George glanced at his watch. "I'm not going in today, so you have plenty of time to fill me in."

"On what?"

"With what's up with you and the lady who you're going to put out of her house."

"Buy."

George shrugged. "Whatever you want to call it. When you want something you don't give up until you've stalked, corralled, and tamed it." He smiled. "You can start with last night at Ms. Saxon's place."

"I wasn't at her place," Matt growled. "We were on the beach and she . . ." Matt glared at George's raised eyebrows. "It's not what you're thinking. We met by accident and when she nearly fainted, I took her home. Lancaster was there."

"Ah," George said with a knowing grin. "The other man."

Matt stood. "Look, I have work to do if you don't . . ."

George held up a hand. "Hold on, just kidding with you. Don't go away mad." He grinned. "I still need you on Saturday. You're not backing out on me, are you?"

"I said I would go," Matt grumbled. He sat back down.

"Good." His tone serious, George said, "She's a beauty, isn't she?"

Surprised, Matt asked, "How'd you know that?"

"It's what you omitted before."

Matt should have known his astute brother would notice something, but he didn't embellish his remarks.

George knew when to stop. He said softly, "Don't lump them in one pot, Matt." He stood and walked to the back door. "I'll call back with that address. Dress casual."

Matt followed George outside and he watched as his brother exchanged a greeting with Andre, who was passing by.

George watched the man until he disappeared. It was hard to believe that the two men were the same age and had been friends growing up.

"He's doing good, George," Matt said in a low voice. He'd watched his brother's expression.

"I know. You've told me. You wouldn't stay away for months at a time like you do, entrusting everything to him and Diane." George looked at Matt. "You've done a good thing, helping him the way you did." He shook his head. "He was a brilliant lawyer. Could've had the whole world by now."

"That's what his father wanted for him," Matt said softly. "He wanted to be Andre."

"And he is, isn't he?" George remembered how Andre

had turned his back on his overbearing father and turned to alcohol. Lost in the underworld for years, Andre was huddled in the doorway of a bar, begging for food when Matt stumbled upon him. Recognizing him as George's old friend, Matt had taken him home. He'd been there ever since.

"Yes, he is."

George waved to Matt as he walked to his car, his smile hidden from his brother. "You're not so tough, Matt," he said. Suddenly he couldn't wait for Saturday. He had to meet the woman who'd put that look in his brother's eyes. "June Saxon, I hope you're a strong woman," he murmured, "because my brother is stalking. Even if he doesn't realize it—yet."

Matt returned to his study, musing over the conversation with George. Small world wasn't the term for it, he thought as the reality of the situation hit. June and Lancaster. The question that had been gnawing at him would be answered on Saturday. Are they a twosome? Immediately, another question arose. Why should he care? But try as he might, Matt couldn't shake the feeling that something was terribly wrong with the woman who'd been on his mind for weeks. *But you're only interested in buying her house, right?* Matt shrugged off the annoying inner voice. He picked up the phone and dialed the number, not giving a second thought to his having memorized it.

After several rings, without an answering machine kicking in, Matt hung up. Telling himself that there could be any number of reasons for her lack of response, he gave up wondering about the Saxon woman and opened his appointment book. Visitors were due in soon and he had to enlist Diane's aid in making preparations. He hated disrupting his laid-back routine to accommodate guests. He was determined as ever to follow through with his plan. But minutes after closing his book, Matt was walking to his car. He had to know what was going on.

Her white Camry was parked in front of the house and Matt pulled up behind it. Satisfied at last to have found her, he didn't realize the relief he felt in knowing she was okay. Lancaster's car was gone from his drive and Matt felt secure that all was well. He wouldn't have left if she were ill, would he? Matt frowned when there was no response to his knock. Silence met the peal of the doorbell. Perturbed, Matt walked around the deck to the back door. Maybe she was in the kitchen. He was about to knock when he saw the door ajar. *Something's wrong.* Without knocking he pushed the door open and went inside.

"June," he called. There was no answer and Matt's mouth went dry. The kitchen was empty and Matt began walking down the hall when he heard a cry. "June?" He walked toward the sound and stopped at the bedroom door where he saw her thrashing in her sleep. He went to her.

"June, wake up," Matt said softly. He sat down on the edge of the bed and shook her shoulder gently. Almost caressingly, his fingers brushed the soft brown skin. The strap of the white cotton tank top she was wearing was off one shoulder and Matt drew in a sharp breath. She was braless and her nipples strained against the thin cloth. "God," he breathed.

"Caleb?"

The name on her lips brought Matt back from a dangerous place. He removed his hand from her shoulder and stood up. "It's Matt Gardiner, June," he said in a low voice.

June opened her eyes. Hazily, she looked up. "Matt?"

"I heard you cry out," Matt said. He'd stepped away from the bed and was looking at her closely. "I came by to see how you were. I couldn't reach you by phone."

"Matt?" June repeated. Trying to make sense of why he was in her bedroom, she tried to sit up but fell back with a groan. "Oh," she said, touching her head.

Concerned, Matt stepped closer to the bed. "What is it?"

"A granddaddy of all headaches," June murmured. "I thought the medication would have kicked in by now, but guess it hasn't." She stared at her visitor. "H—how'd you get in?"

"I saw your car and when you didn't answer the bell I came to the back door and found it open. I followed the sound of your cry. You must have been having a bad dream."

June frowned. "Caleb must have left it open. He went to pick up a few things for me." She stared up at Matt. "Why are you here?" Her eyes darkened. "If it's about the house . . ."

"I was concerned," Matt said tersely. "You weren't exactly standing up straight the last time I saw you." He backed up. "If you're okay, I'll leave."

"Matt, wait," June called. She slowly sat up and then noticed her state of undress. Beneath the covers she was wearing only her underpants. Embarrassed, she adjusted the tank top straps. "Please," she said, as Matt hesitated. "Sit?"

Matt sat in the rocking chair by the window and stared at her. He could see the effort she was making to ignore the headache. "You mentioned medication. You've seen a doctor?"

June started to nod and thought better of it. "That's why you couldn't reach me. Got back an hour ago and must have immediately fallen asleep. I had a sleepless night."

That makes two of us, Matt thought. "Nothing serious?"

"Don't know yet, but probably not." June wondered at the concern in his voice. *Why should he be worried?* she thought. "That's why you called me?"

"Yes."

"Thanks, but I'm sure it's nothing. The doctor will let me know what's going on as soon as he knows. Until then, these painkillers should help." She smiled. "But the pills haven't kicked in yet, so I'm not so sure."

"Perhaps you haven't given them time." Matt stood.

"I'll go and let you get some rest." He hesitated. "Is there something I can do before I go?"

He was leaving and June already felt lonely. "Thanks, no, I'll be fine."

Matt didn't leave.

"What's wrong?"

"The door. It shouldn't be unlocked. You never heard me come in."

"You're right. I'll lock it. Caleb has a key."

Matt's jaw set. "Fine," he said. "Good-bye."

June heard the door close sharply, and before she got out of bed, the bang of the car door was followed by the quick start of the engine. After locking the back door, June went back to bed. She propped herself on the pillows, mulling over her strange visitor. Had he really been so concerned that he'd come over just to check on her health? And why had he left so abruptly, as if he'd thought visiting her was suddenly a bad idea? Unable to come up with a sensible answer and overcome with drowsiness, she slid down under the covers and closed her eyes. But Matt Gardiner's grim face bothered her until she realized that he was fine until she mentioned Caleb. Caleb? Matt Gardiner was annoyed that her neighbor had a key! Or was he jealous? June didn't know that a smile was on her lips when sleep claimed her.

When Matt parked his car, he'd calmed down. *So much for being solicitous,* he fumed. She'd nothing more than a huge headache, and her boyfriend was helping her through it. He could have kicked himself for appearing the fool. Going over there as if to the rescue. "Damn, man," he muttered, slamming the back door, "when are you going to learn?" For once, Kagi didn't greet him and he knew that Diane had let him out to run.

Diane Heath turned at the sound of the door. When she saw her scowling boss enter the kitchen she raised both brows. Her long, thin face was expressionless but she knew that look. It meant beware of the big bad wolf, but for the past five years she'd come to know when to back away and when not to. Now was not a time to watch him hide away in the study. She'd seen a lot of that after his return from Zaire, licking his wounds after that fiasco of a marriage. She guessed that there was a woman behind his present foul mood.

"Hey, Matt," she said. "Hungry? Dinner's not ready yet, but there's cold ham. Want a sandwich?"

Matt realized he was hungry. "Sure," he said. "You go on with what you're doing. I'll make it." She was mixing dough for her mouthwatering biscuits and Matt suddenly didn't want to eat alone tonight. After a few bites of his sandwich he said, "Why don't you make enough for all of us? You and Andre come on over."

"Thanks, but can't tonight. We have a seven-thirty meeting." Diane turned to see the disappointment on Matt's face and she wished she could change her plans.

"Oh, I forgot," Matt, said. Andre still attended meetings for recovering alcoholics, and his wife always attended her family support group. "Maybe another time."

"Bet on it," Diane said. "Seen Bron today?" Thinking about his animals was sure to chase away Matt's funky mood.

"This morning. Any change?"

"No. But Andre took him to Doc Faselli for another shot. He's being made as comfortable as he can be in his condition." She sucked in her breath, and her thin lips pursed in a scowl. "That man oughtta be shot with you know what and put in jail for stinkin'," she said. "Andre said you called your lawyer. What'd he say?" After putting the pan of biscuits in the oven, she turned to Matt, her hands on her hips.

"He'll get to work on it. Said he doesn't expect Sellers's blustering to turn into anything. Bron was healthy when he left here. Faselli'll vouch for his condition." Matt cleaned up after himself and walked to the door. "I'm going out back. See you later."

"Okay." She caught him before he left. "Guests still coming next weekend?"

"Yeah, a couple and their kids from Massachusetts. Be here on Saturday. Guess you can use the same two rooms upstairs."

"Sure. If there's anything special you need, just let me know."

"Will do," Matt said and went outside.

Diane watched him through the window, noticing the relaxed shoulders and his easy stride toward the buildings. Whatever or whoever had riled him up was relegated to the back burner. Satisfied she'd done her bit to put it there, she began tearing apart a head of romaine lettuce.

"Hey," Andre said, looking up at his boss, then inclined his head toward Bron's cage. "He's resting easy, now."

"Hey, Bron," Matt said to the dog, who was too weak to get up but wagged his curly tail and whimpered a greeting. To Andre, Matt said, "Doc say how long?"

Andre shook his head. "No."

In that one short answer, both men knew Bron's fate. Matt patted the dog's back and talked to him in soothing tones. After a while he stood and walked to another cage. "I'm betting on that family to take a liking to this little guy," he said. "How's he doing?" Matt didn't like to name his animals. Prevented confusion when they were sold. Owners preferred naming their own pets. He spoke to the playful pup that lapped up the attention, licking Matt's fingers and making contented sounds. The three-month-old had yet to find his yodeling voice.

"He's good," Andre said. "Ready to go, if everything works out." After a second, he said, "If it's no sale, you've got somebody else in mind?"

Surprised, Matt shook his head. "No. Why?"

"One of the part-time kids has taken a liking to him."

"Oh?" Matt said. The teenagers, who worked at the kennels as dog exercisers, frequently took a liking to the dogs but couldn't afford the basenji. "He wants a pup?"

Andre looked amused. "Only that one," he said. "He's doing a great job in conning his mother into making it a birthday present."

Matt smiled. "Oh, really?"

"Yep."

"Hmm, you guys should have let me know. We could have worked something out."

"There'll be others."

"Well, we'll see what happens next week." Matt walked away, checking each dog as he passed, looking for anything unusual and changes in behavior. He knew all the dogs and their idiosyncrasies and could spot abnormal moods in a minute. That's why he was certain that Bron had not shown signs of illness before he was sold. An hour later, Matt left the kennel, leaving Andre to dismiss the staff and to close up for the night.

Diane's meal of short ribs, mashed potatoes, and braised carrots was delicious and Matt felt lonelier than ever while eating at the kitchen table. The quietness of the house did nothing to help chase away the somber feelings that'd plagued him throughout the day. Finishing his meal he found himself walking around the big house, finally dropping on the sofa in the spacious, professionally decorated living room.

After the house was built, he hadn't the slightest idea of what his tastes ran to for fixing up such a formal space. The decorator he'd engaged asked him endless questions about his lifestyle, favorite colors, how frequently he entertained, and before he knew it he had a living space that suited him. A comfortable room dressed in soft blues and grays and shades of white with dark mahogany wood set in various places against the walls. The silk wool carpet was pale gray.

The room was beautiful and inviting without being stiff and Matt thought that his wife-to-be would love the place as much as he did. Of course, if she wasn't pleased, she could redecorate to her heart's content as long as it made her happy.

Matt made a face at the choice he'd eventually made. *His* wife had never laid eyes on the place. Somehow that thought made Matt glad because he knew now that Carlotta would only have shown disdain for his home. Whatever had made him think that such a glamour girl would have been content to live in this house with him? To take to his dogs, helping him to care for them if that was her wish, or doing whatever it was that made her happy. He didn't care, as long as she loved him and wanted to have his kids.

Only days after the ceremony, Matt believed that he already knew the kind of person he'd married. But he'd chosen to ignore her laughing remark that having babies would ruin her figure and hoped that he wasn't crazy about the little things.

After he had discovered her deceitful ways, her words had helped convince him that he'd married the wrong woman.

Matt turned out the lights and went upstairs to his bedroom. Something must have been wrong with his head, he thought, if he was attracted to such women. All he wanted was a woman who would love him for himself and who was willing to take her chances with their future. Fortunes were lost as easily as they were made, and in crunch-time he wanted a woman who wouldn't flee at the first sign of crisis.

Most men, Matt mused, would say that they wanted a woman like their mother, but that was one thing Matt had tried to avoid. He wanted someone who was honest. His mother had known for years about her husband's affairs and instead of confronting him and leaving or putting him out, she'd turned her head. She'd become adept at playing the society matron, acting the dutiful wife, and hosting fashionable parties.

Matt never knew whether his mother was hopelessly in love with Hank Gardiner or just plain frightened to begin a new life of her own. She'd died when he was twenty-three and he'd always wished that he'd had the gumption to ask her why she'd stayed.

Sleep was elusive in the dark room as Matt's thoughts continued to crowd his mind. As always they went back to June Saxon and how he'd found her that morning looking so alone and beautiful. He'd stared at her as if he were a besotted schoolboy.

Later, when he thought of June's relationship with his ex-wife, he cringed, wondering how in the world he could have thought about her with lust in his heart. He was *this* close to playing the damn fool again over a beautiful woman.

Matt closed his eyes. His one last thought was, thank God, she and Lancaster were having a thing.

Chapter Six

"For the second time during this two-minute, early-morning conversation, I'm fine," June said to Beverly.

"You sure do sound fine," Beverly answered. "Nothing like my brother described the other night. We're worried about you, girl."

"Don't be," June answered. "I'm feeling better than I've been feeling. Those headaches, whatever they're coming from, are gone now. Not even thinking about them. I'm on my way out so can't talk now. Are you coming in after work tonight?"

"No, can't, last-minute things to pick up for tomorrow. We decided to cater a lot of stuff, including the meats, so we can enjoy the party too," Beverly said. "You've got the potato salad covered, and the hors d'oeuvres are mine. Mabel Foods has gone international with their new line of frozen party foods. They've got meat and veggie empanadas, Argentinean style, and beef or chicken Thai satay that is delicious."

"I know. The satay will be a first but I'm sure those tiny slivers of meat on small skewers are great also. Need me to do anything else today? Not a problem, you know."

"Nothing," Beverly said firmly. "Just enjoy your day. From the response it looks like no one turned down the invite, so look for a crowd. See ya."

June was telling the absolute truth when she said she was feeling fine. Yesterday, after she'd fallen into a deep sleep, she'd awakened near midnight, starving and with no aches. She'd eaten lightly, flipped TV channels until her meal digested a bit, and promptly fallen back to sleep. She awakened at seven o'clock, a new person, feeling no aftereffects from the painkillers.

Dressed and ready for shopping, June checked the phone directory, jotted down the correct address, and locked her front door. There was one stop she had to make on her way to town. It was almost nine-thirty and everybody should be up and working, she reasoned. "Too bad if they aren't," she muttered.

June couldn't whistle so she just settled for a "whew!" as she sat at the front gate to Gardiner Kennels. The lacquered wood sign with carved letters was so unobtrusive that one would miss it if not specifically looking for the business. The property was surrounded by high black iron gates, and the huge cream-colored house was set back on a slight incline. There was a small house some distance to the left and she wondered if it belonged to the servants. If there were dog kennels on the grounds they were invisible to the passing traffic. She didn't know what she'd expected to see but this was not her vision of a dog business.

To her surprise the gates were not locked and June, wondering if she should have announced her visit, drove through and parked behind a blue Altima. "Must be his Friday car," June muttered as she got out and walked up the steps to ring the bell.

Carlotta gave this up? she thought. June peered through the side glass panel and saw a long center hall with a gleaming wood floor that was stained a deep tan with red tones. If she could get her old wood floors to shine like that she'd pull up the worn carpet. She loved the look of warm wood in some rooms of the house. About to leave, she saw the figure of a woman approaching.

Diane looked in surprise at the visitor. "Good morning," she said. "May I help you?"

"Good morning, my name is June Saxon. I'm here to see Matt Gardiner."

"Oh," Diane said. "He's busy in the kennels with the vet. Was he expecting you?"

June stepped back. "N—no," she said, turning away from the woman's inquisitive stare. "Perhaps this is a bad time. I should have called first."

Diane saw the disappointment in the young woman's eyes, though she tried to hide her face. *Hmm, so this is the reason for the funky mood for the last couple of days,* she thought. "Ms. Saxon?" she called. "Wait a minute. The doctor is probably finishing up. Why don't you come with me and we'll see?"

June hesitated. "I really don't want to disturb him—"

"Then we can come back here to the house and you can sit and listen to my vacuum until he gets here." Diane held out her hand and smiled. "My name's Diane Heath and I work here."

June relaxed, feeling at ease with the woman who walked beside her with quick, short steps, guiding her around the side of the house. When they reached the back, June stopped in awe. There were three long, enclosed structures that she knew to be the kennels, and a few roofed dog runs. She saw a man exercising a basenji and a German shepherd in a run that was enclosed with a six-foot-high, heavy wire fence.

"Andre," Diane said, "Matt's still with Doc?"

"Yes, but they're almost finished." He looked at June and nodded. "Good morning."

"This is my husband, Andre Heath. He works here as well. Andre, meet June Saxon."

"Hi." June liked the man's firm grasp.

"Wait here, Ms. Saxon, I'll let Matt know you're here." Diane walked to the middle building.

June looked around in admiration. The working operation was not visible from the front of the house. The property extended far back to a copse of trees. She looked at the man who'd turned back to the dogs, and watched in fascination as the basenji who was an older dog raced with the shepherd, up and down the long run.

Andre stopped what he was doing and watched her. "First time here?" he asked, already guessing the answer. He'd never seen her before. When she nodded, he said, "Go take a look in that one." He pointed to the first building. "There's more to see there." He nodded and sprinted down the long run and the animals followed him.

Inside the building, June stared at the many cages, some with brass tags on the doors. She saw young pups and adolescent dogs and a few older basenjis that looked at her silently. All had wrinkled foreheads that gave them a puzzled look. They varied in color but had white feet, chest, and tail tips like Kagi. June wondered where the animal was and realized that he must be the owner's pet and stayed in the house.

Curious, she read the different name tags, noticing that a few had the same first name. Avongara. A beautiful red and white older dog's name was Avongara Dosi. Beneath it were the call name, Dosi, and the sire, dam, gender, and year of birth.

Impressed, June walked the length of the kennel, admiring the animals that now made different, odd sounds and jumped excitedly as she passed. "Amazing," she said.

From the doorway, Matt watched June's absorbed study of his animals. Relaxing against the doorjamb, he crossed his arms and observed her manner when she talked to the dogs and their happy response as she passed. Unsure of what he was feeling, he continued to watch silently, knowing that whatever it was, he was all right with her presence and thought that it was the most natural thing in the world to see her in his space. A long time ago he'd envisioned such a scene whenever he married. His jaw tightened. Carlotta in this space was unthinkable.

Matt watched June's side profile as she stood by a cage. The shapely legs that went up to there, and perfect thighs, disappeared under white shorts. A black T-shirt was tucked inside the unbelted shorts and Matt could see the arc of her curvaceous breasts. He'd gotten a glimpse of the valley that led to the soft mounds, and the thought of touching them crowded his mind once again. She stooped to one knee to talk to a dog, and Matt sucked in a breath, but before she turned at the sound, Kagi bounded past him and raced toward June. He pounced on her back, and unbalanced, she went sprawling on the floor.

"Kagi," June said. "Hi, boy. Where'd you come from?" She laughed, patting the playful dog that yodeled happily. Now that she could see him in the daylight, June noticed that the dog had the same red and white color as Avongara Dosi. Kagi was licking her face and June found it hard to move the strong dog. "Hey, you got me trapped," she said, trying to struggle to her feet.

"Can I help?" Matt was standing with outstretched hand. "Kagi, sit," he commanded and the dog obediently moved away and sat.

"Matt," June said. She took his hand and after he easily pulled her to her feet she quickly withdrew her hand. The warm, strong grip had sent an unexpected surge of excitement through her. She busied herself with brushing her legs and the back of her shorts.

"Kagi is strong for his size," Matt said, watching her curiously. "Did he hurt you?"

"No, of course not. Surprised me, though," June answered, recovering from her giddy feeling. She felt the heat rush to her temples. "Seems when you're around, I'm about to fall, lying flat on my back, or already fallen. Tiresome, huh?"

Matt looked amused. He'd never seen her when she wasn't composed. Except when he'd awakened her in her bedroom. She was fiddling with her car keys and looked anxious to leave. "I haven't found that to be so," he said smoothly.

The silence stretched as they stared at each other. Kagi stopped panting and lay down at his master's feet, an expectant eye on both humans as if wondering who was ready to play.

Finally, Matt said, "You wanted to see me?" Surely he wasn't expecting his offer for the house to be accepted this easily? He almost felt deflated.

"Yes," answered June. "I—I came to thank you properly for your concern. For helping me home and then coming by the next day to see if I was still in the land of the living. Yesterday, I'm afraid I was a little out of it, but I remember your visit and I appreciate it."

"You're welcome," Matt said simply, "but you've already thanked me, though you were a bit groggy."

"I remember," June answered, "but . . ." She hesitated. "But?"

"Before you left I had the impression that you were angry at something I said so I want to be sure that in my groggy state I didn't say anything to offend you."

Offend? Why should Caleb's name on your lips offend me? Matt answered in a light tone, "Angry? No. More like feeling the fool for barging in like that." He smiled. "You could have called the police and we wouldn't be standing here now."

His transforming smile was unexpected and so was the drop in her stomach. The high cheekbones and square jaw were accentuated and the cleft in his chin deepened. His full mouth invited her to trace the outline of his thin mustache. Safely putting her hands behind her back, she turned to go. "No," she said. "You were nonthreatening. Anyway, I have to be going. Busy day ahead, and I'm sure I interrupted yours." She waved her hand. "I'm impressed. This is some incredible operation you have."

"Thank you." Matt was watching her carefully. "You think so?"

"Absolutely," June said as they walked, but then she stopped Matt with a touch to his arm. "Why do some of these dogs have the same first name? And why do you give them fancy name tags if you're only going to sell them?"

Matt knew she was unaware of the slight touch to his arm but he could hardly say the same. She had walked to Dosi's cage, but he could swear that her fingers were still touching him.

"Matt?" June turned, curious at his silence and flushed at his silent appraisal.

"They're a hundred percent African descent." Matt moved closer to her and cast his eyes down to the dog that watched them with disinterest. "Avongara is a tribe in Africa and the prefix is used to identify the purebred African basenji. Sometimes, an unscrupulous breeder will use the name for their American-bred dogs."

"Why?"

Matt shrugged. "For more lucrative salability. Prestige. Who knows?"

"Then a lot of yours are American bred?"

"Most of the ones you see here are. I also have a kennel in Zaire, which I visit during the year." *Is she really inter-*

ested in all of this? "When I get serious buyers, I bring the dogs here."

"Africa? Every year?" They were outside and June looked around the expanse of land. "You look quite successful. Could the average Joe afford one of your dogs?"

"If that's his desire," Matt answered. "The range varies. A thousand for a pup isn't unreasonable."

June stared. "Are you sure you don't have another job?"

"This is it."

"Then I have to take my hat off to you. You sure are an incentive for a body striking out on his own and trying to make it," June said. She was thoughtful as they walked toward her car. *Maybe entrepreneurship isn't half bad,* she mused. If there were people who'd pay a thousand for a pet, surely she could find something to do that would give her both satisfaction and a comfortable income.

Matt saw her glance at the house and knew she was curious at the interior. Before they rounded the corner to the front, he stopped. "Have you had breakfast?"

June looked at her watch, wondering where the time went. "It's ten-thirty, Matt." She was curious. "Don't tell me that you're the workaholic, up at dawn, feeding your animals instead of yourself?"

Matt shook his head. "Hardly. Up at seven, yes, but skipping meals, no. At this hour it's time for refueling. Diane has a second pot of coffee going. Care to join me?" He could see her indecision but felt her excitement. It struck him that more than anything at this minute he wanted her inside his home. He waited.

"I . . . I don't want to impose . . ."

"You're not."

June stared up at him. "You know I'm dying to see the inside, don't you?" Before he answered, she said, "It's so beautiful, and yes, I'd love to join you."

"Thank you." Matt signaled to Andre to call Kagi and

when the dog raced away, Matt led June to the back door and opened it. When she stepped inside, he watched her intently.

"This is Kagi's room," Matt said. "The kitchen is through here." He opened the door.

The aroma of fresh brewed coffee hit June's nostrils, and her stomach made a most disagreeable sound. "Oh, pardon me," she said and then grinned. "I did eat this morning, but you wouldn't know it, huh?"

"Diane's coffee does that." Matt looked at the stove and saw biscuits and ham. He gestured to a door near the dog's room. "You can wash up in there," he said. "I'll go upstairs. Be right back."

He returned before she did and when she entered the kitchen he'd fixed two plates of the food and was pouring her coffee as she sat. "Help yourself," he said.

"This is lovely, Matt," June said after sipping the delicious brew and gesturing at the large room. "No, it's fabulous. Definitely a place where two women could work just fine together." She tasted the biscuit. "Mm. Diane?" When he nodded, she asked, "Does she do all your cooking?"

"Yes, she's my housekeeper as well as Andre's right arm when I'm gone. She's a marvelous woman." Matt was thinking of the determined woman who'd stuck by her husband through his time of anger and pain.

June heard the unspoken thought and wondered about Diane's story. She finished her light meal and pushed away from the table. "That was delicious. Thank you." She'd caught him looking at her in the strangest way—the same look she'd seen in the kennel.

Matt stood, clearing the table in a flash, and gestured toward the hall. "Care to look at the rest of the place?" Now why did he sound as if he had cotton in his mouth? he wondered. But he had to see!

June saw that the same reddish wood ran the length of

the hall, partially covered by a dark blue and white paisley-pattern runner. There were several entrances on either side of the hallway and Matt led her to a room where the door was open.

"This is where I work," Matt said and stood aside to let her pass.

After several minutes, June said, "I like it." She didn't tell him that she could see him working behind the huge desk or napping on the soft leather sofa. It was him. Diane must have just polished the furniture, she thought, because the pleasant smell of lemon oil softly scented the room.

Across the hall from the study was another room and Matt stood by the entranceway while she entered. "The living room." Again he hung back and watched her. Why was it so important that she like it? But deep down in his soul, Matt knew and he was almost terrified of the realization. For weeks he'd watched this woman. At first it was curiosity to see if a Carlotta clone was living so near to him. When he'd dismissed that obnoxious notion, he'd told himself he wanted her property. After meeting her and singeing his fingers on her soft skin, he knew that it was more than that. He knew that he'd scheme to visit her, to be near her. Now here she was walking in his home and he wanted her to stay! He wanted *her!*

June was drawn into the room as if she'd been there before. It felt like home. Her grandmother had a big overstuffed chair that must have been in the family for years. June didn't remember how many different makeovers it'd had before it was finally relegated to the trash. Every visitor had promptly gravitated to that chair to her grandfather's consternation but he'd deferred to his guests. June sat in such a chair. It was white with a faint, pale blue, delicate abstract pattern. The rolled arms enveloped her and she laid her head against the high back and closed her eyes.

Matt stayed where he was. Silent. Observant.

June opened her eyes and glanced at the rest of the room taking in the soft colors that complemented the warm, polished woods. Not how she'd expected a bachelor's room to appear, she thought. She wondered if Carlotta had done the decorating. *Had she really been this close and had fled for fear of running into me?* Her eyes roved the room. Impossible! This wasn't Carlotta by a long shot.

Wondering where her thoughts were, Matt was reluctant to disturb her.

June turned to Matt, who was so still. "It's beautiful," she murmured.

Matt's eyes flickered. He was leaning against the wall, arms folded, but he stayed put. He didn't trust being so near her at this second. When she'd closed her eyes and rested her head back, he wanted to feel the softness of her throat and massage her neck. He'd had the urge to run his fingers through her short black hair. The sparse, faint, silvery strands that ran through it shimmered against the soft colors of the chair, and the one tiny, silvery patch on her temple invited his caress. "Thank you." He didn't trust himself to say anymore.

June got up, reluctantly, and suddenly feeling embarrassed, laughed softly to cover her discomfort. "You'd think I'd bought a ticket for a tour," she said. "I think I made myself at home." She was by his side. "You'd better think twice before you let a stranger in here again. It's hard to leave."

"Is it?" Matt breathed deep. She smelled warm and fresh, like soap.

"Yes," June said, a little breathlessly. She was trying to ease by him. He filled the whole doorway. In the kennel, when she'd smelled his sweat and woodsy cologne, she'd maintained her decorum, but now she threatened to make a fool of herself if she didn't get out of there. "I'd better go," she murmured.

Man or woman could not ignore the electricity that crackled between them as she passed. Matt caught her hand and pulled her back to him. "June."

The raspy voice tore at June's senses as the feel of his rugged hand in hers sent her equilibrium into a tailspin. She was speechless as his eyes bored into hers. If a train were bearing down on them she could not have moved fast enough to escape certain death, just as she couldn't escape his lips, not an inch away. As if they weren't her own, she watched her fingers trace the smooth outline of his mustache and she had the giddy thought that she'd gotten her earlier wish. "Matt," she murmured, then touched her lips to his.

Spurred by his long-denied desire, Matt clasped her tightly against his body and kissed her lips hungrily, devouring their sweet tenderness. Encouraged by her response and his need to touch her skin again, he slid his fingers down her bare arm and winced from the exquisite warmth filling his belly. He touched her neck, throat, and wanting more of her, touched the soft breast that was crushed against his chest.

"Matt," June managed against his mouth. But when his lips left hers she had no desire to leave the warmth of his arms, and flustered, she stepped back.

Dropping his hand from her waist after she'd steadied herself, Matt looked down at her, still trying to come to terms with what had just happened. Was he about to let himself be duped again? No. June was not Carlotta! Not in a million years. *Now what?* he wondered. He could see her confusion and he followed her as she stepped into the hall. At the front door, he stopped her, placing his hand over hers on the doorknob.

"June." When he had her attention, he said, "Was this a mistake?"

"Mistake?" June whispered. "How could something like that be?"

His hand tightened over hers. "Then you felt it too?" he said in a tight voice.

"I've got warm blood, Matt."

Matt smiled. "You wouldn't kid a brother, would you?"

Under that smile, June felt like melted cheese on toast and she could only whisper, "No."

"You and Lancaster aren't involved?" Matt asked in a quiet voice.

I was right, June thought. "Caleb's my best friend. He and his sister Beverly." The relief on his face made her feel peculiar. "Is that what you thought?"

Matt nodded. "It looked that way."

"We've been neighbors since I was eight years old. I have his keys and he has mine." June turned the knob and Matt lifted his hand and opened the door. "See you, Matt." She walked down the steps and was surprised to see he'd followed her.

"When?" Matt asked.

"What?"

"Later? About what time? Dinner?"

June stared. "What are you talking about?" This was Carlotta's ex-husband and he wanted a date! But how could she ignore the kiss that still stung her lips?

"Would you have dinner with me tonight?" Matt asked.

"N—no, that's impossible," June said.

"Impossible?"

"Yes. I have lots to do, and tonight, I'll be busy."

"Tomorrow?"

"Tomorrow? No. I'll be busy then too."

Matt could have guessed that but he said, "Can I call you?"

"For a date?"

"That's the idea."

"Matt, I don't see how we can ... you want my house

... and you were ..." Flustered, she stopped, wondering what was so amusing. "What?"

"It's just a date, June," Matt said, his eyes smiling at her consternation.

"Huh, that's what you say," June retorted. "Look what a cup of coffee turned into."

In a relaxed manner, Matt said, "Then think about having dinner with me. Should be even more interesting."

June got in her car. The blue Altima was gone and she surmised that it'd belonged to the vet. "Good-bye, Matt." She waved as she left him watching her.

"Not good-bye, June." Matt was motionless until her car disappeared. Then he turned, whistling for Kagi. When the small dog bounded around the front of the house, Matt bent and scratched his ears. "She liked our home, boy."

"Having fun, Junie Bug?"

"Incredible." At six-thirty in the evening they were sitting on the back steps of Caleb's porch, watching the crowd of revelers. People had begun arriving at four and were still coming, and from the looks of it the steam wouldn't run out of this party until the wee hours. The backyard was packed as well as the inside of the house where people preferred to escape the sun. The buzz of conversation was occasionally interrupted with screams and squeals and backslapping as old friends recognized each other.

June reached over and squeezed his hand. "You and Beverly outdid yourselves," she said. "This is great. You guys really weren't kidding when you made it a point to enjoy this too." Her friends had hired a bartender and two others who sliced the meats and replenished the food.

"Yeah," Caleb said. "Getting too old to finesse with drinks and all that stuff. Nothing wrong with giving a brother a play."

She leaned over and kissed his cheek. "Thank you."

"It's worth it to see your old smile where it belongs," Caleb answered. He cocked his head and raised a thick brow. "Me and Bev would've done this sooner if we thought this was all it would take to get you back." His eyes scanned the crowd. "Or was it your old boyfriend that did it?"

"Boyfriend? Who?" She saw his pointed look, then laughed. "Wilton? Oh, please. Look at him. Such pompous conceit." June stared at the handsome man, with the mocha skin and deep-set, black, mesmerizing eyes. He was less than five-ten but carried himself as if he were seven feet tall. His nose was held so high up in the air he wouldn't have seen a deadly python crawling at his feet. Even then he probably would have sniffed and kicked it to the curb. "Yet, he's absolutely gorgeous," June murmured.

"He's got a right to be proud," Caleb said. "Did he tell you about his business?"

"Who hasn't he told? Yes, I know all about his fabulous Web site business. Took off like a rocket and he hasn't looked down at the rest of us mortals since. Why couldn't I have done something like that?" The answer darkened her eyes.

"Tsk, tsk, Junie Bug, is that jealousy I hear?" He ignored her thoughts of Carlotta.

"I told you it was going to be like this. I had to tell him I was leaving for my new job in Paris in a few weeks." June looked away from Caleb's disbelieving stare.

"You lied to the man?" Caleb held back the humor that threatened to cover his face.

June flashed him a look. "So, what would you have done to shut up that stuffed windbag?" She made a face. "If I only had one chance to meet your Paris friend, then I know my lie would become true. I'd convince him to hire me on the spot."

Caleb didn't respond to that but said, "I probably would

have been just as creative with Wilton Maitland.'' Caleb
stood. ''Look, why don't you mingle? I heard more cars
pull up. Catch you later, Junie.'' He kissed her cheek. ''Enjoy
the night. It's yours.'' He winked, and then walked away,
moving easily through the crowd.

June went inside, making her way past the crowded living
room and avoiding the equally congested family room.
Caleb's study was empty and she wondered why he hadn't
locked the door to maintain his privacy. She sat in a chair
by the window and spied Caleb greeting some people. A
pretty woman smiled and then introduced her two compan-
ions. When Caleb moved, allowing June to see the two men,
she gasped. ''Matt?''

''No, I'm afraid not. My name is Ivon Raleigh.''

June whirled at the deep baritone voice coming from the
doorway. ''Oh,'' she said. Had she been suddenly transported to fairyland? A bronzed prince if she ever saw one
was staring at her curiously. Where in the world did such
a heavenly looking creature come from? she wondered.

''May I join you?'' Without waiting for a reply, the man
sat casually on the window ledge, not far from June's crossed
knees.

June had never seen the man in Oyster Bay before and
couldn't imagine that he'd been a classmate. Looks like his
weren't easily forgotten. He gave new meaning to the words
tall, dark, and handsome. His heart-shaped, dark brown face
was almost gaunt with hollows in his cheeks that highlighted
his cheekbones. His almond-shaped brown eyes were the
shade that changed colors with his moods and could appear
as cold and black as obsidian. His finely chiseled head was
in profile as he turned to look out the window, and June
liked the way he wore his curly black hair with the long
sideburns. She was almost startled when his eyes found hers.

''What is your name?''

''June Saxon.''

"Ah, happy birthday, Ms. Saxon." He bowed his head. "Then I am your guest, *sí?*"

"Yes," June answered. She hadn't noticed his accent before but could detect the precise speech of a foreigner. *African? Spanish? Yet he injects Spanish into his speech.* "You can say that. My friends are giving this party for me. Caleb and Beverly Lancaster. How do you know them?"

"I am a friend of Caleb's." Ivon watched her with interest. "You are very beautiful, Ms. Saxon." He looked at her in surprise when she appeared flushed. "You are embarrassed that you are beautiful?"

How strange he is, June thought, relaxing under the man's scrutiny. She liked his directness. "Thank you. Please call me June. Are you enjoying yourself?" she asked, hoping that he'd forgotten his question.

"Yes, I am, thank you." His gaze roamed over her and as if making a decision, he turned his head to the wall of books. "A huge library. I wonder that my hardworking friend has time for such pleasing distractions." He stood and strode to the bookcases and studied the many diverse titles.

June watched the man, dressed elegantly in tailored cream slacks and a collared, black, short-sleeve shirt and black shoes. "You don't?" June asked. He glanced at the volumes of English and American literature, African folklore, and mythology; works by African and African-American authors; business and finance books; and several mystery novels. He picked up a book and walked back to his window seat, a curious look in his eyes.

"I miss such as this." Ivon held up the slim volume.

"Langston Hughes," June murmured. "A favorite?"

Ivon nodded. "He saw us as we are. Even today. Very little changes."

"I agree." She thought of a poem that reminded her of her life now, and she smiled.

"You have a favorite?"

"Several," June answered, "but I'm thinking about one that's pretty apropos for my life right now."

"May I ask which one?"

" 'Still Here.' "

"Ah." Ivon nodded, then said in Spanish, "You were hurt."

June replied easily in the same language. "I'm over it now. I'm a survivor, I suppose." He answered that she spoke the language well and continued to speak Spanish. After a while, June realized that they had switched from poetry to fiction to world and social problems, speaking in Spanish and English. Almost an hour had passed in French, the language that they'd slid into with such ease that June had barely noticed, when they were interrupted by car doors slamming.

"Oh," she said, getting up from the chair and going to the window. "I think some of my guests are leaving."

Ivon was sitting in the high-back desk chair and he observed June beneath his changing dark eyes. "Then you must go," he said, standing and walking toward her. "I've enjoyed our conversation, June. Thank you for sharing your birthday with me."

June offered her hand and he gripped it. "I hope you're not leaving yet," she said. "It's still early."

"I'm not leaving," Ivon said. "Go, you must see to the others. I'm afraid I've been very selfish, monopolizing your time."

June left him staring at her with those enigmatic eyes. "What a fascinating man," she said, as she went in search of Caleb. She wanted to know more about the mysterious Ivon Raleigh. Her head down, deep in thought, she nearly bumped into the man who was walking down the hall toward her.

"Excuse me," June said, then looked in surprise. Lord! She'd forgotten that he was here. "Matt?"

"June." Matt stared at June and then at the man who followed her from the room she'd just exited. The man nodded at the couple and without a word passed them and walked outside.

"Happy birthday, June." Matt raked her with a harsh look.

"Matt?"

Chapter Seven

June couldn't miss the look that Matt had given Ivon and then her after he'd surmised they'd been together. *He's jealous!* That idea was still roiling around in her head while she was deciding whether to be pleased or annoyed. That one kiss they'd shared made her his? *I don't think so,* she fumed inwardly.

"You did say that you were busy tonight, didn't you?" Matt said softly, his eyes never leaving hers.

"What?" The slight incline of his head in the direction Ivon had gone left no doubt as to what he was referring to.

"Dinner?"

"Yes," June said. "My party." She stared at him. "I had no idea that you knew Caleb. I—I was surprised to see you pull up."

Matt raised a brow. "That was over an hour ago, June." His voice remained low.

"I—I was engrossed in the most fas . . ." She stopped, wondering why on earth she had to explain to him. "I'm sorry I was so rude to my guests," she said. "If you were neglected, please forgive me."

"Neglected?" Matt's eyes flickered dangerously, but in seconds the anger was gone. "Caleb and his charming sister Beverly are excellent hosts. No, we weren't neglected."

"We?"

"My brother George and his wife. Toi is the invited guest. I'm a tagalong."

After a second of silence, Matt said, "Come. I think you've deprived your guests of your presence long enough." He gently touched her elbow and walked with her down the hall. When they reached the living room, Matt, without a word, kept walking toward the front door and went outside.

Before June could react to Matt's cold behavior and abrupt departure, Beverly grabbed her hand.

"Where have you been?" Beverly accused, her dark eyes flashing. "I wanted you to meet the most fascinating man. He's gorgeous and filthy rich." It was after eight o'clock and had turned dusk. Although many people had gone, a good crowd had left the lawn and the backyard and assembled on the porch and inside the big house. Those who felt the urge to dance were in the living room while others, still catching up on their lives, conversed in small, scattered groups.

Fascinating. That word certainly is being used a lot tonight, June thought. Matt knew she'd been about to describe Ivon Raleigh as fascinating when she'd caught herself.

"Are you listening to me?" Beverly said. "What's wrong with you?" She eyed her friend suddenly, her brows furrowed. "You're not—"

"No, I'm okay, Bev. I met a great guy too. I was looking for Caleb to give me more info on the man."

"Well, he can't possibly be as interesting as my man,"

Beverly said with a gleam in her eyes. ''This one lives in your own backyard, and wait'll you hear who he is.''

Disinterested, June searched the crowd, looking for Ivon Raleigh. ''Really?''

''You know those hors d'oeuvres you've been raving about? Well, the owners of Mabel Foods are your neighbors!''

''My neighbors?'' June look interested. ''But I know everyone around here.''

Beverly waved a hand in exasperation. ''Oh, not neighbor, neighbors. You know, in the general area!''

''Oh, okay, you've got my attention. Who's the handsome, filthy-rich man who deigns to attend my birthday party?''

''There's two of them. The older one is George Gardiner. He's here with his wife Toi, who was in high school the same year as Caleb. And the other one, the handsome guy, is Matt Gardiner!''

June stared at her friend in disbelief, wondering if she'd heard correctly. ''What did you say?''

''Close your mouth, girl,'' Beverly said. ''Floored you, didn't I?'' Her friend was looking peculiar. ''What'd I say to make your face turn green and your eyes turn red? You look like a witch ready to scald somebody in her cooking pot.''

''Matt Gardiner is Mabel Foods?'' June said in a scratchy voice.

''Henry Gardiner and his five sons. He's retired and lives in Florida and the sons run the company. George and Matt live here in Oyster Bay, the others live nearby.''

June made a sound and her eyes darkened.

''What's wrong with you?''

''Caleb didn't tell you?'' June turned a dark look on Beverly.

''Tell me what?''

''Matt Gardiner is the man Carlotta ran off to marry.''

"Carlotta? And Matt Gardiner? Married?" Beverly closed her eyes briefly as if to clear her head. "You never told me?" Her eyes were accusing. "When did you find out?"

June felt weary all of a sudden. The world was full of rotten surprises, she thought. They walked to Caleb's study and closed the door. She explained to Beverly about the unopened letter from the attorney. When she finished she looked at Beverly. "I'm sorry. I thought Caleb told you the whole story. Guess I was too caught up with other things."

Beverly apologized. "I wasn't thinking. You did have other things on your mind. Any word from the doctor yet?"

June shook her head. "Uh-uh. Too soon." She shrugged it off. "Anyway, that is news. The Gardiners. So all this time we've been eating Mabel Foods, the millionaires were our neighbors? Incredible."

"Right? But they're so unassuming and down to earth," Beverly said. "Toi married into the family but she's a fun lady. Her husband is quiet, but has a repertoire of funny stories. Matt? He's gorgeous, June. No wonder your friend went dipsy doodle on you."

June crossed her eyes. "You're excusing her?"

"Of course not," Beverly retorted. "Don't be silly. I just meant that the man is fine and it's no wonder a woman could be charmed by him."

June gave a short laugh. "Guess you're right about that."

Beverly heard the unspoken words. "Something happen between you two?" When her friend remained silent, she said, "June?"

"I like him." June looked at Beverly. "I kissed him and he kissed me back."

"And?"

"We both liked it."

Beverly sighed. "Am I going to get this piecemeal? What happened after that?"

"He wants to see me again."

Tapping her fingers on the desk, Beverly resigned herself to hearing everything, but at the speed of slow-dripping molasses. "And you don't?" She thought for a second, then said, "Because of Carlotta?"

June hesitated. "I had thought that at one time, but no, not because of Carlotta. Last night, I'd decided to see him again, but now? I don't think so."

"Why? The other man you met tonight is more to your liking?"

"No, it's not that. Surprisingly, I never thought about Ivon in those terms, and you know, I think he wasn't romantically inclined either. I didn't get the slightest hint that he was regaling me with his stories because he was hitting on me. We just talked about so many interesting things, including his travels."

"Matt's not as interesting?"

"Oh yes," June breathed. "But in another way. He's so strange. He's cold, warm, hot, and compassionate toward his animals. He's wonderful."

"Is that so? Then why is it that you can't see this *wonderful* man again?"

June turned bitter eyes on her friend. "He lied to me."

Beverly stared. "Lied?" Caleb, who opened the door, interrupted her.

"Here you two are," he said, grabbing June's arm. "This is a party, not a gabfest. C'mon, we want to eat cake." He pulled her from the chair and steered her down the hall to the waiting crowd.

Beverly followed, wondering if her friend knew how she'd sounded when talking about Matt Gardiner. In all their shared talks about relationships, she had never heard her call a man wonderful in such reverent tones, and realized that June was falling hard. But she knew that there was no way that June would tolerate dishonesty in someone so close to her. What had Matt Gardiner lied about? she wondered.

Matt caught his breath when June entered the room. He ignored the glance his brother gave him and watched the woman who was stealing his heart. He realized he'd acted the fool when he'd walked away from her. Why couldn't she spend time with other men she found fascinating, because surely that's what she'd been about to call Ivon Raleigh?

The man had looked vaguely familiar to Matt, but it was George who'd pointed out exactly who the man was and appeared surprised that Matt had never met the wealthy Paris banker during his trips to the city.

"I never knew June and Beverly in school. They're both lovely women," Toi Gardiner said to her husband. Her bright eyes were her prettiest feature, round and black and lit up when she smiled. Her pixie-cut hairstyle framed her dark beige face. "I think it would be great to have them over to dinner sometime, don't you think?"

George glanced at Matt, who was eyeing June. "As guests because you enjoy them or because you want to match them up?" His gaze followed his brother's.

Toi gave an observant look at her husband and her brother-in-law, who was strangely quiet. She looked at June cutting her cake and talking animatedly with her guests. She had the kind of laughing eyes and smile that could brighten a cloudy day. Toi watched Matt and wondered why her infectious radiance hadn't infected him.

George saw his wife's perplexed look. "Uh-uh," he whispered. "Don't go there. Not yet." He took her hand and folded it under his arm. "Tell you later."

"We're about ready to call it a night, Matt," George said. "What about you?"

"You two go on. I'll follow in a while."

The two men walked behind Toi as she said good night

to some friends. In a low voice, George said, "Have you two spoken tonight?"

"For a minute," Matt answered, warily.

"You're going to change that before you leave, right?"

"Hope to."

"Good idea," George answered. "She looks like a special lady."

Matt nodded.

"Hope she's not the one who got away."

"It's not like that."

"Then I think you should do something about that. Quick." George walked away, leaving his brother staring at June.

"So, what'd you think?" Caleb said to June. It was close to midnight and they were outside on the porch waving to the last guests as they drove off. "We done good?"

June smiled. "It was great. I haven't enjoyed myself like that in Lord knows when. Thanks again, Caleb." She leaned over and kissed him on the cheek.

"Not a problem, Junie Bug. You know that."

Though the porch light was dim, June caught the gleam in her friend's eye. "So what are you looking so pleased about? Did I miss something here, tonight? A new woman in your life, maybe?" she teased.

"Congratulations, lady," Caleb said, unable to contain himself any longer.

"On what?" June couldn't help but be infected by his big grin and she smiled.

"Your new job."

"Come again? I knew we should have hidden the cognac."

"In Paris. You've got the job if you want it."

"Caleb Lancaster, what are you babbling about? Your friend called you?" June held back a squeal of disbelief.

"Better than that. He let me know before he left tonight." He burst out in a big laugh. "You were interviewed tonight, June. Ivon loved you."

June's jaw dropped. "Ivon Raleigh!"

"Yes." Caleb lost the smile and spoke quietly. "That's the way he wanted to meet you. Spontaneous reaction."

"Incredible! Unbelievable! But I loved that man, Caleb. You painted such a horrible picture of him." *The French. The Spanish. The accent.* "I should have guessed!" June hugged her knees and rocked back and forth. "I've got the job!"

"The way I described him is the way he is," Caleb said firmly. "Don't go getting stardust in your eyes when you get over there. The man is a taskmaster."

"I'm not afraid of hard work. You know that."

"And romantic ideas?" Caleb asked.

June scoffed. "With him? Not on your life. We didn't even go there. Not once."

"Good. He's a confirmed bachelor and I don't want you getting hurt." He smiled at her and said, "He'll be faxing all the particulars to me in a day or so but he said for you to prepare to leave in two weeks for about a ten-day stay. You'll actually be starting after Labor Day when he gets back in town."

"Two weeks?" June could have burst with joy. "I think if I get up from here, I'll be walking on a cloud."

"Don't worry, I'll catch you."

June looked at him. "You've been doing that for a long time with me and Beverly, haven't you?" Her eyes softened as her heart filled with affection for her friend.

"What are big brothers for?" Caleb asked softly.

A lump stuck in June's throat and she stood up. In a

choked voice she said, "I'll see if Bev needs anything before I go. Good night. See you tomorrow?" She hurried inside.

The wait staff had picked up and cleaned the kitchen, leaving it spotless. June found Beverly rearranging the leftovers in the refrigerator.

"Thanks, Beverly," June said, giving her friend a big hug. "It was the best."

"Only for you, girl," Beverly said, returning the hug. She turned out the light. "I'm going upstairs to crash. I'm beat." She smiled at June. "You did enjoy yourself, didn't you?"

"Tremendously."

"Caleb told you?" Beverly's eyes twinkled.

"About Paris?"

"Yes," Beverly answered. "So the fascinating man was Ivon Raleigh." She hugged June around the waist. "I'm happy for you, sweetie. You deserve it."

"Thanks. I'm looking forward to it. Just that it's still so new."

Beverly had one foot on the stairs. "Do you think that you may change your mind about going?"

"Why would I do that?"

"Because I think you're beginning to have feelings for Matt Gardiner."

June's eyes clouded. "Had, Beverly. Past tense."

Beverly gave her a long look. "Sure about that? Have you spoken with him again tonight?"

"No. I never saw him again. So many people," she answered.

"You have two weeks," Beverly said. She kissed June on the cheek. "Sleep on it. You'd be surprised what a new dawn brings. Sweet dreams."

June went out the back door and saw Caleb talking to Matt. She looked from one to the other.

"Matt will walk you home, June," Caleb said. He shook

hands with the other man, turned to June, and said, "Good night." He went inside and turned out the kitchen light, leaving the back in semidarkness.

"Matt. I thought you'd gone."

"Can we talk, June?" Matt stared down at her with a penetrating look. "I know it's late, but I must apologize."

"That's not necessary."

"Ten minutes?"

June started across the grass. "It's not going to take me that long to open my back door."

Matt kept in step with her. When she put the key in the lock he stopped her from opening the door. "You avoided me for the rest of the evening knowing I wanted to apologize for my rudeness. Why?"

"Don't touch me." June moved her hand from under his on the doorknob. From the bright floodlight, she could see the puzzled look on his face. "I don't know what makes you think that I'd want to have any more to do with you after your lies."

"What lies?"

Her laugh was without mirth. "You told me that breeding dogs is your only job."

"It is."

June shook her head. "Here I was admiring the evidence of your success so much, the determination and the courage that it must have taken, that I was considering taking another stab at doing something again. I thought it incredible that you jumped out there to do something so far out as breeding a practically unheard of dog!" She flashed an angry look. "You didn't have a care in the world if you failed. Mabel Foods was your safety net. How many other starving entrepreneurs have such a velvet cushion?"

Matt stepped back, surprised at the hurt he heard in her voice, and then realized the pain from his ex-wife's dishonesty had resurfaced. "I wasn't being deceitful," he said quietly.

"Oh, what does it matter?" June said impatiently. "Thank God, my prayers have been answered and I'll be far away from here. Maybe I'll be surrounded by hardworking, honest people, and what a breath of fresh air that will be."

"Far away?" Matt's brows knitted. "What do you mean?"

"I've accepted a job in Paris. I leave in two weeks."

"Paris?"

"Yes." June's face clouded briefly. "Good night, Matt." She went inside and closed the door with a firm click.

The sound of the lock slipping into place was so final. Matt walked slowly around to the front of the house where his car was parked. Almost numb with her confession, he shook his head in disbelief. "Paris?" Matt whispered.

Once before, he'd foolishly lost his heart in that city of lovers. Must he return to be reminded of his past folly? But he knew as long as June remained there he would be returning; to bring back the woman he loved. Reliving yesterday, his body reacted as if she were sitting beside him. Her smiles of delight at his animals and the contentment he'd felt when she was in his home: the feel of her lips and her sweet scent were making him squirm. No, he wanted her. Had to have her. He couldn't chance not ever having her in his life. "She belongs here, with me."

Then I think you should do something about that. Quick. George's words burned in his mind. "You've never been more right, brother," Matt muttered.

Matt turned out his bedside light and prayed that his plan would work. If it failed, he couldn't entertain thoughts of the dismal future.

* * *

June awoke the next morning to the insistent buzz of her front doorbell. "Eight o'clock," she said as she hurried from the room belting her robe. Startled at seeing the well-known catering truck parked out front, she peered at the man who was weighted down with two tall metal containers in each hand. He looked pleadingly at her to open the door.

"Delivery for Ms. June Saxon." He indicated one container. "Hot stuff." As if wondering when she was going to admit him, he added, "And heavy."

June stepped aside. "The kitchen is down the hall."

"Everything's been taken care of," the man said on his way out the door. "Just leave the containers on the front porch. They'll be picked up. Oh, the note's on top." He hopped down the steps.

If not dinner, breakfast? Matt.

Before June could react to the note, the front doorbell rang. She opened it to Matt.

"Good morning."

June couldn't tell from his voice or his enigmatic expression how he was feeling. Expecting to breakfast with her or being shown the door. His idea of a peace offering was unique and what did she have to lose by listening? Besides, the aroma of the coffee was tantalizing her taste buds. She stepped back.

"Good morning, Matt. Come in, please." But he stayed where he was. "What's wrong?"

"I apologize."

"Accepted. Breakfast, instead of dinner, is fine. Please come in." Matt nodded and she stepped aside to let him in. When he walked by her she caught the scent of his fresh-smelling woodsy aftershave and closed her eyes briefly. What was she doing to herself?

Matt caught glimpses of the rooms as he walked down the long hallway. The big square kitchen was as he'd imagined it

and would suit his needs, perfectly. Very little would have
to be done to ready it for what he had in mind.

June saw his discreet inspection but chose to ignore it for
the moment. She gestured to the table. "Would you unpack
please? I have to brush my teeth. Excuse me." She made
a hasty exit, escaping his frank appraisal of her contours
underneath the light cotton robe.

"Certainly," Matt said. "No hurry." He busied himself
with opening the first of the two tall aluminum towers. He
was thoughtful as he laid out the food. She'd accepted his
apology for his rudeness, but not for what she thought was
his deceit. Her cold, aloof attitude was the same as when
he'd first appeared, making an offer for her house, and Matt
understood how much she was still suffering from her former
friend's betrayal. Last night he'd promised to do all in his
power to help her overcome that fiasco in her life, but he
knew it was going to be one of the hardest things he'd ever
attempted to do in his life. He had to win her trust before
he could win her love.

June did a quick wash-up, changed into shorts and a T-
shirt, and, in slippers, padded to the kitchen. She stood in
the doorway, looking in amazement. "All of that was in
those?" She waved at the containers.

"Brown's Catering does do it all," Matt answered, noting
the slogan on a tag that hung discreetly from the handle.
'We do it all.' "Come. It's still hot." He waited for her to
join him before he sat.

"A real Sunday get-down breakfast," June said as she
poured coffee in both their cups. The containers had held
hot and cold stuff. There were butter, peach and strawberry
preserves, milk and cream, mixed fruit cups, orange and
tomato juice. Waffles and pancakes still held steam, and the
smell of the spicy bacon and sausage patties teased the
nostrils and tempted the palate. There were scrambled eggs
and grits. The maple syrup was warm.

June chose hot corn bread over the biscuits, buttered and slathered it with the peach preserves. "Mm," she said. "There's something to be said about choices." She decided on the eggs, waffles, and bacon while they were still hot.

Matt heaped his plate with some of everything except the grits. "I didn't know what you liked," he said simply. "Now I do." He was intent on lightening and sweetening his coffee, and didn't acknowledge the look she'd flashed him.

They ate in silence, savoring the tastily prepared food.

Matt, sitting across from her at the breakfast table, gave June a heady sensation. One part of her welcomed his presence as if it were so natural; the other part rejected him as the enemy. He wanted nothing from her but her house. *But he never lied to you about that.* She ignored the inner voice.

Both were on second cups of coffee. "That was delicious. Thank you," June said.

"My pleasure." Matt saw the wary look in her eyes. She was still suspicious of him. "This room is as I imagined," he said. "It's big, functional, but homey." Where could he start to begin to put her at ease?

June sipped her coffee. "It's home," she answered, eyeing him over her cup.

Matt didn't miss her meaning. Unwilling to go there, he said, "You've lived alone since your grandmother died?"

"How did you know that?" She answered her own question. "Oh, you're a Gardiner."

"Don't," Matt answered. He finished his coffee and set his cup down softly, but gripped the handle.

June shrugged. "You're right. What's the use?" She looked around the bright, yellow and white, newly decorated room and could feel the presence of her grandparents. "My father was born in this house," she said. "When I was eight, my parents were killed. My grandparents raised me here."

"You miss them." He saw the softening of her body and

heard the wistfulness in her voice. He realized then how much friends meant to her.

"Yes. They were my family and this has been my home. I can't remember any other." June gestured. "Everything I learned about cooking I learned in this room. I baked my first apple pie from scratch when I was eleven. Boy, what a mess, but Grandma Belle kept about her business, said I had to finish what I started." She grinned at the memory.

Matt relaxed as she relaxed. "How'd it turn out?" he asked.

"Terrible! Grandpa raved over it but I didn't miss him trying to discreetly spit out bits of apple core and seeds. It was a sugary, gooey disaster." The memory made June chuckle softly.

"How do your pies taste now?"

"Delicious," she answered proudly. "Even with that cantankerous old oven, me and Grandma turned out some pretty decent meals. Grandpa would have it no other way. He loved his food." June saw Matt's glance at the appliance. "Oh, not that one. I finally got rid of Grandma's old iron horse, last year when I received some money from ..." She stopped short of mentioning Carlotta's name.

Matt knew that it was his money that had bought her new stove. He tried changing the subject but she stopped him.

"I know why you're here, Matt. You want this house and I know you're going to do all in your power to get it." June sat back in her chair and crossed her arms against her breasts, tucking her hands beneath her elbows. "I expect that we won't be acting so civilly toward each other in the future, so I'm going to give you the grand tour that I know that you want, and then we can get it on, so to speak." She hesitated briefly. "Friday, after seeing your business and your home, and yesterday, learning that you came from wealth—my curiosity is strained. Why did Carlotta leave you?" June saw his easy manner change to one of wariness, and the sudden dark look of anger in his eyes startled her. *Does he still love her?* The thought was unsettling, and June's hands clenched into fists.

It was a long time since Matt had willingly spoken of his ex-wife. Looking at the hurt in June's eyes and realizing that he and Carlotta had put it there, he was determined to absolve himself of her suspicions of an alliance with her former friend.

"There's something about me that I want you to know, June."

"I'm really not interested in learning about you, Matt." *Liar!* She wondered if he could see the evidence of her lie.

Matt studied her. After a long pause, he said, "If you want to satisfy your curiosity, hearing my story is part of it."

June met his unwavering gaze. She rose and gestured to the hall. "Can we sit on the porch?"

"I'd like that," Matt answered and followed her. He sat down in a chair on the porch and stretched out his long legs, crossing them at the ankles. The view of the as yet unoccupied beach held his attention. From across the road he'd seen her many times and wondered who the person was that had sat in this very chair countless times as he'd watched. She'd never paid him or anyone else the slightest mind, as she had been lost in her thoughts. It was a place to be calm and meditative. *But you want to take it away from her!*

"Matt?" June saw the frown crease his forehead. He turned to her and she knew that he'd been thinking of her.

"I had my marriage to Carlotta annulled, three months into the union."

"Annulled?" June was flabbergasted. "You?"

"Carlotta and I dated off and on, whenever her runs brought her to Paris and our paths crossed." Matt's mouth twisted into a grim line. "Whenever I didn't see her, I missed her."

"Matt, you don't have to tell me—"

"I want to satisfy your curiosity," Matt answered. He held her gaze.

"Okay," she answered. She steeled herself against hearing him admit that he loved Carlotta. Why did she put herself into these torturous situations? She knew that the man who was sitting across from her was about to confess his love for another woman; the man that she was hopelessly falling in love with no matter how much she denied it. The only way she could stop from playing the fool was to flee to Paris. She silently chanted, *Think Paris, June,* over and over while she stared into those mesmerizing, dark eyes.

"Carlotta thought she'd married a wealthy man."

Astounded, June said, "But you are!"

Matt shook his head. "She only saw the trappings of what she thought to be my wealth. She saw a man she thought lived in Paris, able to lavish her with—well, someone who wasn't caught up in a nine-to-five situation, traveling frequently between Paris and Zaire. She had illusions of riches and prestige."

"She never knew what you did?" June was amazed.

Matt smiled at her expression. "When Carlotta married me, she never knew what I did for a living."

"Incredible!" June whispered. And *that* was the woman she'd chosen as a business partner?

"Growing up with my family, working in the business during summers, I knew I didn't want Mabel Foods to be my chosen career." Matt's voice lowered as he remembered. "My mother knew. My father did too, but he laughed at me as if branching out on my own was unthinkable. His sons had a calling, he said. To follow in their father's footsteps." He brushed a hand over his eyes. "I stopped working at the plant in the summer and worked as a seasonal in the post office, even during college. I studied business and marketing, and after graduation I worked at the post office full-time while breeding my dogs part-time.''

''You lived at home?'' June asked.

''Yes. My mother refused to let my father deny me a roof over my head, knowing that I didn't have the proper place to care for my dogs.''

''How many did you have?''

''Two.'' Matt grinned. ''For breeding. I had to start from somewhere.''

June smiled. ''Your mother was supportive.''

''Yes. If not for her, I wouldn't have progressed as quickly as I did.'' His eyes held a shadow. ''She gave me a hefty monetary graduation present. I was able to travel to Zaire and set up a small operation there. I brought back another purebred and my business was jump-started.''

''Your father never interfered?''

Matt shook his head. ''No. After he saw my determination he and my brothers let up, just teased me after that. When my mother died when I was twenty-three, it was an inheritance that made me independent. But I stayed with the post office until I was twenty-seven. I'd put all my money into the business, and the steady job was a security blanket.'' He held her stare. ''I didn't want to have to go to my father or draw on other income.''

''I—I didn't know,'' June whispered. ''I accused you—''

''How could you know?'' Matt interrupted. ''But you're right. Any fall *would* have been broken by falling back on my other assets.'' He saw her unasked question. ''I don't deny that I'm independently wealthy. I have a more than generous income from my share of the family business.''

''But you didn't use it,'' June said.

''Not then, because I worked hard. My mother believed in what I was doing, and besides proving to myself that I could do it, I owed her.'' He paused. ''But after I was established and making a living, I did use my personal income to build my home.''

June was silent as she reflected on his confession. After a moment she said, ''Did you ever tell Carlotta about your job?''

''Yes.'' A smile caught the edges of his mouth. ''I thought I would have to resuscitate her after I explained. Now she's beset with the stigma of having married a civil servant.'' He couldn't hold back the chuckle. ''When I told her where my permanent residence was and that I raised dogs for a living, I really thought getting a medic for her was a good idea.''

June smiled. The scene must have been hilarious. ''You didn't gloat, did you, Matt?'' But she could see the glee in his eyes, however brief.

''For a minute,'' Matt answered truthfully.

June thought that for all the anguish of the past year, it was worth it to envision the perfect, beautiful Carlotta Graham eating humble pie and walking away with egg all over her flawless face. A soft chuckle escalated into a big grin and her eyes danced. *If she only knew!* June caught Matt's look. ''Thank you,'' she said simply.

Matt nodded gravely. Though June understood where he was coming from, she was still unaware of his major agenda. It would take more than a few breakfasts to accomplish the impossible: to get her to forgo Paris and stay here with him. Two weeks wasn't nearly enough time to convince her that the man who was trying to disrupt her whole world was also the man who'd fallen in love with her.

Chapter Eight

Joggers, walkers, and a few sun worshipers disturbed the serene quiet of the sunny beach. June watched the activity with interest, vaguely wondering if her residence in Paris would be close to the water. Or would she have to travel for hours to catch a whiff of the ocean breeze or feel the sand beneath her feet? She stirred, realizing that the man who was sitting at her elbow could provide all she needed to know about the distant city. June felt his gaze and she turned to meet his stare.

Matt would have bet on her thoughts. "You love this place," he said in a low voice. "Why are you going away?"

"I do and it's my home." Her look was direct and she was certain he hadn't missed her meaning.

Matt understood but wasn't baited into going there. "Why Paris, June?"

"To work. I've gotten used to eating and clothing myself and keeping a roof over my head." June saw the brief shadow cross his face and was annoyed with herself for regretting her sarcasm. *I'm the one struggling to survive*, she told herself. "Last night I was offered a position that I'd be crazy to turn down," June said.

"Ivon Raleigh?" Matt knew without a doubt that the wealthy banker was June's new employer. *Why did that make him feel his purpose was already defeated*?

"Yes." June looked surprised. "Do you know him?"

Matt shook his head. "We've never met, though I've heard he has many business enterprises." He was curious. "You don't intend to return to the airline?"

"No. I'm not physically fit to their liking."

Matt remembered her dizzy spell. "You're not ill?"

June raised a brow at his concern. "No. I'm fine. At least that's what my doctor tells me, pending some test results, but there's no reason why I shouldn't look for other work."

"How will you be employed by Raleigh?" Matt tried keeping his voice normal. *Test results*. Since his mother's long illness and subsequent death, those words always loomed as ominous.

A twinkle appeared in June's eyes as she splayed her hands. "Do they still use the term 'gal Friday'? Anyway, that's how I see myself though I'm sure my official title will be executive something or other. I'll be the all-around office manager, hirer, firer, and I suppose whatever else needs cleaning up."

Matt frowned. "You won't be part of the banking business?"

"No. As I understand it my duties concern his enterprises." June lifted a shoulder. "It's a challenge, I suppose. Anyway, I'll find out more about it when I get there in two weeks. After ten days I should have a pretty clear idea of what I'll be doing." She smiled. "Can't be all that bad, though, since travel is part of my job."

"Travel?"

"To Africa." June smiled. "Who knows? We might meet across a crowded room once or twice."

Matt didn't return the smile as he turned from her animated face and sparkling eyes. Her sudden effervescence was a startling change from the subdued woman he'd breakfasted with. And all it took was talk of her new job. With a man she found to be fascinating. She sounded happy and excited about her upcoming adventure. *With a new life and career, why should she return? Will Paris entrance her so that she begins to call it home?* His thoughts made him feel as if he'd been roundhoused by the fist of Evander Holyfield.

"What happens after ten days?" Matt's voice sounded normal though his throat burned with the strain of keeping it even.

"It's only an introduction. I officially start after Labor Day." June hugged her chest and settled back, closing her eyes. "I can't wait, Matt. Things are finally falling my way, after . . ." She opened her eyes and looked at him. "Well, you know . . ."

"Yes, I know."

June wondered about the sudden tightening of his jaw.

"How long do you intend to make Paris your new home?"

"If I don't get fired, at least two years," June said. "Right now I can't think of a thing about Paris that I wouldn't like." She looked away from the grimness in his eyes. "I need this to work for me. Otherwise . . ."

"What?"

"It's—just something I need to do for me."

"Why is making it in Paris so important to you when you haven't given any thought to finding other employment here?" Matt waved a hand in the empty air. "What about your interest in franchises?"

June stared at him. "Oh, my *little venture?*"

Matt winced. "That was said in anger."

"But from the heart."

"Yet you meet a man at a party and after one night and one hour in his company, you're ready to take off to God knows what?"

"What concern is it of yours?" June answered hotly. "If it hadn't been for your wife we wouldn't be sitting here having this conversation."

"I'm not married."

"Well, you were, and what a fine pair. One didn't know what the other was getting and it served you both just right that you got fooled!"

Matt glared at June. "*I* got fooled?"

She didn't miss his meaning. "Touché," June said. Suddenly, the humor of the situation got to her. A smile touched her lips.

"What's so amusing?" Matt couldn't help but be infected, and felt himself smiling.

"Us." June's eyes twinkled. "We're fighting." She winked at him. "If we keep this up, we're going to have to be so inventive in finding ways to say we're sorry." She tilted her head toward the interior. "Although I must say your apology this morning was simply delicious."

"As was yours, Friday," Matt said.

June blushed at the memory of their kiss.

"Have I embarrassed you?"

"A little," June answered. "What happened in your house was unexpected."

"But enjoyable?"

"Well, it certainly wasn't the worst experience I've ever had," June retorted.

"I'm glad for that, because I certainly did enjoy our kiss." Matt smiled. "If you're off in Paris, how can we know that we won't find more of such visits as enjoyable?"

"Why would we want to? We're in opposing camps, aren't we?" June felt warm to the tips of her toes, but couldn't turn from his riveting gaze.

Matt reached over and took her hand. "Do we have to be?"

The heat in his eyes trapped June into immobility, and she was powerless to stop him from rising and slowly pulling her to her feet. She waited expectantly for his lips to claim hers as they had two days ago. His nearness evoked memories of his powerful kiss and being enfolded in his strong embrace. Already her body was responding to his touch as, shameless, she pressed into him, her arms sliding around his waist. When his lips brushed hers, June moaned her pleasure.

Matt sucked in a breath as his lips captured hers, savoring the same sweetness as he did before. If he'd been tentative in his actions, her reaction to him erased all doubt that she wanted him as he wanted her. Her arousal hardened her nipples into ripened buds beneath the thin cotton of her shirt.

June gasped when she felt the caress of Matt's hand on her breast. She pulled away from his grasp. "We can't do this," she whispered.

Matt felt deprived at the abruptness of her move. His breathing was heavy as he stared down at her. "Why not?" His voice was thick with desire.

"Because, beca . . ." Her voice faltered.

"Because there is no good reason, is there?" Matt said. She was backing up, and he followed, catching her hand and pulling her back to him and into his arms. "Is there?" He bent his head and kissed her again. When he felt her response, he lifted his head and stared into her eyes. "There can't be," he murmured.

When she felt his lips again, June squirmed from his arms. This time she moved far from his reach. Her breath came in spurts as she said, "It's not right."

Matt didn't pursue her but moved to the rail and sat down. "I thought we had this conversation." His stare was unwavering.

"I know," June said softly. She leaned against the door-jamb and folded her arms. "I feel as if there's a barrier between us."

"You're saying that a relationship is impossible?"

"Ye—yes," June answered.

"You're wrong."

June shook her head. "Not about this. It's just something that I feel."

Matt held her gaze. "Are you saying that we don't have feelings for each other?" He watched her struggle with answering his question. "Because I think we do, June. The way we met and the reasons why are not important. It stands that we have met and there's something going on that neither of us planned." His voice softened when he saw the fear and uncertainty in her eyes. "Why do you want to deny it?"

June couldn't understand why she felt trapped. Flustered and exasperated, she sat down and crossed her knees. One foot swung back and forth in a nervous gesture.

Matt saw an explanation coming and he joined her, taking his same seat but remaining silent.

"I must go away, Matt," June said in a low voice, not trusting herself to look at him. She stared at the sun-dappled water. "Staying here would be copping out. Not giving myself a chance to see what I'm made of, to see if I can excel at something. Now that I have this opportunity, I can't let anything stop me."

Matt's heart dropped when he heard the anguish coming from the depths of her soul. He wanted to hold her here. Deprive her of her dream. What if his arguments convinced her to stay? Would she learn to hate him? He turned brooding eyes on her. "Not even if you think that we might have something together?"

June shuttered her eyes against the hurt she saw in his

and realized that he cared for her. She straightened her shoulders and looked at him squarely. "I can't."

The silence between them widened as both stared ahead, lost in their own thoughts.

Matt stood and walked up and down the porch, head down as if contemplating the situation. His amble took him around the deck, and when he returned he sat down on the railing and faced June. He braced himself with the palms of his hands.

"Will you listen?" Matt said as June watched him curiously.

June nodded, wondering why he looked so at ease, the hurt and anger gone.

"You will be leaving in two weeks, returning ten days later, and starting your new job in September. Right?"

"Yes."

"Then as I see it, I have the rest of the summer to make you change your mind about returning to Paris in September." Matt's tone was even, but his stare was penetrating.

"Why would I change my mind?"

Matt smiled. "The obvious answer is that you would want to. Because you would find something here that was missing before."

"You?" June returned the smile.

"Us," Matt corrected.

"A relationship?"

"Yes."

"And how far is this relationship supposed to go?" June asked, a whole lot of skepticism in her voice.

"Who can answer that, June?" Matt said, mildly.

"Then I'm supposed to put my needs on the back burner until this 'relationship' runs its course?" Her eyes narrowed dangerously. "And after my dream job is gone?"

"I'm not asking you to do that," Matt said.

June laughed, then said, "No, you're just asking me to

have a summer fling with you. Then when the bloom is gone from the rose, and the north wind blows, you make your escape and leave me to my own devices.'' Her smile widened. ''Who knows? Maybe Mr. Raleigh would have chewed up and spit out another assistant by then and I'd wind up in Paris after all.''

Matt folded his arms and waited for June's laughter to subside. When she looked up at him, a cynical smile still on her face, he said, ''I never asked you to give up your dream, June. I would never ask that of anyone.''

June heard the sincerity and wondered why she'd thought the worst of him. ''I believe you.'' She held his stare. ''But I can't entertain your plan. I'd be helping you to thwart my own plans for the future.''

''Then wouldn't that mean that we've discovered that we have something going on?''

''Yes.''

''Then I'd say that you stayed because you wanted us to be together. Correct?''

June looked pleadingly at Matt. ''Please don't.''

''Why not, June?''

''Because I do like you. I'm denying it as we speak, but I do care.''

''And that upsets you.'' Matt's statement was confirmed by the misery in her eyes.

''Because I want more than anything to prove myself,'' June whispered. ''You can relate to that.''

Matt weighed her words. ''Then if it turns out that we both care deeply you will still leave to prove yourself?''

June nodded. ''I have to,'' she murmured.

''I see,'' Matt said.

Another silence.

Matt wanted to catch her in his arms and never let go. More than ever, he knew that he was in love with June Saxon and he wanted her in the worst way. How it happened so quickly, he'd never question and probably would never understand. But he would never admit to being responsible for the permanent look of sadness in her eyes, because falling in love with him prevented her from following her dreams.

Hearing his heavy sigh, June looked at Matt to find him with the saddest look she'd ever seen on his face. It quickly disappeared when their eyes locked.

Matt sat in the chair next to June and took her hand. "Okay," he said resignedly.

"What?" June asked, suddenly feeling empty. "Giving up so easily?" Hadn't she wanted him to?

Matt shook his head. "Not giving up," he answered. "Just taking it a bit slow." Still holding her hand, he said, "Suppose we let things coast, take a natural course, so to speak? No pressure, and we'll just see."

"But ..." Slight pressure on her hand made her stop.

"For two weeks, at least?" Matt said.

"And after that?"

Matt lifted a shoulder. "Then we'll see what happens when your ten days are up."

"What happens during the two weeks?"

Matt shrugged again. "Getting to know each other. Dinner. You visit me. I visit you. You know. Dates."

"Dates, huh?" June smiled.

"I believe that's the way it works. Have things changed since my marr ... since, well, in the past year or so?"

"No, Matt, things haven't changed." She tilted her head. "And after the ten days?" A smile tugged at her mouth.

"More of the same until September?" Matt didn't let go of her hand.

June feigned a deep, ponderous pose. She answered, "I think I can live with that."

Matt saw the next question coming and silenced her with a finger to her lips. "Don't. We'll let September take care of itself. Agreed?"

June was nearly breathless. She wanted to kiss the finger that so gently feathered her lips. Instead, she caught and held his hand. "Deal."

The telephone rang and interrupted any further discussion as June excused herself and went to answer the phone.

"So when is he leaving so I can come over and find out what's going on?" Beverly said excitedly.

"Beverly?" June's eyes narrowed. She went to the back door and saw her friend waving from the kitchen window. "So you're spying on me now?"

"Nothing of the kind," Beverly said huffily. "You owe Brown's driver for waking me up. Of course when I saw the Mercedes and that gorgeous hunk striding to your door, I could hardly go back to sleep, girl. Caleb's been trying to make me mind my own business but I'm having conniptions over here. So what's up?"

June couldn't help but tease her friend. With a devilish wave, she said, "We had a delicious breakfast and now we're talking. Don't call me. I'll call you. See ya." She let the curtain drop and with a smile on her face, joined Matt on the porch.

Gorgeous hunk is right, she thought. Matt was standing against the porch beam, watching the beach scene. The short-sleeve, collarless, yellow T-shirt was tucked into faded jeans that hugged his trim physique. The man was firm and solid, as she already knew when she'd wrapped her arms around him. Twice. She was caught staring when he turned around.

"Problems?" Matt asked.

"Uh-uh," June said. "Everything's fine. Just that maybe we'd better get Brown's canisters ready for pickup. If it's the same driver, I don't want to be caught unprepared."

Matt frowned as he followed her to the kitchen. "Did he say something wrong?"

"No. I was just surprised."

After placing the canisters on the porch, June took Matt's

hand and led him back inside the house. "I think it's time, don't you?"

"For?" Matt looked inquiringly at her.

"The grand tour," answered June. "We can start on this floor."

They started in the kitchen, where June showed Matt all the hidden cabinets and closets that still held a lot of her grandmother's old cooking utensils and pots that never seemed to wear, and ended up in June's sitting room.

Matt studied the quiet pastel-colored room with its eclectic mix of old and new. Hanging plants and potted herbs decorated the windowsill. So like her, he thought. Cool, fresh, and bright. A faint scent of lavender mingled with the fresh-cut flowers in a glass vase on the table. "From your garden?" he asked, indicating the handsome array.

"Uh-huh," June murmured.

Matt nodded in appreciation. "You did a great job with this room. Relaxing."

"I like it," June said. "Ready for the rest?"

"Right behind you."

"I don't come up here much," June said. "In fact, it's closed off in the winter. Saves heat. In the spring I cleaned and dusted so it's not too musty smelling."

Matt paused on the landing. "I had no idea it was so big." There were several varnished wood doors and the walls were covered in green floral wallpaper. "How many bedrooms up here?"

"Three. I moved downstairs, as you saw." June stood back and watched Matt walk down the hall.

"May I?"

"Sure."

Matt opened doors to several closets, a bathroom, and the bedrooms, taking his time inspecting them all. When he walked back to June, she was smiling.

"Do I amuse you?"

"A little. I could see the wheels working," she said. "Does it suit your needs?"

"Perfectly," Matt answered.

"How could it not? It's a grand old house." She walked downstairs. "I think my grandparents expected to raise a brood in here."

"There was just your father?"

"Yes. Grandmother Belle could never have anymore." She frowned. "They never got over losing him."

Matt heard the sadness in her voice. "You must have been a very scared little girl losing both parents at once." They were in the kitchen and June had poured tall glasses of ice tea.

"I was. But love and kindness helped me through that." She smiled and inclined her head toward the back door. "And friends."

"The Lancasters."

"Yes. Seems like they've always been there." June sipped her tea. "What about you, Matt? How was it growing up with four brothers? I can't imagine!"

"Wild." Matt grinned. "That's what my mother called it. Threatened to refuse to pay the ransom if we ever got kidnapped."

June laughed. "She sounds like she had her hands full."

Matt's eyes clouded. "She did. But as time went by, she let the nannies play a big role in keeping us in check." He didn't mention his mother's withdrawal when her husband's philandering became the town's worst kept secret.

They walked to the front porch, and the beach sounds drifted to their ears as both watched the activity for several seconds. "It's a gorgeous day," June said. "Surely you didn't intend your apology to extend over half the day. It's nearly noon. I don't want to put a damper on your plans."

Lazily, Matt turned to her. "No?"

"Of course not!" Suddenly she felt embarrassed. "I have,

haven't I? Why didn't you say something? You could have looked at the place some other time.''

''I did have plans, but they're still salvageable.''

''Thank goodness,'' June breathed.

''But only if you agree.''

''What do you mean?''

''Have dinner with me tonight?''

''Dinner?''

''Yes.'' A hint of a smile tugged at his mouth. ''That last big meal of the day?''

''But . . .'' June was at a loss for words.

''Unless I'm interrupting *your* plans.'' He looked at her inquiringly.

''No, I hadn't planned on anything special,'' she answered. ''Probably help Caleb and Beverly eat up the leftovers.''

''Probably?'' Matt pinned her down. ''Then it wasn't anything definite?''

''N—no. It's just expected, I guess.''

''Oh.'' Matt turned away and after a second said, ''Would you have dinner with me tonight?''

June hesitated, wondering if she was making a mistake. But hadn't she agreed to his step-by-step plan? *It's only for two weeks.* She turned when he called her name.

''Its just dinner, June.''

''Only dinner?''

''Certainly,'' Matt answered. ''Unless there's something you wanted to do afterward.'' Other possibilities flitted across his mind.

How could she resist the light in his eyes? June nodded. ''What time?''

''I'll be back for you at five-thirty,'' Matt said.

''That'll be fine. I'll be ready.''

''See you then.'' Afraid of scaring her off, Matt refrained from kissing her again though he wanted that more than anything at the moment. He settled for the warm smile she gave him and walked down the steps.

June watched until his car disappeared. "Now what could I possibly want to do afterward?" A devilish smile was on her lips when she went inside the house.

The back doorbell pealed incessantly as June went to answer it. "What? Did you stick a pin in it?" she said, exasperatedly, as she opened the door.

Beverly flew past her and sailed into the kitchen. "Well, you shouldn't have taken an eternity to let me in." She plopped down in a chair and crossed her arms and legs. "Okay, what *happened?*"

With an exaggerated sigh, June sat down. "I told you," she said. "We had breakfast and talked." She ducked the daggers shooting from her friend's eyes.

"You amaze me." June was sitting in Matt's living room in the same big chair she'd admired on Friday. She took another sip of red wine and set her glass down on a mirror coaster.

"Do I? In what way?" Matt tasted his own wine as he stared at her. Since he'd picked her up and brought her back to his house, he'd been unable to keep his eyes off her. Even when she joined him in the kitchen and watched as he'd pulled apart lettuce for the salad and chopped tomatoes, he'd almost nicked his fingers while sneaking looks.

Yesterday, she'd been a vision in her yellow dress. When she'd danced, the hem swirled above her long, slender legs teasingly showing glimpses of shapely thighs. He'd watched the watchers and had become jealous. But today, the sleeveless, V-neck, black sheath she wore did equal justice to her curves and he had developed a strong will not to run his hands over her smooth shoulders and to kiss the softness of her throat.

"Dinner," June answered, aware of his intense looks from the time she got in his car. "Watching you move around the kitchen like it's second nature." She inhaled the savory aromas that wafted down the hall. "I'm surprised."

Matt shrugged. "I've been on my own for quite some time. Messing around in the kitchen was necessary if I didn't want to become a junk food addict." He smiled. "But I have to admit I had a lot of help from critics who let me know what worked and what didn't."

"Oh? You have great friends if they were willing to knock your experiments."

A grin spread over Matt's features. "They couldn't let me know in so many words," he said. "I got the message when they ran away as fast as their four feet could carry them."

"You experimented on Kagi and your shepherds?" June's mouth fell open.

"Not Kagi," Matt said. "I didn't have him then. But, my shepherds were quite willing to join me for a free meal." He laughed. "They survived quite healthfully, I think."

June laughed. "Amazing."

Matt stood and retrieved their empty wineglasses. "I believe the roast is ready for carving. Hungry?"

"Famished. Lead the way," June said.

Instead of taking her to the kitchen, Matt led June to the formal dining room where he'd set the table with fine china and crystal.

"This is lovely, Matt," June said, admiring the decor. The color scheme was carried through from the living room. Light blue and cream damask covered the dining room chairs, complementing the light oak contemporary furniture. The same fabric draped the windows over sheer white curtains. The carpet was the same plush gray. As Matt pulled out a chair for her, June protested. "Can't I help with something?"

''Uh-uh,'' Matt answered. ''First-time dinner guests don't do a thing,'' he said, seeing that she was seated comfortably. He winked as he walked away. ''But that doesn't say what happens the next time.'' Grinning, he disappeared.

June stared after him. *The next time?* she wondered. The more she thought of the idea of dining like this with Matt, the more she liked it. ''A girl could get used to this,'' she murmured. Matt was at her elbow and she wondered if he'd heard. But his expression told her nothing as he held out two bottles of wine.

''Which do you prefer?'' Matt asked. ''Either would go equally as well with the meal,'' he said.

''Then whichever you open will be fine,'' she said of the red Bordeaux and Chianti.

Matt returned pushing a cart laden with dishes. He put the roast loin of lamb on the table, then the rest of the dishes as he removed the covers. He poured wine in their flutes and then sat. He raised his glass. ''Promise this won't be your last?''

June's eyes twinkled. ''Before I even taste everything?''

''Guaranteed, you won't run. Everything's been tested in the past. I can make this meal with my eyes shut.''

''Tested, huh?'' June looked skeptical.

''Not by my animals,'' Matt said. ''My brothers and their wives gave these dishes the green light.''

June touched her glass to his and sipped the wine. ''Okay. I'm game. There's nothing much I can do about it right now, seeing as how I'm starved.''

''Then let's not delay,'' Matt said. He set the crystal flute down and started to carve the meat.

Curried rice and a fragrant casserole topped with tomatoes tickled June's palate as she filled her plate with the steaming vegetables. She tasted white potatoes, zucchini, eggplant, carrots, and onions. The lamb was as soft as butter as she bit into a piece of the generous slice Matt had placed on her plate.

They enjoyed the superbly prepared meal over light conversation; neither wanting to delve into areas each knew would raise the ire of the other.

"Simply delicious," June said, after taking the last bite of her dessert.

"Thank you." Matt sat back, watching her enjoy the coconut custard pie.

"Don't tell me this came from your oven too."

"One of the plant ovens, I believe," Matt said solemnly.

"This is Mabel Foods?"

Matt nodded.

"I had no idea," June said. "Impressive."

"Would you like some more? Another cup of coffee?"

She shook her head. "You're kidding me, right? I'm about to bust my seams now."

"Really?" Matt looked as if the idea wasn't half bad and he would have welcomed watching such an event.

June saw the look and smiled. "But that's not going to happen," she said.

"Unlucky me?" Matt said easily.

" 'Fraid so." June was as relaxed as she'd ever been, especially since the last few months. So much so, that she'd kicked off her shoes during dinner, relishing the feel of the deep carpet under her feet. The sudden disturbing thought that she felt at home bothered her. *At home?* Matt's touch on her hand startled her. She hadn't realized he'd moved so close.

"Frowns?" Matt said. He brushed a thumb across her forehead, smoothing the wrinkles. "Headache?"

June's lashes fluttered against the soft touch and the intake of her breath was softly audible. "No," she murmured, "I'm just fine." She wanted to rest her head against the roughness of his hand for the rest of the night.

Matt took her hand and pulled her up. "Come. I think you'd be more comfortable in the living room."

"Where's Kagi?" June asked as she once again slipped her shoes off. She hadn't heard the dog moving about since she'd arrived. This time, she and Matt both settled on the big sofa.

"I sent him on a sleep-over with one of his friends."

"Oh?" June laughed softly. "That sounds interesting."

"He's in fine company." Matt watched the silvery strands in her hair shimmer in the soft light. He reached over and fingered the tiny cluster of silver on her temple.

"Family trait?" Matt asked. She was too young to gray.

"I'm the lucky one," June answered. "It skips a generation. My grandmother was silver by the time she reached forty."

"She must have been a beauty," Matt murmured. He brushed his lips against her temple.

"She was," June, breathed, heady with his clean male scent. His fingers were tracing the contours of her shoulders, moving down her arm to her hand and sliding back up again. She shivered.

"Cold?" Matt whispered in her ear.

"Rather the opposite, I think," June managed.

"Is that so?" Matt said softly against her cheek. "Let's see."

The feel of his lips on hers so gently, tasting, exploring, then strong and hard, made June twist herself into his arms, wrapping her arms around his neck. His tongue was involved in a game of tag with hers, searching, then conquering as June surrendered herself to the sweet devastation of the recesses of her mouth.

What she'd felt on Friday was nothing compared to what her body was feeling now, June thought. She welcomed the gentle touches to her breast, the kisses on her throat, her eyes, and her nose. June buried her face in his neck and kissed him there. His reaction brought a yelp of pleasure and she knew she'd found an erotic zone. The realization pleased her as her tongue darted out to taste him.

"God, June," Matt blurted. His breathing was heavy as he nibbled her earlobes and then reclaimed her lips. Matt's thoughts took him beyond passionate kisses on his sofa, and his body's response to her was telling as they found themselves sliding into a reclining position.

June closed her eyes. She wanted him to love her, and all cautious thoughts were nonexistent as she mentally submitted to him. Later, she would wonder just how far things would have gone had not fate intervened.

"What the . . ." Matt's head shot up at the sound of tires screeching on the drive. He eased himself off the sofa, frowning at the unusual sound that disturbed the quiet Sunday evening. No one drove like that on his property. He looked down at June, who looked as perplexed as he did. "Excuse me," he said and went to the window. He was in time to see Andre's car going through the gates. Just then the back doorbell rang. He turned to June. "Something's wrong."

"It's Bron," Diane said to her worried-looking employer when he opened the door. "He was barely breathing and Andre caught Doc at home. He said he'd meet them at the office, pronto."

"Did you see Bron?" Matt asked huskily.

Diane nodded.

"That bad?"

"It won't be long," she said softly.

Torn between saying good-bye to his old breeder and staying with June, he wondered how he could leave her now.

"Hello," Diane said as Matt's guest appeared at the door.

"Hello, Diane."

Matt turned to see June watching him with bright eyes.

"It's okay, Matt," she said. "Go on. I'll be okay."

"Are you sure? It might be a while."

"Hurry," June said with an encouraging nod.

Walking to the front door, Matt planted a swift kiss on her temple as he brushed by. "Wait for me," he murmured.

Diane watched the exchange and a subtle smile appeared on her lips. When June turned to her the two women stared at each other with appraising looks.

June met the other woman's stare with unwavering eyes. An age-old inexplicable something that happened between women where men in their lives were concerned passed between the older and younger woman. One the nurturer, the other the lover.

Wordlessly, they entered the kitchen, where Diane broke the silence. "I'm going to clean up this mess and put on a fresh pot of coffee. He'll need it."

Without asking, June began to help. She didn't miss the knowing look on the older woman's face. "I know," she said softly.

Chapter Nine

Before June knew it, days had passed, and with mixed emotions she realized that there were less than two remaining. She was leaving for Paris on Sunday. As promised, Ivon Raleigh had sent her tickets and an itinerary for a ten-day stay. Excitement filled her more with each passing day. Time was elusive, as she began her preparations.

Early on the Monday morning following the memorable evening with Matt, the house painters had arrived to prepare the exterior. While they worked outside, she was busy inside, pulling out clothes and inspecting them for suitability, wondering if Paris summers were cool or hot. Casting a critical eye at the garments laid out on her bed, she decided that there wasn't very much there to choose from, and a shopping trip to the city had been necessary. Although Long Islanders with all the fabulous stores and outlets at their disposal had no need to travel to Manhattan to shop, it was much easier to take the Long Island Railroad to the city where June had met Beverly, who'd taken an afternoon off. When they'd finished, June was pleased with her new wardrobe. She'd never been a designer clothes freak, and the few stunning pieces June did own she had to thank her friend for.

Now as June dressed, preparing for her date with Matt, she eyed the new garments and was satisfied that she'd made the expenditures. Making an appearance as the new executive looking like a shabby country cousin would hardly do. Her thoughts stirred a memory and she realized she'd just emulated Carlotta's warped thinking. *Putting yourself in my place, you wouldn't go to your man with a yard of bills and a few rags on your back.* Those were Carlotta's words.

Perturbed by the association, June pushed the thought away, knowing she was nothing like her former friend. She wasn't going to Paris to snag a husband but as a take-charge executive who needed to look as impressive as her haute couture employees. It would be hard enough arriving carrying the stigma of the Ugly American, but there was no need to look the part.

Thinking about Carlotta left a sour taste in her mouth and June shifted her thoughts to more pleasant ones. Matt Gardiner. The very thought of leaving him brought a sadness to her heart and she wondered how in the world she was going to make an impressive showing to her new employer. Especially when she knew her mind would be a thousand miles away in New York. How does a woman knowingly leave the man she loves for an indefinite period, years, maybe, possibly so that he could find love with another?

Although they had not voiced their deepening feelings, June knew that the bond between them was strengthening into something more than just a truce and friendship. An unspoken agreement not to bring up the sale of her house to him had been established from the beginning of their "relationship." She found him to be a warm and caring

person, interacting with his workers with respect and his
animals with quiet authority.

She'd watched him work with the dogs and she'd taken a
few of them through their exercise paces. She was a frequent
visitor and found herself looking forward to exchanges with
Diane, who was a very observant and intelligent woman.
June had the warming feeling that her presence was welcomed. Especially from the friendly Kagi, who yodeled
excitedly when she appeared.

Today and Saturday. That was all the time they'd had
left. A smile tugged at her mouth. She wondered what inventive idea Matt would come up with this time to give her
more reasons for returning home from Paris after ten days—
and staying. She'd never forget two of the days they'd spent
together after Bron's death. Knowing that the loss of the
once-prized animal had cut deeply, she admired his efforts
to keep his promise. The first day they'd driven over the
endless, beautiful countryside to Cold Spring Harbor, where
many of the fine old houses were built in the mid-nineteenth
century by whalers. On Main Street, they enjoyed a delicious
luncheon at a quaint restaurant where Matt pointed out that
Paris had nothing on this small café with its red and white
checkered tablecloths. He'd even laced his conversation with
butchered French phrases that had June bursting with
laughter.

The second date had ended with dinner at an elegant
French restaurant. The Victorian setting was romantic, quiet,
and unobtrusive and the food was delicious.

At two o'clock, June was waiting on the front porch. At
Matt's suggestion to dress casually, she'd selected a white,
short-sleeve cotton batiste blouse tucked into cream-colored
slacks with a bronze-tone slim belt and matching flat shoes.
When he drove up she went to meet him.

"Hi."

"Hi, yourself." Matt's admiring glance took in all of her

before he bent to kiss her cheek. "What's that gleam in your eyes for?" he asked, tilting his head back with a scrutinizing stare.

June smiled. "Just trying to figure out what side of Paris in New York you'll be showing me today."

Matt took her hands and pulled her into a close embrace. His eyes were teasing. "Don't you like surprises?" he murmured in her ear.

"Sometimes," June breathed, squirming at his touch. How could she leave this man?

"Good," Matt said. "Me too. But this is a two-day happening. Tomorrow is the last I see of you for a while and I want to make it memorable. Ready?"

"Ready," June answered, tasting her lips where he'd brushed them with a kiss.

Matt noticed her inquisitive look when he drove in the direction of his house. "No, it doesn't start here," he said. "More visitors are coming today and I want to meet them before we leave. They should have arrived by now. Then we'll be on our way."

"Oh, that's good. I hope they have a successful visit. Which of the dogs did you have in mind for them?" Last weekend she'd met the family who'd stayed for two days, selecting and bonding with a basenji pup. The wife she hadn't cared for, considering her to be too bossy and controlling, but the two boys, at five and seven, had been adorable. She was glad when the pup had taken to them and they'd left quite happy with their new family member. She also saw how relieved Matt had been to see them go. He'd had to play host and Diane had done double duty, cooking and cleaning.

For the first time she'd seen his dedicated scrutiny of his buyers. His desire to send his animals to a good home involved long hours of explaining the care and attention the dog needed and their personality traits, especially the destructive tendencies of the pups. The basenji washed itself like a cat and there was no doggie smell, so a daily rubdown with a hand glove would suffice for cleanliness.

June admired his professionalism and concern that his buyers were happy, but not at the continued disruption of his household. June sympathized with his need to house strangers anywhere else but under his roof.

"Care to meet them?" Matt asked as they got out of the car. "Shouldn't take long. It's a man and his nine-year-old son from Philly. Andre is taking care of the preliminary introduction and other things. I'll be pretty busy the rest of the weekend." He caught her hand and squeezed as they entered the house.

"Sure," June said, her body responding pleasantly to his touch. She expected to see Diane moving about in her efficient, assertive way, but the house was quiet. It was after two and normally she would have the kitchen filled with delicious aromas in preparation for dinner.

"They must be with Andre out back," Matt said. He went through Kagi's room and out the back door, wondering why Diane had let the animal out. The playful dog only got in the way of the workers in the kennels.

They found the visitors in one of the buildings where a particular area was specifically designed for pet and potential owner. Matt saw Andre and Diane standing back. Both had crossed arms and identical looks.

June watched Matt's handsome features turn into a frown as he stared at his friends, and she saw the silent exchange between Andre and Matt. "Something wrong?" she asked softly.

Andre left his wife's side and walked toward them. He acknowledged June and to Matt, said, "These two are a joke." He jerked his head in the direction of the fenced-in area where a carrot-topped young boy and a beefy-looking man were interacting with a pup.

"What's wrong?" Matt asked, his body stiffening. He

trusted Andre's instincts as well as his own when it came to perceptions of other people. He looked at the pup that was uncharacteristically sitting quietly, but looking expectantly at Diane as if wondering when he was going back to the refuge of his cage. The boy, his father's spitting image, was pulling on the dog's snoot and loudly telling it to make noise. The father was laughing his encouragement and making sounds like that of a baby crying.

Matt's eyes darkened at the spectacle. "Did you explain anything at all yet?" His voice was hollow.

"Yes, but you can see it went over their heads," Andre said. "The guy said he's satisfied that his son likes the pup and they don't need two days of this orientation stuff." He rolled his eyes. "They'll just leave with the pup in the morning."

"Is that a fact?" Matt's voice was deadly. "Have they taken their bags inside?"

"Not yet. Diane just let the kid use the bathroom, but they've been in here the whole time." A satisfied look settled over Andre's rugged features when he saw Matt's jaw tighten.

Matt touched June's elbow. "Wait here. I won't be long."

June nodded and watched his long strides bring him within inches of the fenced-in area where he invited the man and boy to step outside. When Diane went inside to get the pup and carry it away, June could see an exchange taking place between the two men. Matt was speaking so softly she couldn't hear him but could guess at what he was saying when he pulled out his wallet and offered the man some money. The man, who towered at least four inches over Matt and was a hundred pounds heavier, brushed Matt's hand away so forcibly that bills floated to the floor. Spouting an obscenity, he advanced toward Matt.

Andre walked purposefully toward the two men. When

he reached them, he stared unflinchingly at the visitor, who ended his blustering and stepped back.

With the speed of a buck during hunting season, the man, with his son in tow, stormed past June so that she felt her slacks rustle with the breeze. Angry gray eyes in a mottled red face crackled with fury.

Matt was by her side and June not only felt his anger, but could see the cords in his neck jutting out and his temples pulsing.

"You go on," Andre said to Matt in a low voice. He gestured to the animals that were excitedly crying and yodeling. Even the shepherds were barking. "We'll settle things down in here."

Disgust evident on his face, Matt swept the room with his gaze, but he knew that Andre and Diane would have the animals calmed in short order. He nodded. "You got it. Check with you when I get back."

"I take it that's the last of them?" Andre said in a dry tone.

"He's ignorant, not stupid," Matt, said tight-lipped. "See you later."

June slipped her hand in Matt's as they walked in silence toward his car. Words weren't necessary. The way he gripped her hand told her volumes. They drove away in silence.

As they rode, June couldn't miss the tightened jaw. She could see his effort to adopt his usual relaxed manner of driving, but his hunched shoulders were a dead giveaway of bound tension. Although they engaged in conversation during the drive, his input was polite but distracted.

After an hour, Matt parked and opened the door for June. He took her hand as they walked toward the building, and before entering he gestured to the sign atop the roof. "Don't let that mess back there spoil this for you," he said. "I want you to enjoy yourself."

June looked up. "Oh, Matt." LONG ISLAND'S ONLY PARIS REVUE DINNER THEATRE. The red, white, and blue animated neon sign twinkled with Can-Can dancers. She squeezed his hand. "I don't think there's anything that can spoil this for me," she whispered. "Come. Let's both enjoy."

During the revue, Matt's mood lightened up, and he laughed and smiled in all the right places, but June sensed it was more for her pleasure. The evening of fun and romance he'd planned had been tainted by his visitors' boorish behavior. His valiant effort to drop his dark mood for her was endearing and she wished she could help.

The applause for the talented actors and dancers was genuine and June expressed her pleasure at the performances.

"So, you think that I won't find the same quality show in Paris?" June teased as she buckled her seat belt.

Matt looked at her solemnly. "Nah. Too commercial."

June smiled because she saw his relaxed manner and knew he'd gotten past his anger. She leaned over and kissed his cheek. "Thank you," she said. "I'll remember this while I'm away."

"There's something to be said for ulterior motives," Matt said, gravely. He gave her a sideways glance, but said no more.

"Would you like to come in?" June asked after he'd parked and walked with her to the front porch. At ten o'clock the warm night beckoned to be prolonged.

Matt caught both her hands and backed up to the railing where he propped himself on one hip. He shook his head. "You know I want to, but you have an early day tomorrow, remember?" He kissed her lips. "I'll be here at seven A.M. sharp."

"I remember," June murmured, tasting his lips.

"Good," whispered Matt. "Thought you might be backing out."

"What? And always wonder what other sights and sounds

of Paris I've been missing in my own backyard? Not a chance." She nibbled his ear and heard him inhale sharply.

"Okay, Miss, that's enough. Inside with you," Matt breathed.

June chuckled. "All right. But you're a hard taskmaster." She gasped as he pulled her into his arms and held her tightly.

"I miss you already, you know." Matt spoke huskily against her hair.

Hugging him around his waist, she laid her head on his chest. "I miss you too."

Neither wanted to break the embrace, and silence ensued for a moment. Finally Matt untangled her arms and, holding her at a distance, said, "Don't oversleep."

"I won't," June answered, watching as he hesitated by the steps. She knew what was on his mind. It was the one thing that had been unspoken between them since the episode in the kennel.

Matt and June each knew the other had thought about the issue, but neither was willing to broach the volatile subject of the sale of her house to him.

June breathed in deeply. "Matt."

Turning at the seriousness of her voice, Matt peered at her in the bright porch light. "What is it, June?"

"What are you going to do about future visitors?" she asked softly. She met his direct stare. "I know it's been on your mind all evening." Waiting for his response was like anticipating the sound of a feather landing on a bed of cotton. For June, time stood still.

"It has." But Matt knew the real question. Without breaking eye contact he moved a step closer to her. "You know the answer to that, June. If anything, my desire to buy your property has escalated. If that doesn't happen, then I'm looking at changing my philosophy on how to conduct my business. My animals and my customers need that orientation period. With my success rate after all these years, I'd be a fool to change now.''

June's shoulders slumped. Sometimes the truth was hard to accept but she'd seen for herself what obnoxious strangers he had to deal with. *But, where would that leave me?* she wondered. How could she accept his offer to uproot herself to God knows where?

The doubt on her face pained Matt and he knew his abruptness had hit hard. But there was no way he could stand here and lie to her.

''June.''

''Right now, I don't know how to respond to that,'' she answered. From his look, she knew they were experiencing the same mixed emotions. ''My grandmother always said that things looked brightest in the morning.'' Their eyes locked. ''Maybe during the night something bright and miraculous will come our way. See you at seven?''

He was blanketed with relief. ''Do you mean that?'' His voice was thick with emotion.

''Of course I do. Good night, Matt.'' June unlocked the door.

''Tomorrow at seven.''

When Matt drove around to the back of his house and parked the car, he was surprised to see Andre and Diane leave their house and walk toward him. His instant thought was that another dog was sick. Whatever happened, it had the couple on tenterhooks to have watched impatiently for his return.

''Don't tell me they've come back,'' he said dryly, referring to the man he'd ordered off his property. ''Am I being sued again?''

''Kagi's gone.'' Andre didn't mince his words, knowing that nothing would soften the blow of the pet being lost.

''What are you talking about?'' Matt gestured toward

the eight-foot-high nylon fencing that separated the kennels from the house. "The gate was left open?"

"It's my fault," Diane said. "This afternoon, I didn't stay with the boy while he used the bathroom. I told him to close the door behind him and join us in the kennels." She looked disgusted with herself. "Kagi probably ran off as soon as he was let outside. I didn't have a clue until I noticed the back door ajar."

Matt frowned remembering that earlier he'd thought the dog was with the workers in another building.

"He's been gone that long?"

"Looks like it," Andre answered. "We've been all over the neighborhood and walked the beach but no one's seen a stray matching his description."

"Let's go inside. Standing out here isn't accomplishing anything." Matt unlocked the door and walked through his pet's small area and into the kitchen, hoping that somehow the animal had gotten locked up inside one of the rooms in the big house. His penchant to explore was inherent, and sticking his nose in where it didn't belong could get him in a world of trouble.

Diane saw his quick glances. "He's not inside. I've checked everywhere," she said softly.

"I know you have. Just a thought." He could see the effect the dog's disappearance was having on her. "Stop beating yourself up about this. It won't help and it'll just hasten my plans to change things around here." His eyes darkened. "I've been pussyfooting around long enough."

Andre's lashes flickered but he said, "Is there anything else you'd like us to do tonight?"

Matt shook his head. "No. It's obvious he hasn't been found," he said. "His ID tags have all the information, and if he wasn't stolen we would have heard something by now. We'll just wait. In the morning I'll take a walk around. If he's hurt and lying off the road somewhere, he can't call attention to himself by barking.''

After Diane and Andre left, Matt sat in his study, finding it hard to keep his mind off his pet. If he was stolen, he could only hope that Kagi was taken to make some kid happy. The other alternative of theft for animal atrocities darkened his thoughts and he pushed them out of his mind, instead turning them to tomorrow and June.

It was unfair to wait until morning to call her, especially since she would have to get up so early. She'd only agreed to the date because he'd promised to have her home early, so that she could have some time to pull together any last-minute preparations for her trip. Now there would be no time at all spent together before she left.

But before he turned in, he'd have to call his brother George to cancel the use of George's yacht and the special preparations made for the French chef to regal her with breakfast and lunch. Deep down in his heart, Matt knew that June would not turn down the job and that when she returned in ten days, she'd spend the rest of the summer making plans to leave for her long-term employment overseas. *So why are you beating a dead horse?*

"No reason at all," he muttered as he reached for the phone to call his brother. "Why am I kidding myself?" With all the enticements of her new job and accomplishments, June was as lost to him as if they'd never met, and the sooner he realized that, the sooner he could get on with his life.

June was too keyed up to sleep. While walking on the near-deserted beach, she wondered if tomorrow would be the last time that she and Matt would be together as friends. There was no way that he would change his way of doing business. His plan to house customers elsewhere was paramount. Although sleep-over customers averaged about twice a month, still the inconvenience and the disruption of his privacy were becoming telling. Those buyers who lived in the city had no compunctions about taking two days out of their lives to acquaint themselves with an animal that would become a daily part of their households.

Looking across the road, she noticed that Caleb had returned home. He'd spent the last week in the city working on some of the firm's problems but had assured her he'd be home to drive her to JFK airport on Sunday. Beverly was planning to meet them there.

Leaving brought mixed emotions, and June wondered if this would be her last summer at home. At least for the next few years. Her yearlong feelings of self-doubt and inadequacy appeared to have dissipated after she'd learned Ivon Raleigh wanted her. When she realized that by being herself she'd earned his admiration and respect, her self-esteem had risen by degrees. She felt that the man knew what he was looking for and had found it in her in just one hour of conversation. The easy way in which they'd conversed, speaking on topics of every description and in different languages, led her to believe that they would have a fine working relationship together.

Her only problem, which was merely a minor dilemma, was what would she do with the house during her absence? Selling it to Matt was not an option. She would have to have a roof over her head when she returned to set herself up in some other type of entrepreneurship, whatever that turned out to be. Still, letting the house sit idle would be detrimental to its health. Although Caleb would be in and out checking on things and watering the plants and flowers, the stale smell of unoccupied premises would permeate the structure for months to come.

It was nearly eleven o'clock and the night air had turned cool. Rubbing the chill bumps on her arms, she began to walk back home when she heard a sound. Startled, and suddenly nervous about being out alone so late, she hurried down the beach. There was no one in sight and June felt relieved. She'd rather take on a roving pack of dogs than to encounter a band of two-legged animals that would pose more of a threat to her personal safety.

The noise was coming from near the water's edge. Reluctant to ignore what might be a baby's cry, June paused, a sense of déjà vu overwhelming her. The night that Kagi and Matt had come into her life, she'd heard a similar sound.

Expectantly, she looked about for Matt but the beach was deserted. This time the faint cry ended in a plaintive wail. A basenji, she thought. She'd been around the animals enough in the last weeks to become attuned to their strange ways of communicating. She'd come to know Kagi's cry of frustration when his master wouldn't let him have his way. This cry was almost the same but fraught with pain.

Checking to see that she was the only human in the vicinity, she took a deep breath and hurried toward the sound. Her heart was pumping when she saw the bundle lying in a heap, unable to move. As she moved closer, a small sound that could only mean joy was emitted when the animal recognized her.

"Kagi," June said, kneeling down beside the dog. "What's wrong, boy?" she cooed, knowing the soothing sound of her voice would help calm him. "Let me see," she continued. The dog was whimpering and trying to lick her hands as she felt him for bruises. His quivering body was wet and sand-covered and didn't appear to show any injuries. But when she touched his leg and his foot he cried loudly. "You're hurt, boy," June crooned. Unable to see very much, she picked the dog up carefully. "Let's get you home."

"Oh my God," June cried. She was sitting on the edge of the bathtub where she'd washed the dog off. His body was covered with welts and his foot looked as if it was crushed. At first she'd thought that he'd been run over by a car, but she knew that wouldn't account for the bruises on his body. Each mark looked as if it had been deliberately delivered. "You've been beaten." There was no other explanation. Since she'd unclogged the wounds of the sand, some of them began to bleed, especially the foot. Realizing the bleeding had to be stopped, she patted the dog dry as gently as she could and wrapped the foot in gauze. Folding him in a bath sheet, she carried him to the bedroom where she placed him on her bed. At this hour the only veterinarian office that she knew of on Main Street would be closed. Matt would have to get over here quick. She hurriedly dialed his number.

After ending the call to George, Matt sat in his study, reflecting on their conversation. His brother was disappointed that Matt was canceling Saturday's plans and didn't spare his words when voicing his opinion. When Matt had casually dropped by George and Toi's one evening with June, the three had hit it off. Since then, his sister-in-law never missed an opportunity to ask about June and hinted that she'd like to see her more often. George was equally as inquisitive, causing Matt to be inwardly pleased that his family liked her. Sometimes he found himself comparing his family's reaction to June Saxon to what it would have been toward Carlotta Graham had they ever met his ex-wife.

The ringing of the telephone interrupted his reflections and he looked surprised to see June's name and number on the caller-ID display.

"Hello." Concern filled his voice. Was she ill?

"Matt, I have Kagi. He's bleeding and needs a doctor," June said quickly. "Can you come for him?"

As calmly as he could Matt asked, "Where is he bleeding and is it flowing?"

"His foot looks like it was crushed. The blood is trickling now. I wrapped it with gauze."

"Crushed?" Matt swore. He thought rapidly. "June, the bleeding I can handle in an emergency, but the injury sounds too serious for me. It would save time if I met you at the vet's office. Can you handle him?"

"Yes, just tell me where." After taking down the information, June hung up, bundled the whimpering dog in the bath towel, and hurried from the house.

Almost two hours later, June and Matt were standing by their cars outside the doctor's office. After assuring Matt that Kagi would sleep through the night, Dr. Faselli had driven back home.

"Do you think the surgery will prevent crippling?" June asked. Matt had been reluctant to speculate while the doctor operated to save Kagi's foot.

"Doc says we can only wait and see." He leaned against his car and rubbed his fingers against his throbbing temples. "Thank you," Matt said.

"You've already done that," June answered. When he'd taken the hurt dog from her arms the look of gratitude in his eyes had nearly made her cry. There had been no need for him to thank her as he did while they sat quietly in the waiting room. She touched his arm. "You'd better go and get some rest," she said. "Kagi'll be looking for you first thing after the anesthetic wears off. You can call me later to let me know how he's doing. I'll be home."

Although Matt had explained about Kagi's disappearance, he'd never told her that he'd already canceled their date for tomorrow in order to look for his lost dog, and now she was telling him herself that he had more important things to do.

He caught her hand and kissed it and then kissed her lips. "That's for understanding," he murmured.

After responding with a quick hug, June looked up at him. "What's mystifying is, where's he been all these hours?" She was perplexed. "If the doctor thinks he was run over by a car, why didn't the driver stop and bring him to a vet? And surely he would have been spotted creeping along the road."

"That's hard to answer. It's possible that Kagi ran in panic before the driver could get to him." Matt frowned. "Then again, it's possible that the foot was injured intentionally, by being smashed with a heavy object. He was definitely beaten. Doc said those bruises were viciously inflicted, judging from the wood splinters he extracted."

"My God," June whispered. "The poor dog must have hidden himself all this time, terrified of running into anyone."

"Could be, or he might have been trying to find his way to your house since he couldn't find his way home."

"I didn't think of that," June said. "That stretch of beach is so familiar to him." She thought for a second. "Do you think that someone was trying to steal him and he was able to escape?"

"I've thought about that possibility," Matt said.

The sound of his voice brought June's head up sharply. "You think it might be your customer from this afternoon?"

"I'm thinking that way," Matt said softly.

"How awful! What kind of man is he?"

"The kind that shouldn't ever own an animal." He scowled in disgust. "And to think that he's teaching his kid the same kind of cruel behavior to animals." June shivered and he guided her to her car. "Go on home and get some rest. I'll call you when I leave here tomorrow."

Before getting in her car, June hugged him tight and kissed him. "I'll be there."

Matt followed her home. When she turned on her lights, she waved and he made a U-turn and drove home. The anger that seethed within him was evident from the taut skin of his knuckles as he gripped the steering wheel. If he thought that his dog was injured because he'd insulted a customer by paying him to get off his property, Matt only hoped that the man was already home in Philly.

It was after two A.M. when Matt was finally calm enough to drift into a deep sleep. He thought he was dreaming when he heard his German shepherds barking. At the same time he heard the pounding on his door and he was downstairs in a flash, opening the back door.

Diane was in tears. "Matt, fire. Andre's trying to put it out alone. Come get him out of there."

"What? Did you—"

"I called for help already," Diane flung over her shoulders as she ran away.

The heart-stopping smell of smoke filled Matt's nostrils as he rushed barefoot to the kennels. "Damn," he said, angered at the sight. The fire had nearly consumed the building closest to the Heaths' cottage and had eaten half of the small wood-frame house. The flames had not yet reached the other two kennels.

"The dogs," Matt shouted to Diane when he caught up to her. "Are they all out of there?" Some of the dogs were running excitedly back and forth, nipping at his heels.

"Oh, thank God," she breathed, seeing her husband run into the middle kennel. "Yes," Diane shouted. "You help Andre. I'll start on the last kennel." She disappeared.

Matt could see Andre running from cage to cage, freeing the dogs, who instantly ran outside. "Is that the last of them?" Matt shouted, as he reached his friend.

"Yes," Andre said, spitting smoke from his mouth. His eyes were bloodshot and his hands were singed. He ran from the building and Matt followed.

Unheeding the spreading fire in the cottage, all three worked quickly to free the other animals. They were in the midst of freeing the last of them when the fire trucks pulled into the driveway. Matt instructed them where to connect the fire hose.

Matt, Andre, and Diane quickly corralled the frightened animals to the front of the house out of the way of the firemen who worked frantically. The fire had not touched the remaining buildings but had totally destroyed the first building and was fast burning the house. Suddenly there was a shout and the firemen ran from the cottage seconds before the explosion shattered the air.

"Oh my God," Diane shouted. She hid her eyes in the shelter of her husband's broad chest.

Matt stood stoically, watching his world go up in smoke. It was when he turned to walk away from the sight that he hopped off one foot, crying out in pain. Holding to Andre, who'd caught him when he stumbled, he lifted his foot. "What the . . ." he said in surprise and disgust. He never realized that he'd stepped on a piece of metal that had embedded itself in the sole of his foot.

"Christ, man, that looks mean," Andre, said. "Hope you're up on your shots. Come on, Diane. Help me get him to the house. He needs a doc."

Leaning on his friends, Matt fumed as he limped inside. When he was sitting at the kitchen table he looked up at Andre. "How did it start?" he asked.

"The alarm woke us up. The hall outside our bedroom door was thick with smoke. I didn't see the fire until I made my way to the kitchen." He shook his head in disgust. "I tried to put it out with the fire extinguisher, but it had gotten too much of a hold. That's when Diane shouted that the kennels were burning and we ran outside."

A frown lifted Matt's eyebrows. "But how could the fire spread from your house to the buildings that quickly? Or vice versa. There's hardly any wind." His eyes narrowed.

Andre and Matt stared at each other, and Diane grabbed at her chest in disbelief.

"That man!" Diane whispered.

"There were two separate fires," Matt said knowingly.

The curse Andre emitted was barely audible as the knuckles in his big hands whitened. His light eyes glinted with anger. "Guess he didn't like the odds this afternoon," he said in biting tones.

"Well, the man was crazy," Diane said excitedly. Her eyes were just as bright as her husband's. "The nerve of him using the N word and calling Matt uppity when he was offered reimbursement for his travel expenses! But for him to come back here and try to burn us out? He's got to be insane!"

The two men stared at her. "Then why torch the cottage and not the big house?" Andre mused.

"Because you were the one who was about to knock him senseless."

Matt sized up his friend. "Makes sense to me," he said, a smile tugging at his mouth.

The captain came through the opened door and spoke to Matt. "Sorry the house was lost. If it hadn't been for the gas explosion we could've saved part of it. The rest of the property is secure and we're hosing down this house now." He started to leave, then with a look short of being accusatory, said, "The inspector will be around tomorrow to confirm my findings."

Matt looked the tired man squarely in the eyes. "There were two fires, both deliberately set."

"That's right," the captain said in surprise.

"Captain," Matt said evenly. "There's not enough insurance in the world that would make me burn down my own property."

After the chastened man left, Matt looked down at his throbbing foot. "Damn," he muttered.

"That needs attention," Diane said. "You sit tight while we secure the dogs; then Andre'll drive you to the hospital."

Before Matt could respond, George and Toi burst through the door.

Relieved to find his brother safe, George expelled a deep breath. "What the hell happened here?"

Chapter Ten

At twelve-thirty in the afternoon, Matt was in his study, scowling at his bandaged foot that was propped on the ottoman. Incensed that he couldn't move without hopping about on the arm of someone or using the crutches that he'd been supplied with, he was feeling as frustrated as a toddler on a tether. He'd just finished brunch and his brother had gone to refill his coffee cup.

When he and George had returned from the hospital at six in the morning, George and Toi had refused to go home. They and the exhausted Heaths slept soundly in the guest rooms, while the sun was beaming strongly through his windows before Matt was able to drift off to sleep. Unable to try to make it up the stairs to his room, he'd slept on the big chaise longue in his study. The smell of breakfast had awakened him.

George returned with two steaming mugs of coffee and handed one to his brother. He took a sip and then grinned. "Not like you to have to depend on others, huh?" His smile broadened. "Get used to it. It'll be a while before you can put your full weight on that foot. Unless you're bargaining for some serious trouble."

Matt grunted and drank his coffee. "What are you still doing here? You could have left with Sutherland and Reuben." When he'd returned from the hospital, they'd been there, helping Andre and Diane sift through the rubble of their house. Though he'd expressed his gratitude they'd sloughed it off. The brothers, although they had their differences of opinion, never failed to come to the aid of each other. Before he left, Sutherland had taken it upon himself to get Matt's insurance papers from the neatly organized files and take them home. He'd insisted on getting the claims process started. Grateful, Matt let him handle it. He would have enough problems convincing the fire inspector of the fire's suspicious origins.

George looked out the window when he heard a car engine. He dropped the curtain and sat back down. "Diane's finally taking Andre to get those hands looked after. From what I could see he was still fussing." He turned a studied gaze on his brother. "What are they going to do?" he asked quietly.

"I don't know," Matt answered. He rubbed his temples. "Everything they owned was lost."

"He's a proud man."

Both men knew that his homeless situation was eating away at Andre, and accepting Matt's hospitality for even one night grated on him.

"What does he expect me to do, throw him out on the street?" Matt said, shooting a disgusted look his brother's way. "They have to stay here. Where else can they go? Not to his father!"

George snorted. "He'd leave Diane and live on the streets if that were his only option."

"My point exactly," Matt said.

"What about Diane's mother in Hempstead?" George volunteered.

"That's not an option. Three adults in a one-bedroom apartment? You want them to go stir-crazy?"

George gestured helplessly. "Then what would you suggest? I'm stumped." He cocked a brow. "One thing I do know, that man is not going to be happy living under another man's roof. What is he going to do? Pay you room and board? You can't ask him to do that, and he's not going to take your charity."

Toi, who had been standing in the doorway listening to the two men, sat down next to her husband on the sofa. She sighed and slipped her hand through her husband's arm. "You're both right, you know," she said. "You're thinking about Andre and how proud he is, but what about his wife? Helping her try to salvage what she could broke my heart." Her eyes misted. "She doesn't even have a change of underwear."

Squeezing his wife's hand, George kissed her temple when he felt her shiver. He'd always told her that she was a soft touch but in this case her concern was justified. "We'll think of something," he said. He winked. "But for now, since you like to shop so much, why not take Diane on a spending spree when she gets back? She's a practical woman and she won't object to a change of clothes for herself or her husband."

Matt eyed the two people that he loved trying earnestly to help solve his problems. He nodded in agreement at his brother's suggestion. "That sounds like a good idea. I'll take care of Andre if he acts stubborn over the whole thing."

George stood and pulled Toi with him and walked to the door. "You'd better close your eyes for a minute," he said to his brother. "You look tired. I'll hang around outside with the mutts until Andre gets back." He paused. "Have you called June yet about all of this?"

"No," Matt said. "I was supposed to call her about Kagi's condition, but with this mess . . ." He shrugged. "Besides, she'll be busy getting ready for her trip tomorrow."

"Trip?" Toi said. Her eyes glittered. "Oh, that's right, she's leaving for Paris, isn't she?" She looked at her brother-in-law with interest. "Surely you're not going to let her leave without saying good-bye?"

Matt waved a hand. "I'll call after Doc Faselli leaves. He should be here in an hour to check the dogs over and remove the carcasses." His eyes shadowed. Two of the young pups had died from smoke inhalation. "At that time he'll give me a report and I can tell her everything."

"That's still hours from now," Toi said. "Why don't I give her a call to let her know that she'll be hearing from you later on? She's got to be wondering about Kagi."

George looked bemusedly at his wife. He put his arm around her waist and steered her from the room. "Catch you later, man," he called back to Matt.

"Ouch," Toi said as her husband pinched her waist.

"Okay, I can hear the wheels turning," George said. "What's up?"

Waiting until they were out of earshot, Toi whispered, "Rent!"

"What are you talking about?"

"June can rent her house to Andre and Diane until she gets back," Toi said excitedly. "I'm sure she would feel better if someone were living there, looking after the place for her."

"Oh, you're so sure, are you?" George said, shaking his head at the suggestion.

"Yes, I am," Toi said firmly. "I know she would." She reached for the phone and dialed the operator. She smiled sweetly up at her husband. "Care to make a bet?"

George groaned. "No," he answered. "You sound too

sure of yourself.'' But he hugged her waist and kissed her cheek. ''Go for it.'' He went outside.

After her husband left, Toi replaced the receiver. ''On second thought,'' she muttered, ''this might best be done in person.'' She grabbed her purse from a kitchen chair and hurried from the house.

By two o'clock, June had given up waiting for Matt's call. She'd slept late but had still gotten everything accomplished in preparation for leaving tomorrow. Just in case she and Matt unexpectedly went out, she didn't want to cut their time short by rushing back home. One large Pullman was packed and sitting by the front door, and her carry-on was in the bedroom, open and waiting to catch last-minute toiletries. She spent the last few hours cleaning out the refrigerator and scrubbing the bathroom. The house smelled clean and fresh and June was satisfied that when Caleb came over to check on things, he wouldn't be chuckling over her housekeeping talent.

June was relaxing in the kitchen with a cup of hot tea when the front doorbell rang. She smiled and patted her hair. *He came after all.* The presence of Toi Gardiner standing on her porch startled June. Her mind raced. ''Matt?'' she whispered, her mouth suddenly going dry.

Toi knew instantly that she was looking at a woman in love. *Brother-in-law, you're a fool if you let her go.* ''Oh, June, now I am sorry that I didn't call first. Matt will be okay.''

June only stared. ''Will be?'' She still couldn't speak normally.

''May I come in?''

''O—of course. Please.'' She led the way to the kitchen. ''I was just having some tea. Would you like some?''

''Please,'' Toi said. After June set the cup before her and

then sat down, she touched the perplexed woman's arm. "There was a fire at the kennels this morning. Matt got a piece of metal stuck in his foot. He had it stitched up and is home being waited on. Much to his chagrin, I might add."

"Is he all right?" June whispered.

"Yes. As long as he won't be hardheaded and insist on hopping about getting in Andre's way."

Relief poured through June, making her body feel like a tub of Jell-O. "The dogs," June said. "Andre and Diane? The property?"

Toi knew that she was right about this woman who was overwhelmed by the news. Although in June's presence only twice before, she knew the woman was sensitive and genuinely caring toward others. And it wasn't due to her customer service training as a flight attendant. Toi could hear the unspoken love and concern for Matt. With that realization a further embellishment of her plan began another reel of film in her mind.

After explaining about the dead animals and the lost kennel, it was when she talked about the complete loss of the Heaths' home that Toi watched June's face very carefully.

"They've lost everything?" June sat in disbelief. "Oh my God," she whispered. "What are they going to do?"

"That's why I'm here," Toi said softly. "Please listen to my suggestion."

Matt's mood was foul as he slammed down the receiver in the middle of the message. For the fourth time today, he'd called June, and had gotten her answering machine. Since the vet had left and he'd eaten lunch, the house was quiet. The only disturbance was at three-thirty when Toi returned infuriatingly chipper. She'd gone home and changed and was back ready to take Diane shopping. She'd brought dinner for him and told him to relax in front of the boob tube and that everything was taken care of for the night.

"Where's Andre?"

"He's gone to take care of some business."

At nine P.M. the sound of a car awakened Matt. "About time somebody got back here," he muttered. Expecting to hear the back door, he was surprised to hear the front door opening and then footsteps in the hall. "Diane?" he called.

"Hello, Matt. How are you feeling?"

"June?" He stared, his eyes doing a double take and his heart flipping cartwheels. It was as if he hadn't seen her in ages. How was he going to get over her leaving? A dark scowl covered his face.

"My, my, aren't we cross tonight." June saw the plate of food that he'd hardly touched. "Toi said you were cranky and might not have eaten. Would you like me to fix you something light?"

"You've talked to Toi?" Matt growled. He still couldn't believe she was there.

He lay there, in shorts and T-shirt, his muscled arms tanned, and his legs extending an invitation to touch. She could almost feel the tactile sensation of the wiry hair under her fingertips. What a gorgeous man! She wanted to run to him and hug and kiss him senseless. She wanted to love him madly!

Instead, the epitome of nonchalance, June shrugged off her cotton cardigan and tossed it on the sofa. "Uh-huh," she answered and sat down, relaxing as if she'd done this a million times before. "While she and Diane were shopping, I showed Andre everything he needed to know about the house. Then we went to the supermarket where we shopped for the foods he and Diane like to eat. I introduced them to Caleb and the other neighbors on the block so they wouldn't be uneasy with strangers in my house." An easy smile touched her lips. "Toi said she'd call you in the morning.

But not too early." Her body language was unmistakable and her dark eyes sent a message for lovers only.

"Not too early?" Matt didn't miss the emphasis and his heart was a trip-hammer as he caught her look. *Dare I believe?*

"Uh-uh. I told her my scrambled eggs aren't half bad."

His body was telling his head that he was receiving the signals right, but still treading lightly, he said, "What about Diane and Andre?" His voice nearly failed him.

June crossed her legs causing her skirt to hike up to show shapely thighs. She swung her foot. "They're spending the night at my place. You know, getting used to being alone there."

The sound in his throat escaped in a growl and if he could move fast enough she'd already be in his arms. Matt's eyes bored into hers. "Come here."

June demurred. "Is it safe?"

"Safe?" Matt smiled dangerously. "Are you afraid to come see?"

Unwilling to playact anymore, gliding swiftly to the chaise longue, June knelt and caught his hands. "Oh, Matt," she murmured, kissing his face. "I was so scared." She looked at the heavily bandaged foot. "Is it going to be all right? I'm so sorry." Unable to hold back her emotions, her eyes filled with tears.

Matt pushed himself up and caught her into his arms. "It's okay," he murmured against her hair. "Everything's going to be fine, sweetheart. Just fine." He held her until he felt her shoulders relax. When she was still, he kissed her forehead and with one finger tilted her chin and planted kisses on her wet eyelashes. "Better?"

After a moment, June nodded. "I'm the one who's supposed to be consoling you," she said, still teary-voiced. "Look at me."

Matt's groin tightened. "Believe me, you are, sweetheart."

They were silent for several minutes. Matt stroked her short curls. "So Toi single-handedly did my thinking for me, and you are her accomplice, huh?"

June hugged him, inhaling deeply. He smelled like hospital, spice, and warm male. "Do you mind?" she murmured, liking the feel of her cheek against his broad chest. When he talked his rumbling voice tickled her ear.

He kissed her hair. "If Diane and Andre are all for it, then how could I object?"

"They'll be fine," June said. Matt squirmed, trying to adjust his leg, and she sat up. "You must be exhausted. Can you make it upstairs with my help or will you sleep down here?"

"Who said anything about sleep?" he said huskily. He chuckled at her shy squirm. "Short of tumbling down the stairs and bringing you with me, I'd better crash here for the night." He pointed at the crutches lying on the floor. "I haven't mastered those yet."

June reluctantly extricated herself from his arms and rose. "Okay, tell me how I can help you. Which is your bedroom? I'll bring you some pajamas. You'll sleep more comfortably." She picked up the plate. "Do you want something special before you turn in?"

Matt smiled at her take-charge manner. "Yes," he said softly.

"Okay," she said. "Let me get rid of these and I'll be right back." After carrying the tray to the kitchen she returned. "Now what's that special thing you want?"

"You."

June was sitting on the edge of the chaise longue and the sexiness of that one word sent spasms of heat through her body. How could she deny herself any longer? What if he'd been badly hurt? Or worse? The thought of losing him forever sent shock waves through her. There was no way that she would get on that plane without loving this man. "I want you too," she said.

Matt kissed her, long, deliberately, and hungrily. Her hand on his bare thighs sent a wave of heat through him that scorched his insides. Suddenly, he pulled back, aching with frustration. There was something else he needed from upstairs besides pajamas.

"What is it, love?" June saw the frown cloud his handsome features.

If he'd wanted her before, her endearment seared his soul. In the two weeks that they'd dated, kissed, and cuddled, she'd never once used love words. She was looking at him with such concern he couldn't stand not taking her this minute and to hell with protection. He needed to be inside of her before he exploded.

"Matt?" June murmured. "What is it?"

"My condoms are upstairs," he said abruptly.

"Tell me where," June whispered in his ear. "If I take too long it's because I'm changing." She indicated a small canvas satchel by the door. After standing and eyeing his shorts, she said in a smoky voice, "If you need help with those, I'll help you."

Rapidly, Matt told her where to look. "I can manage. Hurry back," he rasped.

"I won't be long." June walked to the two window walls and closed the drapes. She dimmed the room, leaving the desk lamp on.

"June," Matt growled.

Finding the condoms with no problem, she searched until she found his pajama drawer, and then used the guest bathroom to freshen up and undress. Alone in the house with the man she loved, June felt uninhibited slipping into the short, pale blue batiste spaghetti-strapped chemise set and padding about in bare feet.

When she reached the study she could only gaze at him, mesmerized by the sight of his bare chest. He'd covered himself from the waist down with the large multicolored throw that had been flung over the chaise longue. Even in the soft light she could see the desire for her burning in his eyes. Her glance touched the small pile of clothes on the floor. Realization of being enfolded in his naked embrace made her gasp.

Matt stared at her when she quietly appeared in the doorway. She was worth the eternity he'd waited. He held out his arms and she came to him. Burying his head in the softness of her throat, he whispered, "You're so beautiful. I want you more than you'll know, June Saxon."

He claimed her lips, covering her mouth hungrily. Savoring the sweetness of her, he sought to prolong his intense need. How long before he would have her again? But her passionate response and her delicate fingers on his nipples, burgeoning them into rock-hard pebbles, thwarted his intention to move slowly. He was ready to devour her, but when she pushed aside the cover and tentatively trailed her hand down his thigh to fondle his erection, he moaned from the sheer pleasurable pain.

"Oh," June exclaimed unexpectedly as she grasped him, and embarrassed at her schoolgirlish surprise, dropped her hand. She felt his hand guide hers back to his pulsing sex and he whispered, "I want you too." The cover fell to the floor, and emboldened, she stared at this beautiful man.

Matt willed his body to obey. He wanted to plunge ahead, to satisfy his aching loins, but realized she needed this time to be comfortable with him. Her hands caressed him slowly, then moved to the tender flesh of his inner thighs, and he squirmed from the ecstasy of it. While she was busy with her tantalizing explorations, he lifted the chemise over her head. Her breasts were firm, beautiful, and inviting. He tasted each one, savoring the nipples like tender, sweet, brown berries.

The feeling that swept through June when his warm tongue teased her nipples sent her over the edge. She could feel the slippery wetness between her thighs, and when his fingers caressed her there she weakened like a kitten. "Matt, love, I want you," she murmured. She slipped off her panties and laid her full length on top of him. "Oh God, you feel so good." She moved her hips up and down pressing into his erection, torturing herself with the pleasurable feeling.

Through the excruciating pain, Matt managed a smile. He could sense her feeling of power over him as the giver of pleasure but one who was also yearning to receive. For seconds he let her do with him what she would, but when he felt her spread her legs to accept him, he caught her hand.

"The packet," he rasped. "Where is it?" When she felt on the floor for it, he took it from her hand and tore open the wrapper. She took the condom from his hands and whispered, "I'll do it."

Moving adroitly, Matt adjusted their bodies until she was beneath his hard body and he entered her. From the moment her feminine lips sheathed him in their warmth, he was lost. "Sweet June," he gasped.

Instinctively, June's hips arched, seeking to experience the full joy of him. Alternately moaning and overcoming breath-stealing gasps, she felt herself being transported to a place she'd never been. If not for his ear-tingling murmurs of desire she'd have believed she was spinning in a world beyond her comprehension.

The intensity and fiery passion with which she met his powerful thrusts sent an undeniable spiral of knowledge to Matt's brain. The woman in his arms was not having a sexual encounter; she was giving her love to him. Whether it was his male ego or weeks of his deep unspoken feelings

that made him soar, he returned her love, unleashing his
pent-up emotions until their love flowed.

Shuddering from the huge tremor that coursed through
her body, June slumped, her arms falling to her side, her
weightless legs sliding limpidly from his legs.

With no room in which to lie comfortably beside her,
Matt eased himself from her slender body and carefully
swinging his feet to the floor he sat up.

"Matt, your foot. Where are you going?" June reached
out and caught his hand.

Finding the throw, he spread it out on the floor, then eased
himself on top of it and pulled her down beside him. He
brushed her kiss-swollen lips. "It's only pressure on the
sole I have to watch." He hugged her. "And I'm not walking
anywhere, my sweet." He kissed her again. "I just don't
want to let you go."

June snuggled in his warm embrace, tucking her head in
that soft space between his shoulder and his chest. She
relished his nakedness and allowed her hands to roam over
his hard contours. Their bodies were damp from their torrid
lovemaking and she shivered a little but was unwilling to
move. Leaving his own body exposed, Matt covered her as
best he could with the edges of the throw.

They lay in silence, each wondering what the other was
thinking about their wondrous display of love.

"I meant what I said." Matt's voice was low but it livened
the still room.

"What, love?"

"I don't want to let you go."

"But you have me," June dreamily murmured. She
planted gentle kisses on his chest.

"Do I?" He was sliding his hand up and down her back,
lingering on all the delicious contours.

"What do you mean, Matt?" His intense voice alerted
June. Were they speaking about the same period of time?

Matt propped himself up on one elbow and peered down at her. "I don't want you to go—ever." His look was unwavering. "I'm in love with you. I believe I have been for a long time."

June went still. *What is he saying? He sounds so—so permanent!* She eased from under his arm and moved to the safety of the chaise longue, where she sat and stared down at him. *Safety!* That was how she thought of the moment. She needed shelter.

"Don't run from me, June." He felt her inner struggle.

June reached for her chemise and slipped it over her head. She felt so vulnerable.

Matt could almost hear her thoughts. "What are you thinking?" He looked around for the pajamas she dropped when she came into his arms.

Picking them up, June handed them to him and he slipped into the short-legged bottoms. "Ever is a long time, Matt." Her voice was just a murmur.

"I hope so." He stared up at her.

June turned away from that intense gaze. Finding the rest of her lingerie she slid into the panties and went to turn on the lights.

He blinked at the flood of light, then eased himself up and onto the chaise longue. "Do I frighten you?"

She shook her head. "Confuse is a better word."

"Believe me, that wasn't my intention." Matt didn't miss her screaming body language. She didn't return to him but sat on the edge of the sofa. He was reminded of a fragile bird ready to spread its plumage and take flight.

"Do you love me, June?" Matt asked quietly.

Yes! Yes! Yes! Why are you doing this to me? She barely nodded her head.

"Ever means forever," Matt said, watching her carefully. "Will you marry me, June?"

The tears that were waiting behind her lids to fall now

cascaded down June's cheeks. "Why, Matt? Why are you doing this, now?"

"Because I love you and I don't want you to leave me forever." Matt held out his hand to her but she didn't move. A crooked smile touched his lips. "I want to hold you but if I try using those wooden legs to get to you, I'll make a fool of myself falling flat on my butt." He tilted his head. "Is that what you want? Me at your feet?"

June smiled. "For what you're asking of me that might not be such a bad idea."

For all his outward calm, Matt began to breathe easier. She was teasing him, and how bad a sign could that be? He began to slide to the floor.

"Matt," June said, rushing to his side, but she was too late. He was flat on his butt. "What are you doing?"

"Obliging you," he said.

June chuckled and joined him. "You're such a determined cuss."

"It's one of my faults." He wrapped his arm around her shoulder and pulled her close.

"Do you always get your way?"

"Most of the time." He kissed the top of her head. "But I don't know about now. You haven't answered my question."

She slid her arm around his waist and emitted a deep sigh. After a long moment of silence she asked, "Have you ever heard anyone use the word 'smitten'?" She didn't really want an answer and continued. "My grandparents were smitten with each other. 'Smitten with her charms right from the start' my grandfather used to tell me. Grandma told me the same thing about him. They were incredibly old-fashioned for the twentieth century but were never ashamed to let me see how much they loved each other."

June sat up and looked into Matt's eyes. "I was smitten with you the first time I saw you in Denton's office. I didn't know who you were, but one glance at you had my heart doing flip-flops. If I hadn't been called into that office when I was, I would have been trying to seduce you in nothing flat.'' She responded to his squeeze and gentle kiss to her forehead.

''What about after we met?'' Matt asked.

''Then, I was all huff and puff and full of fire,'' June answered with a chuckle. ''But the conflagration had already started deep down in my soul. I think it'll burn inside of me forever. I'm so in love with you.''

Matt closed his eyes and hugged her, almost squeezing the breath from her. ''God, June, then tell me you'll marry me,'' he said in a ragged voice.

Breathless, June held him tightly. She shook her head. ''I want to,'' she managed.

His heart froze. ''Does that mean no?'' He couldn't look at her. When she kissed his eyes open he saw the pain in hers. ''Answer me.''

''You know what you're asking me to do,'' June said. ''Yet you still want me to give in, never to see what I can be. What I can accomplish with my life.'' She made him look into her eyes. ''Like you did.''

The poignancy of her words twisted his insides like a corkscrew. ''I already know what you are,'' he rasped. ''A beautiful, intelligent woman who has love in her heart and can do anything she wants to do. Be anything she wants to be. Right here in New York. Who doesn't need Paris, France, to show what she's made of.'' His eyes flashed. ''Hell, if you want to manage something, Sutherland can give you a department to head. You can do that and still live here as my wife!''

She lay quietly against his chest, listening to his argument. When he finished, she could feel the beat of his heart. For the first time June realized he was scared to death. He really believed that she'd leave and never look back. He was afraid of losing her.

When she stirred out of his arms, Matt touched her hand. "You're leaving me?" His voice was harsh.

June admired the control he exhibited in not using his hand as a vise to hold her. Willing to let her leave him in the middle of the night, yet dreading it if she did. She smiled and patted his cheek. "For a few minutes, love. Where's the linen closet?"

He relaxed with a near inaudible sigh. "I'm frozen in one position. Would you hand me those? I need to move." When Matt was on his crutches he hobbled awkwardly beside her to the foot of the stairs. "The first door to the left of the guest bathroom." He watched her walk slowly up the stairs, then turned and made his way toward the kitchen.

Matt was still in the small bathroom when June finished preparing a plush pallet on the floor with sofa cushions and fluffy pillows and lavender-scented sheets that freshened the room. In the kitchen, she boiled water for instant coffee and warmed some biscuits she found in the bread box.

"Hungry?"

Matt watched her butter a biscuit. She had put on a short cotton robe, and the sight of her dressed in lingerie sitting at his table did something to him. Just as he'd needed to see her reaction to his home, and had seen her as the lady of the house, the need for her to be with him always filled him with a fierceness that scared him. Instinctively he knew that forcing an answer from her now would be the mistake of his life. Tonight, he'd made her his, and he wouldn't lose her. Knowing what he had to do, he sat down, bit into a biscuit, and sipped the hot coffee.

June was silent as she ate, but watched Matt thoughtfully. She realized he'd done some heavy thinking. His words confirmed her thoughts.

"I pressured you, June, and I apologize," Matt said. "But no matter what happens I never want to lose you. There must be a way to work this out."

"I don't want to lose you either, Matt," June replied in a soft voice. She got up and went to him and kissed his mouth, warm and tasting of coffee beans. "But I know you're tired and should sleep. Can we discuss this in the morning?" She handed him his crutches.

Instead of starting down the hall, Matt propped himself up and cupped her delicate face in his big hands. He kissed her hungrily, his tongue reaching deep inside her mouth. When he lifted his head and saw the look of passion swimming in her eyes he felt himself becoming erect. "Everything you say and do amazes the hell out of me," he growled. "Every second I find something else to love about you."

June pressed herself into his arms and wasn't surprised to feel his erection against her belly because her own loins were on fire. She moved her hips suggestively against him.

"Don't do that," he warned, suddenly cursing himself for starting what he couldn't finish.

"Or what?" she asked huskily.

"Or nothing. You know I don't have any more condoms down here."

June writhed her hips again. She slipped her hand in her pocket and pulled out the little square packet. "I do," she murmured and grinned at the stifled sound in his throat. She held on to his arm, as he made short work out of the hobble down the hall. "Do you think you can stay awake, though?"

"Just watch me," he muttered, tossing his crutches away as he sank down on the pallet.

June started to turn out the lights when he called her name. She turned to see his eyes burning with desire.

"Leave them on and come to me," Matt commanded. When she was kneeling beside him he caught her shoulders and began to undress her. "I want to look at the woman I love. It's got to last me a long time." He pushed the robe off her shoulders and lifted the gown over her head. As if delaying his pleasure, he used both hands to fondle and caress her breasts as his gaze swept over them. The nipples tautened into pebbles under the gentle brushing of his thumbs. He bent and kissed them, drawing one and then the other deeply into his mouth. Her cry of delight tortured him. Matt lifted his head and stared into her eyes. ''At least, for the next ten days,'' he grumbled.

June's eyes misted when she understood what he was saying. He wouldn't deny her. ''Love me, then, sweetheart.'' His warm fingers on her belly as he caught the elastic of her panties sent erotic waves of anticipation pulsing through her already wired body. In seconds the wispy fabric was over her hips and down her legs. Naked, she lay down and watched him gaze at her from head to toe. He was making love to her with his eyes.

''I love you too,'' she murmured and shuddered at his first touch to her tingling flesh.

Chapter Eleven

Paris, France

Sleep was elusive during the last hour of June's flight as excitement flowed through every pore. From the moment she settled in her seat at JFK airport, her mind had begun churning with myriad ideas and possibilities. She'd slept for some of the seven-hour flight but much of her wakefulness had been filled with such stirring soul-searching that she'd felt the relief of her seatmates when she did drift off to sleep.

There wasn't any doubt that part of her excitement was due to the beginning of a challenging venture in Paris. But the rest stemmed from what she'd learned about herself during the last six hours, the summation of which was that she'd had her head buried in the sand; if not for months, then years, since her Grandma Belle had died and left her the house. She realized that she was going so far from home to find a niche for herself when there was really no need! She'd asked herself the same question over and over: Could she really be successful and happy at the same time? Successful in a new career and happy because she was in love. Could she have it all? She'd told herself that happy endings were fodder for fairy tales. Didn't one always have to sacrifice something?

The ultra disturbance that was spinning like a whirligig inside June's stomach had been precipitated by a remark made by Diane on Sunday while they conversed in June's kitchen. During the long plane ride she'd played that conversation over in her mind.

"You really like it, don't you?" June said.

"Like it?" Diane said. "Are you kidding? I love this big old house. Reminds me of the rambling barn I played in when I was a kid. Every summer me and my sister were shipped off to my great-aunts in rural Georgia." She winked. "They were spinsters who shared a home and I think they just wanted cheap child labor for a few months."

June smiled. "Bet you loved it though. Just like I love this house so much. It has that welcoming feeling that you don't find much in so many modern structures." She remembered where she spent the night. Except one other place she'd visited.

"I know exactly what you mean. I felt that the minute I stepped on the front porch." Diane smiled. "No wonder Matt wants . . ." She hesitated. "Forget that," she said.

"No, that's okay. It *would* suit Matt's purposes perfectly." June chuckled. "But it's my home."

"Well, if it were mine," Diane said, "I sure would find a way to live here and make it pay for me too." Her glance swept the big kitchen. "It has all the potential for a bed-and-breakfast." Her eyes twinkled. "For me, that is. My husband is hardly the chatty type to be breaking bread with strangers every morning."

Nodding in agreement, June said, "He's more private than others. Nothing wrong with that."

An affectionate look crossed Diane's features. "No, there isn't," she said softly. Then she gave June a quizzical look. "So you never really considered doing something like that yourself?" She shrugged. "Sure beats sitting in traffic to and from a nine-to-five every day."

"No, I haven't." After a second, June said, "Diane, you know ten days are going to just fly by. Have you and Andre made plans for when I return? I mean . . ."

"When you kick us out?" Diane was immediately apologetic. "Oh, honey, you know I was only kidding." She reached across the table and touched June's hand. "You have the biggest heart of anyone I've ever met. We can't thank you enough." She looked weary as she assessed their situation. "No. We really haven't thought beyond today. But I guess we'll have to start looking for an apartment to rent."

"You're perfectly welcome to stay here until you find a place. There's more than enough room," June said.

"We'll see," Diane said. "We'll see."

Loud laughter stirred June, and she glanced out the plane window. Nothing but white and gray clouds greeted her. She closed her eyes and her thoughts swam again.

. . . *find a way to live here and make it pay . . . It has all the potential of a bed-and-breakfast.* Diane's words taunted her. *Now why couldn't I see that for myself?* she wondered.

June could see herself weeks ago when she'd first encountered Matt Gardiner and listened to his off-the-wall pronouncement that he'd wanted to buy her house. She'd been incensed at his arrogance. And all the while Matt had the right idea. He saw what she couldn't see. But that was then. She *believed* she could run her own business and not rely on a partner. Who knew? Down the road she probably would have been pushed to buy Carlotta out when she didn't pull her weight in the laundry franchise. Like any other new venture, the work would be hard and entail many long hours. There was a mountain of research to be done but she knew she would do her damnedest to make it work.

June was tickled that she and the man she loved would be working together in a roundabout way. Certainly, her first customers would be Matt's customers. If *that* wouldn't be a challenge! Starting such a venture in her own backyard would surely equal if not surpass the intrigue of Ivon Raleigh's offer.

Although most of the passengers were stirring, preparing for the early morning landing, June feigned sleep, unwilling to invite the chatter of her seatmate, a talkative widow who was a worldwide traveler. June was still as she listened to her body and sighed gratefully. There was no sign of the throbbing headache that had hit her on Sunday. When she'd boarded her flight at JFK airport in the late evening, remnants of it had lingered and she had remembered what had instigated it.

When June had awakened in Matt's arms early in the morning, she found him propped on one elbow staring down at her. Opening her eyes must have surprised him because his expression became quickly guarded, but she felt his angst. She pulled him down beside her and they clung to each other and after making love they talked about their feelings for a long time. Afterward, Matt found that by putting slight pressure on his heel he could maneuver up and down the stairs. They were in his bed when they heard sounds outside and realized that Andre had arrived and was discreetly going about his business in the kennels. They'd made love again.

At noon, June left. It was while driving home she'd felt the first sensations of the headache that made her pull over until the first pangs passed. The doctor had warned her of what to expect. The tightening of her neck and head muscles felt like a viselike band around her head. Days before, she'd learned that she was one of those unfortunates who suffered from tension headaches. The doctor had commented that she was more fortunate than others who had to endure migraines, and that her condition was not as serious as the chronic headache sufferer who experienced unrelenting pain nearly every day. Hers occurred randomly and the doctor said that she could go for long periods without having a headache, but to expect one whenever she became distressed or felt a deep sense of anxiety.

June knew that it was her heavy emotional feelings about leaving Matt that had affected her so deeply. Even though they'd talked for a long time, sharing their fears and cares about the future, he'd kept his promise not to pressure her for her answer.

Now at nine A.M. Paris time, after deplaning and enduring the customs ritual, she was waiting at the luggage carousel, grateful that she was headache free. All that she craved was immediate transport to a bed, a big fluffy pillow, and sleep. But Ivon had informed her that someone was meeting her and had described the area where she was to wait. With her Pullman in tow, she walked toward the designated spot but stopped short when she spied a familiar figure. *Carlotta Graham!*

Openmouthed and incurring the wrath of travelers who had to sidestep the rude woman blocking traffic, June pushed her way to a window wall of stores and just stared. She clenched her hands willing herself not to get another headache, because if nothing else the stress and anger seething inside her would surely bring on a humdinger! She rubbed her temples as if daring any kind of pain to surface. But for insurance she hurried inside a notions store and bought a bottle of water, then downed two painkillers. If her first day in Paris would land her in jail for pummeling a woman to death, then so be it. June wasn't leaving with anyone until she faced that witch. The picture of her and Carlotta going at it like two mud-wrestlers brought a wry smile to her lips. She hurried forward.

Carlotta was sitting at a table in the outside space of a small café. June watched as the flight attendant, who was sitting with her, got up, waved, and walked away. It hit her then. Carlotta was in uniform. She was working?

In all the weeks that had passed since she learned that Carlotta was no longer married, it had never dawned on June that the woman would have returned to work. A woman with such conniving instincts would certainly have snared another wealthy man, even if it meant being a mere paramour. But returning to the air? Unthinkable!

June held back the laughter that was bubbling up in her throat when she remembered where she'd slept the day before. The woman had held liquid gold in her hands and like silt had let it flow through her fingers. June sobered quickly. If her former deceitful friend hadn't shown her true self to her husband, then June would never have crossed paths with the man she loved. Thinking about him made her almost as limp as a wet noodle, and as she approached the table the wrath in her soul was replaced with a sense of peace.

"Hello, Carlotta." She sat down. "Do you mind?"

Perturbed when out of the corner of her eye she saw a figure approaching her, Carlotta wished that her coworkers would quickly go about their business. The only person she wished to see on her days off was the American businessman that she'd met last month. He was finally meeting her, promising to spend the next two days together. *About damn time*, she fumed. She looked up. Her face contorted into a kaleidoscope of colors and images. "June?"

"It's me." *Oh, payback is sweet!*

"W—what are you doing here?" Carlotta's eyes skimmed the other woman. *She wasn't in uniform. Which carrier was she with?* "Y—you're working international now?"

"You might say that," June said, relaxing in her chair. *Whoosh!* With those words and the stunned look on Carlotta's face, June felt vindicated. If she never heard those words, "I'm sorry," from her former friend it wouldn't matter. Everything was going to be all right. The woman that she'd known was still beautiful but there was something missing. Instead of an air of chic confidence there was a look of desperation in her eyes. And she appeared worn—no, used, June thought. All used up. The first hint of a woman's classic beauty fading was the overuse of makeup. Rosier cheeks and heavier eyeliner overshadowed the once flawless skin and beautiful contours. June started at the woman's strident voice, filled with sarcasm.

"Well, have you looked me over to your satisfaction, honey?" Carlotta drawled. She appraised June with a critical eye. "My, my, have we come into money, dear? You look so . . . rich!"

Does love do that? June suppressed a malicious retort. "In a manner of speaking," she demurred. "But what about you? Marriage to a wealthy man wasn't what you thought it'd be?" She looked pointedly at the bare third finger of the left hand.

"Hah! Wealthy?" Carlotta waved her manicured fingers in the air. "That didn't last long, honey." She narrowed her eyes. "Why else do you think you never received any more money after I promised to reimburse you? Do you think I'd make a promise like that and not intend to keep it? I was broke!" She rolled her eyes. "I was the world's biggest fool," she spat.

That you are. "Really?"

"What do you mean, 'really'? Yes, really!" she snapped. Her eyes narrowed. "I'd think that after what happened you'd want a piece of me the first time we met again."

Carlotta studied June carefully. "You almost look . . .
beatific. Don't tell me you went and fell in love with the
boy next door. What's his name? Caleb something?"

"I've told you a million times before that we're childhood
friends. Nothing more. Romance between us has never been
a question." She held Carlotta's gaze. "That's something
you probably wouldn't understand, though. It's all about
friendship."

"I get your point, honey." She laughed. "Guess I screwed
us up for good, didn't I?"

June gestured indifferently. "I realized that we were all
surface, and you never truly comprehended the meaning of
friendship. You don't matter to me anymore." She glanced
at the bare ring finger again. "But I am curious to know
what happened to the great love of your life."

Carlotta laughed. "Guess you're entitled to some explanation seeing as how I reneged on my promise. But one day
you're going to get it all back."

June held up a hand. "Waiting for another ship of riches
to dock at your feet? Spare me, please. I'm only interested
in how you went from fairy tale princess to working girl."
Wickedly, she waited to hear the grandiose explanation.

An unpleasant smile curled Carlotta's lips. "I dumped
the fraud of a frontin' phony. Wealthy businessman? You
know what that guy did? Dogs! He was a damn dog breeder!
And before that he was a postal worker! He actually expected
me to live in Long Island, of all places, to help him raise
his mutts!" She swore. "Living my dream life in Paris?
Forget that! Humph! Making me believe that he lived here."

"Made you?" June said softly. Her eyebrows raised a
notch.

"Well, what fool would fly across the water as much as
he did, from New York to Paris to Africa? He stayed abroad
more than he did at home. So what was I supposed to think?"
She swore. "Come to find out he made this a stopover to

visit with some old man who's gotta be a hundred at least and lives just as many miles away from the city. A damn country bumpkin.''

''So you only assumed that he was a wealthy Parisian?''

''What would you think?'' Carlotta snarled. ''Long Island!'' She looked at June curiously. ''You live on Long Island. You may have heard of him although it's quite possible you haven't with all those little towns running into one another. Cross the street and you're in a different zip code.'' She chuckled. ''Gardiner Kennels. That's the name of his business. To think that once I was Mrs. Matt Gardiner.''

''You're divorced now?'' June asked, trying hard to maintain her serenity. His name on this coldhearted woman's lips made her want to smack the disdainful smirk off her face.

''Annulment actually,'' Carlotta said airily. ''As if it'd never existed. Good riddance.'' She looked at her watch, then glanced around the room irritably.

June could only guess what or whom she was waiting for. In an amused tone she said, ''I'd better go. I'm being met.'' She stood up. ''Forgive me if we don't shake hands and say meaningless clichés to each other. Suffice it to say that my curiosity is assuaged and I do hope we never meet again.''

Carlotta laughed. ''You never did bite your tongue, did you?'' She lifted a thin shoulder. ''Now you can do the same for me. My curiosity is piqued. What are you doing here?''

''Working.''

''Here? In Paris?'' Carlotta's jaw went slack. ''Doing what, may I ask?''

June looked across the room where she was supposed to meet her guide. A woman was holding a placard with her name printed in large black letters. ''I'm with Raleigh Enterprises.'' She picked up her shoulder purse and caught the handle of her Pullman. "Good-bye, Carlotta. Try to have a decent life." She walked away with a confident stride.

"Raleigh Enterprises. Ivon Raleigh?" Carlotta spoke to June's back. "Well, I'll be damned."

The woman who was waiting for her was looking expectantly around the room, and as far as June could tell there wasn't the slightest sign of impatience on her face. From this distance she could see that the woman was a stunner, and June wondered where she fit in Ivon Raleigh's scheme of things. If her boss had to go outside his country to hire personnel, then she must be one of those clichéd beauties without brains, June thought, and breathed, "Lucky me."

"*Bonjour. Je suis* June Saxon." She extended her hand. "*Excusez-moi, j'ai été retardee par une affaire importante.*" June hoped her tardiness would be forgiven.

Laraine St. John took the proffered hand. "*Bonjour, madame Saxon, ne vous en faites pas. Mon nom est Laraine St-Jean. J'espère que votre voyage s'est bien passé.*"

"*Merci.*" June thanked the woman for dismissing her apology and inquiring about her safe journey. In French she said that the ride was long but safe and was certain that the horrible recent air tragedies were on the minds of many an air traveler all over the world.

Laraine nodded gravely. "*Oui,*" she answered. She discarded the cardboard placard as they walked briskly outside the building, then looked curiously at the pretty American. "Would you prefer to speak in English? I don't mind." She spoke English.

"I would like that," June answered in her native tongue. She returned the woman's frank appraisal. "Thank you." They stopped beside a long black limousine whose driver was standing beside it. As the two women approached he opened the door.

"Monsieur Raleigh sent his car for you. Thank you, Micah." The driver nodded and handed both women in the car and once behind the wheel, guided the big limo easily into the steadily flowing traffic moving slowly from the airport.

The glass partition separating the driver from passengers was closed and June sensed that her guide had requested it be so beforehand. She wondered what the woman wanted to tell her in private. Although Laraine St. John was the epitome of politeness and cordiality, June could detect a reticence that was nearly imperceptible. Training as a flight attendant had fine-tuned her senses to the idiosyncrasies of the human species, and her natural curiosity set the wheels turning, leading her to believe that maybe she wasn't sitting next to an airhead after all. The well-modulated voice interrupted her thoughts.

"You speak French excellently," Laraine said, appraising June coolly.

In a bland tone, June replied, "A requirement of the job," and continued to observe the passing scenery.

Obviously perturbed by the cool response, Laraine realized that although her manners were impeccable this stranger had picked up her negative body language. Her eyes clouded. Of course, Ivon would not hire an imbecile to work so closely with him, she thought.

"That was a silly remark." Laraine said. She smiled ruefully at her gaffe. "I know that you are an excellent linguist, as Monsieur Raleigh requires. Are languages part of your heritage?"

June recognized the silent concession in the tone and the shifting of the woman's body into a more relaxed pose. She shook her head. "Both my parents were African-Americans as were my grandparents. I learned early on that I had an affinity with languages. My grandmother noticed my fascination with Spanish-speaking TV programs and how I'd tried to pronounce the words, so she encouraged me by buying videos in Spanish and French. By the end of high

school I'd learned to read and write in both languages."
The look of admiration in the other woman's eyes helped
to soften her tone. "If I may ask, what about your excellent
English? I detect an accent, but it doesn't sound French."

"I'm told that," Laraine said easily. "Attending college
in California helped create my English accent. I inherited
the language of my parents, speaking my native French and
later Spanish and English. My mother is Spanish and French
and my father is French and British." She shrugged. "The
whole world has become one gigantic melting pot, I think."

"That's so true," June agreed. Laraine's mixed heritage
accounted for her pale beige skin with a slight rosy tinge.
Her light brown hair shone with natural red highlights and
her hazel eyes changed with the light from green to gray.
She wore her hair severely pulled back in a bun but June
could see the wave pattern and guessed that when loosened
it would tumble in a curly mass to her shoulders. But the
style suited her flawless, classic heart-shaped face.

The car's moving at a snail's pace for several minutes in
the heavy traffic gave June pause to check out her surroundings. Both the driver and Laraine looked unperturbed by the
delay and June remembered that she was in a foreign country
and not on New York time. She settled back though she
wondered about having her first meeting with her employer,
disheveled, sleepy, and hungry.

Noticing the flicker of worry that crossed June's features,
Laraine said, "We will be arriving before too long. You
will have time to freshen up and get a bit of rest before your
meeting with Monsieur Raleigh."

"Thank you," June murmured, admiring the astuteness
of Laraine St. John. As she listened to her make small talk
about the passing scenery she couldn't help but feel she was
right in her minute assessment of Laraine. *She resents me.*

Impressed by Laraine's professionalism, June was fascinated with the deft and thorough responses to her questions

about the city. After nearly forty-five minutes, June wondered why, with this woman in Ivon Raleigh's employ, *she'd* been hired.

Guilt swept through her. How was she going to tell Ivon that she no longer needed his job? All she wanted was to get on the next return flight and start planning her life— back home where she belonged! But he'd placed his trust in her so completely. She'd be as heartless as Carlotta if she threw cold water in his face at their first meeting. He'd gone to great lengths in searching for that one person he thought could work alongside him compatibly.

There was no time to dwell on her thoughts as the car moved at a quickened pace down a less crowded street. Surprised to pass through iron gates and around a circular driveway only to stop in front of a huge house, June raised a brow. She was expecting to be driven to one of the glitzy hotels that dotted the city. The door was opened and they were assisted from the limousine.

"Thank you, Micah," Laraine said after the man deposited June's luggage on the flagstone walk. "About two hours." The man nodded, and as he drove away she turned to June, who was gazing at the massive stone structure. "This is Monsieur Raleigh's home when he's in town. You'll be his guest for your stay." She turned toward the house as the door opened.

June watched an older, pasty-faced, white-haired man approach with a dignified step and she held her giggle. Surely, she was not in a movie. And surely, this was the butler, dressed in a somber gray suit, tailored to perfection with a pristine white shirt and a black bow tie, the corners standing at attention. The expression he wore was in perfect sync with his very proper attire. In an old whodunit movie he would mostly certainly be the least likely suspect.

"Percy, this is Ms. June Saxon. Ms. Saxon, Percy. He is

Mr. Raleigh's butler and will take care of your luggage."
She spoke in English.

"Ms. Saxon," Percy said, speaking in heavily accented
English. "Welcome to Raleigh House." He grabbed the
handle of her Pullman and nodded at Laraine. "Ms. St.
John." He turned and walked away.

Raleigh House. June suppressed another threatening giggle. She'd never stayed in a house that had a name before,
but had half expected to hear Chateau Bordeaux or some
such, nothing so mundane as Raleigh House!

Laraine stood in the wide foyer as Percy walked up the
wide staircase to the second landing. "I'll show you to your
room but let me familiarize you with this level. You will
be visiting here often when you return in September. Meals
are served in the dining room over here." She opened sliding
wood double doors that opened into a large formal dining
room with country French decor. The wallpaper with its
white background and prominent green vines was airy and
inviting. "When Monsieur Raleigh takes his meals in he
prefers a more conversational seating arrangement with no
more than six." She'd noted June's look at the small table
for such a large room. "For more formal dinners the table
extends to accommodate sixteen."

June took the tour encompassing the kitchen, a maid's
room, a small study, a guest bedroom, and an almost bare
room to seat waiting visitors. She made the appropriate
appreciative comments wondering how much input Ivon had
in the decorating scheme. She'd gotten a different picture
of the man in that one hour they'd talked. He was sophisticated, a little arrogant and distant, but hardly projected the
warmth she felt in his home. When she entered his office
that was smaller than the study, she saw the man she'd seen
in New York. It was quite austere in decor. The floor was
bare but the oak wood flooring shone like glass beneath two
burgundy-colored square Aubusson rugs. The desk bare,

except for a pewter lamp, was modern glass and chrome, unlike the warm woods indicative of the other rooms. It was almost a shock to the senses and in comparison, tacky. There were two black file cabinets, a high-back leather chair, and two straight-back chairs for visitors. A small desk and chair were in a corner and June supposed it was for a secretary since there was a computer. The room was less than inviting and June was in a hurry to leave.

As Laraine closed the door and led the way up the stairs, she said, "Monsieur Raleigh prefers not to conduct business at home. But sometimes it is necessary."

"Very noticeable," June murmured.

"There are four bedrooms up here. The master suite is down there."

Three of the bedrooms, June noticed, were together at one end of the hall and the master bedroom was all by itself at the other end. *Not surprising*, June mused.

"This is your bedroom."

"How lovely," June said as she immediately felt welcomed in the homey room. It was dressed in ivory, pale green, and mauve, and she felt like kicking her shoes off and comforting her tired feet in the mauve carpet that was inches deep. Her luggage was on a rack that was at the foot of the bed. "I'm sure I'll be quite comfortable."

"I think you will be," Laraine said. She turned to the big-boned woman with an angular, red-blotched but pleasant face, who appeared in the doorway. "Hello, Margaret." After making the introductions, she added, "Margaret is the housekeeper and will see to your needs while you're here. Just let her know what you require and she will oblige." She exchanged a few words with the gray-eyed woman who left with a nod to June.

"Margaret has prepared a light meal for us. I'll wait for you in the dining room." She turned to go.

"Laraine," June said, stopping the other woman at the

door. "Do you have a moment?" She saw the woman's light green eyes darken with curiosity. "Please, won't you sit?"

"Why am I here?" June said in an easy voice after sitting on the queen-size bed while Laraine sat in the green wing chair by the window.

"I don't understand." Laraine looked away briefly, then lifted a delicate shoulder.

"I think you do. I could have easily been put up in a hotel, which is what I expected," June said. "Why in Mr. Raleigh's home?" She made a gesture that encompassed the house. "I suspect he values his privacy." Something she couldn't detect flickered in Laraine's eyes but was gone in an instant and June had "something is rotten in the state of Denmark" feelings.

"Monsieur Raleigh wants you near for the next ten days," Laraine said, fixing her gaze on June. "As you know, his businesses are separate from his work in the financial institution of which he is president. His offices are not far from here and he expects neither you nor himself to endure traffic to and from a hotel whenever he wants to meet with you. Most of your orientation and duties will be discussed here in the comfort of his study. I will familiarize you with the staff and the operation of the three enterprises that you will be overseeing."

June was curious. "What is your position with Raleigh Enterprises?" She had thought *she* was hired to be the all-around gal Friday.

Laraine dropped her gaze for a moment, then stared at June. "I have been in Monsieur Raleigh's employ since I returned home from college ten years ago."

Ten years! June had thought that Laraine was younger but realized she was the same age or a few years older. She'd been a young woman fresh out of college and probably landed the job of her dreams working with the prestigious

Raleigh Enterprises. She couldn't help wondering in what capacity.

"I was twenty-two," Laraine said, watching June's expression.

"Oh," June said, sorry now that she'd been so blunt. She was suddenly taken aback at the look of sadness that appeared briefly in the woman's eyes.

Laraine said softly, "I'm a store manager." She held June's look. "Since the airport I've sensed your curiosity about me."

"I am curious," June, admitted. "Store manager?" She waved a hand. "You appear to be doing what I would be doing for Mr. Raleigh," she said.

Laraine crossed her legs and clasped her hands over her knees. "I manage the ladies' boutique."

Again there was that sad look. June waited, wondering what she'd walked into.

"I know every aspect of the businesses; the ladies' boutique, the china and crystal shop, and the antiques store." Laraine released her knees and relaxed against the chair back. "The latter two have been in Monsieur Raleigh's family for years. I started in the antiques shop. The boutique was my idea and since its opening only eight years ago has expanded significantly. Under my management it has become highly successful."

Aware of the pride in the softly spoken words, June remarked, "You sound pleased."

"I love fashion." Laraine's face brightened. "Four years ago, I was able to convince Monsieur Raleigh to begin an African line of merchandise." She shrugged. "I knew it would be a tremendous hit. Paris has always attracted the diverse traveler. My garments are haute couture and are sought after by the African woman working and living in Paris." She paused. "Once a year, in August when the city sleeps, Monsieur Raleigh travels to Africa where he selects

the finest fabrics for the next year's line." Her eyes clouded.
"As his personal assistant you will accompany him."

June observed the woman. Deciding to play a hunch, she
said, "Were you ever offered the position?" *May as well
get it out in the open,* she thought.

"No."

"Why?" *The man can't be a chauvinist,* June thought,
or otherwise *she* wouldn't be sitting here.

"There—are circumstances." Her lashes flickered.
"Monsieur Raleigh believes I am needed here."

June saw the unguarded look of sadness and then the veil
of professionalism that returned when Laraine stood up. She
rose also. "Wait. Please."

Laraine, who was nearly the same height as June, gave
her a direct stare. "Yes?"

"Did you want the position?"

"Yes." Laraine's look did not waver. She said, "I'm
sure you'll want a few moments. Please join me in the dining
room. There are matters I'm instructed to discuss with you.
After our meal, I must leave." After a slight hesitation she
left.

June sat back down on the bed, feeling very much like a
thief. *Then why doesn't Laraine St. John, who seems the
epitome of confidence and efficiency, just tell the man?* June
wondered.

Hours after their light fare and Laraine's departure, June
returned to her room, filled with curiosity. Apparently, Laraine had second thoughts about speaking so freely with a
stranger and had cloaked herself with the same professional
demeanor she'd worn at the airport. During the meal Laraine
had been meticulous in choosing her words when explaining
the week's itinerary. Her unwillingness to share anything
more of a personal nature was more telling than her silence,

and smelling a mystery, June's inquiring mind was working overtime. Beverly would call it downright nosiness. Thoughts of her friend brought sudden pangs of homesickness.

Pondering whether to venture out on a quick walk of her own, she nixed the idea, tickled at the spectacle she'd make sleepwalking down the street.

Laraine had told her that Ivon would be returning very late and extended his apologies that she would be dining alone on her first evening in Paris. So much for the nightlife of Gay Paree, June thought, and began to undress. After showering she donned a silk, floor-length nightgown. Her drooping eyelids begged for sleep and she prayed that the housekeeper would let her sleep through the dinner hour. When she pulled the coverlet back the scent of lavender assailed her nostrils, bringing sweet memories.

Since she left home, Matt had never been out of her thoughts, especially when she'd excitedly searched for the right time and the proper words to tell him about her impending venture. She couldn't wait to hear his reaction and wished that she could see his face go through all kinds of comical changes. The way she was bubbling inside, there was no way that she could keep from blurting out the news the first time she called him.

The sweet fragrance conjured up stark images of their last intimate moments together. They'd made love on lavender-scented sheets, and the visions sent a shower of fireworks through her. A moan escaped and, embarrassed, she glanced around as if someone could have heard.

Giving up the notion of sleep until she heard his voice, June picked up the phone and dialed the infinite amount of numbers required for international calls and hoped she would not get the answering machine.

''Hello.''

"Toi?" Instantly surprised, June was hit with a wave of worry. It was only ten in the morning there. "Is Matt okay?"

"Calm down, honey, everything's fine over here," Toi said with a chuckle. "George and I are trying to give a hand. How about you?" Then she said, "Don't bother answering that. I know I'm not the one you want to talk to. Hold on. It'll take a few minutes for Matt to get here. He's outside with Andre."

June heard the breathlessness in his voice. "Matt," she said accusingly, "what are you doing outside? Should you be—"

"I love you too, sweetheart," Matt interrupted, grinning like a fool at the sound of her voice. He was glad he was sitting and that Toi had gone back outside after helping him inside to the kitchen, because his body was telling on him.

"Oh, baby, I love you too," June whispered. "I miss you so much."

"You do?" Matt answered, willing his insides to be still.

"Of course I do," an indignant June sputtered.

Matt softened his voice. "I know you do, sweetheart. I miss you more and I'm counting the days."

"Me too," June said, swallowing the lump in her throat. Then brushing off a pending flood of melancholia, she said, "You're so out of breath. Should you be doing so much walking around?"

"I'm not walking," Matt answered. "George brought me a wheelchair so I'm maneuvering around pretty well. This is my first real look at the fire damage and my opinion is needed on a few things."

She heard the anger and knew he was reliving the horror. "Any news about how it started?"

"Arson, as we all suspected. An investigation into identifying the culprit is under way with my friend from Philadelphia as the leading star."

"How are Diane and Andre?" June asked, taking his

mind off the arsonist. If Matt were within spitting distance of that man the fireworks would rival the Fourth of July.

"Better. They're trying hard to make the best of the situation." Reflecting on his friend's dilemma, he said, " 'Thanks' doesn't say much for what you did for them, June. Diane is crazy about your house and Andre is grateful for his privacy. I think he likes the idea of not being on the property twenty-four-seven."

Diane loves my house and I love her for lighting a fire under me! June knew she looked silly with a smile as wide as a toothpaste model in a silly commercial. She tried to talk calmly. "If not for Toi, it wouldn't have happened."

"That's true." Matt hesitated. "Makes me wonder what's going to happen when you return."

"I know exactly what's going to happen." June couldn't contain herself any longer. "Matt, I—" His husky voice interrupted her.

"Tell me, sweetheart, what do you think of the City of Lights? Is it everything you expected?" Matt wished he were the one showing her around, and cursed his carelessness. Before the injury he'd toyed with the idea of spending an evening with her in Paris. "Which hotel did Raleigh set you up in and did he insist on a room with a view?"

"I haven't seen those beautiful lights yet." She chuckled softly. "And I'm in Raleigh House with a breathtaking view of a beautiful garden."

"Raleigh House?" Matt frowned. "Can't place it. Which arrondissement is it in?"

She smiled. Like a Parisian, he would know all the districts. "I believe Laraine said it's the seventh. Raleigh House is Ivon's home and where I'll be staying for the next ten days. Before I leave, Laraine will take me to look at a few neighborhoods in which she thinks I'd like to apartment hunt in September, but it really won't be necessary because . . ." She stopped when she heard the whisper of breath that froze the airwaves, and chilled her ear.

"You're Ivon Raleigh's house guest?" Matt gripped the phone.

"Yes." An uneasy feeling crept through June. "What's wrong, Matt?"

"Who is Laraine?"

"His employee. What is wrong with you?"

"Did Raleigh inform you of this . . .arrangement before you left?"

Arrangement? Why did he sound so—so suspicious? "No." Fear touched her chest like spidery fingers. "What are you thinking, Matt?" Her voice was barely a whisper.

"I don't remember reading about the economy going to pot over there," Matt said evenly. "I'm finding it difficult to understand why you're being denied the luxury of a fine Paris hotel on your first visit."

June waited until her heart stopped pounding, then breathed deeply. "It's convenient that I stay here, Matt."

"For whom?" Matt said softly.

June bristled. "Ivon has irregular hours. I haven't even seen him yet. I'm dressed for bed and probably will be asleep when he does get home! This arrangement is easier for both of us." She frowned and her body, once so wired, was now as deflated as a wind-tattered sail. Her big announcement was like bitter herbs on her dry tongue. Her voice was cool. "Is your mind out there in the kennels?"

Dressed for bed? In another man's home? Was it only a day ago that she'd dressed for bed in his home? And lay in his arms soft, warm, and love-drenched.

What was he thinking? Matt rubbed his temples wishing he could recall every word he'd said. He'd angered her with his sarcasm and she had every right to call him a dog. "June . . ."

"I don't believe we're having this conversation." June

was silent for a second, then said, wearily, "Take down this number. You can call me here anytime." When he did, she said, "Right now, I think you have a lot on your mind and must be exhausted. I know I am so I'm going to sleep. Goodbye." She hung up the phone.

Stunned, she sat on the edge of the bed. "What happened?" she whispered, as if by magic her fairy godmother would appear with a crystal-clear explanation and soothe her bruised ego. Was that the man she loved and what in God's name was he accusing her of? The ludicrousness of his silent recrimination brought a harsh laugh.

For the last few hours she'd been dead on her feet and he was insinuating that she was locked up in a torrid seduction scene. Did he think she was like his ex-wife? The devastating thought froze her laughter. *No!* "Does he even know who I am?" June whispered. The thought was sobering and she had to take a long look at their whirlwind weeks together, which culminated in their declaring their love. Had it all been too fast?

A minute ago June had seen a new side to Matt that caused her to wonder what else she'd missed. A man's jealousy was common enough and she immediately dismissed it. *She* would wonder about *his* staying in a strange woman's house for ten days! But suspicious insinuations without merit? She realized that the deceitful Carlotta had wounded Matt badly. Sadly, the wound was deep and still unhealed because he'd fortified himself with invisible armor—against her or any other woman who sought to penetrate it. He steeled himself against future hurt no matter what the cost!

It had taken June all of seven hours on a plane to rearrange her future with an excitement that could hardly be contained. Now there was a void. She'd been ready to fly home to Matt to begin planning their future, one that dismissed the possibility of a long-distance affair, or worse, a transatlantic marriage. Reluctantly and with a heavy heart she realized that with what had just happened, her plans would have to be made without him.

June was determined not to allow a bruised heart to deter her from taking an embryo of an idea and watching it grow to fulfill a dream. Her only regret was that she had to disappoint the one man who'd seen in her what she couldn't see in herself: a drive and the ability to succeed. Telling Ivon Raleigh that Paris wasn't where she belonged would be one of the hardest things she would ever have to do in her life.

Chapter Twelve

Matt sat at the table watching George scrape the dinner dishes and put them in the dishwasher. Toi had left hours ago to go shopping with Diane after reviewing the cooking and cleaning schedule with the housekeeper.

"Women," George said with a wink, and then sat across from Matt. He pushed a mug of coffee and a huge slice of chocolate cake in front of his brother.

"Whose?" Matt said after tasting the moist confection.

"All of them," George said grinning broadly. "Yours, mine, and Andre's."

"Mine?" Matt looked inquisitive.

George laughed. "Don't give me that innocent look. Yeah, yours, but I'll get to that in a minute." He ignored his brother's indifferent shrug. "What I mean is, why did Diane have to buy new stuff when June said to use everything in the house? And Toi hiring a new housekeeper for you until Diane gets it together? The setup's not going to last two weeks before they're going to have to move!"

Matt busied himself with the coffee and cake. "Beats me. Guess there's nothing like having your own."

"Seriously, what are they going to do? Any plans?" George looked mysterious. "My wife has some ideas."

"I don't want to know," Matt said. "But then again, she usually comes up with some winners."

"I know," George said proudly. "She's my woman after all, ain't she?" Then, "No kidding. What are the Heaths going to do?"

"I have an agency looking for something that'll be a little more permanent," Matt said.

"You're looking?" George frowned.

"We'll see what turns up," Matt said, offhandedly.

"You know what I mean. I thought we agreed that Andre doesn't take charity."

"It's not charity," Matt said with impatience. "They can call it a loan if it'll make them feel better." He drummed his fingers on the table. "They've talked about buying a condo or a co-op one day. This'll just nudge them a bit sooner." His voice turned bitter. "That man nearly got his hands burned off trying to save another man's property and way of life. Time he had his own to make the same sacrifices for if need be. He's more than earned a second chance."

"Knowing you, it'll happen and Andre will think it was his own idea." He looked at his brother with admiration.

Matt grunted and started to reach for his cane. George had it delivered with the wheelchair and Matt found that he was able to get around less clumsily. His brother's voice stopped him from struggling to his feet.

"Whoa there. I ain't finished yet." His eyes twinkled. "Now about *your* lady. After you four-wheeled it in here this morning with a Cheshire Cat's grin, you returned with a mouthful of sour balls. Want to talk about it?"

Matt looked at his watch. "Too bad six is too early to tell your kids a bedtime story," he drawled.

George shook his head. "Gina and Jade are like their mother when it comes to shopping. They'll probably close up the mall with their aunt." He planted his elbows on the table and steepled his fingers. "So what happened?" he asked softly. All teasing was gone.

Resignedly, Matt imitated his brother's pose and his face twisted in a grimace. "She called me a dog!"

George found it hard holding back a surprised grin but he managed superbly as he asked, "So what'd you say to earn that distinction?"

"For God's sake, he set her up in his house!" Matt exploded.

Letting the words sink in, George finally shrugged and said, "Sounds like a convenient plan to me. Did she explain why?"

"Yes." Matt glared.

"You didn't agree and told her so."

"Right." He couldn't believe George's cool assessment of a situation that he thought to be ludicrous.

"If you're likening Ivon Raleigh to our father you're way out of line." George's voice was sharp. "He's an astute businessman and from what I've heard is a dyed-in-the-wool bachelor." He jabbed a finger in the air. "We've talked about the red tape involved in working in a foreign country. I don't care how much pull and money the man has; he's got to be bending over backward to get a work permit for her. What man in his right mind would put himself through that just to seduce a beautiful young woman? There must be hundreds right under his nose that he could choose from."

The reference to their father turned Matt's face into a stoic mask. He listened in silence.

George lowered his voice when he saw the tightening of Matt's jaw. "If Raleigh didn't see the potential in June as his right hand, I can't see how a man would go through hell to get her over there to play games. Stop thinking with your emotions.''

Matt held George's gaze. ''There aren't hundreds like June,'' he said quietly.

A long whistle from George followed his brother's words. He was sympathetic when he said, ''You want her back.'' After Matt's look he added, ''Okay, okay, I mean you don't want to hear about her returning to Paris in September.''

''You're a smart man.''

George smoothed back his hair. ''Whew, that's heavy, man. You're not giving her a chance.'' He cocked a brow. ''You're not pressuring her, I hope.''

''I asked her to marry me,'' Matt said. ''She'll give me an answer in two weeks.''

''And to hell with what she wants, huh?'' George stood and threw his brother a look of disgust as he cleared the table.

''What's eating you?'' Matt growled.

''You're blowin' it, man,'' George said.

''By proposing?''

''No. By pushing her into a corner. From what I've seen, she's no Carlotta. She's a woman who'll work with her man to an equitable solution to any problem. Even if it means a long-distance relationship for however long it takes.'' His eyes narrowed. ''Bet you never even thought of that. You just let your mind wallow in the toilet and had the nerve to lay it on her.''

Matt was taken aback by George's vehemence. He'd been happy when June had made such a hit with his family but he hadn't realized the extent of George's feelings. Or Toi's, for all the help she'd been. He watched as his brother wiped the countertop, then dried his hands.

''You're leaving?'' Matt asked as George passed by, clapping him on the shoulder.

''Yeah, man.'' He looked around. ''You should be okay

for the rest of the night. If you need anything, Andre can get here quicker than I can. Come lock up behind me."

Matt followed him to the door. "Thanks," he said gruffly.

George shrugged. "I've done a dish or two in my day," he said with nonchalance. "Don't mention it."

"That's not what I mean and you know it." He gave his brother a steady look.

A twinkle in George's eyes brightened his whole face. "You're a smart man," he said, echoing Matt's words. "Don't blow it. Talk to you tomorrow." He closed the door with a firm click.

An hour later, Matt was in the study still reflecting on George's perceptive words and how much sense they'd made. *Guess having the love of a good woman all these years made him like that,* he mused. His expression grew serious. If he wasn't careful he *was* going to lose the one woman that he'd go through hell for, all because of his insecurities and lack of trust.

She's no Carlotta. George was right and Matt knew deep down that he'd feared that déjà vu would happen all over again, thinking that he was in love, then losing out to a world of glitz and glamour. No, he thought, that would never happen with June.

But when Matt closed his eyes he couldn't help but remember June's last word. Her "good-bye" hadn't sounded like "good night." It'd been so final.

June awakened slowly, acclimating herself to her strange surroundings. She'd slept long and hard but didn't wonder why she still felt restless, because Matt had appeared in several of her dreams. Before last night, seeing his image would have made her ecstatic.

She'd searched her heart and soul for a long time until, weary, she'd closed her eyes. Now visions of a fickle-minded female waffling over decisions hounded her and she thought a shrink's couch would come in mighty handily, though she quickly lost that thought. With great effort, she buried the sadness that had brought tears to her eyes the night before.

In a philosophical frame of mind she threw off the covers, mentally shedding any melancholia. She went to the window to look at the Paris sky on her first real morning in the old city. It was barely seven o'clock and the sky was still a hazy gray, but she relished her view of the beautiful garden below and was grateful to be able to start the day with a sense of serenity. She wasn't of the delusion that she'd be spending hours on one of the few white benches that offered solitude, but before she left she would have to visit if only to meditate. When she flew home her mind would have to be composed before she met Matt. One look at his handsome face and pain-filled eyes would break her heart but she knew for her own sake she had to be strong. It meant her future.

Besides, she thought, with her employer jumping through hoops to get her here, she couldn't betray his confidence in her, at least not at their first meeting. She decided not to break the news to him immediately because she didn't know in her own mind how to formulate her words. She turned away and with a resolute step walked to the bathroom, shedding her gown as she went. As she showered, an old refrain played a tattoo on her brain. *Today is the first day of the rest of my life.*

Dressed in a smart cotton and linen-blend gray suit with a collarless V-neck white blouse and black patent sling-back shoes, June answered the soft knock at her door. Margaret announced that after breakfast she was to meet Monsieur Raleigh in the study.

As she ate, June was grateful for the time alone, unwilling to have her first meeting with Ivon over breakfast. As nervous as she was she would probably upend her plate in her lap or make some other such clumsy move. Although it had only been a couple of weeks since she'd seen him, she remembered vividly his commanding presence. Fortyish, thinning hair, gray temples, at least six feet tall and slender, his almond-shaped cool black eyes were his best feature. Sharp, and all seeing, she wondered how she'd react to one of his arctic looks.

It was just before nine o'clock when June rose and walked confidently to the study. The door was open and Ivon stood at the window, his arms folded across his chest. He turned when he heard June's step.

"*Bonjour,* Monsieur Raleigh."

Ivon observed the young American woman. She was everything he remembered and he knew that his sixth-sense decision to hire her was still working perfectly. He was rarely ever wrong in making judgments that affected his life. For a moment his eyes clouded. All except one. He walked toward June's extended hand.

"*Bonjour,* Mademoiselle Saxon." Her handshake was cool, firm, and confident. In English he said, "We are so formal? In Long Island I was Ivon and you were June. May we continue the informality?" When she responded with a nod, he continued. "You needn't speak French for my benefit. I am comfortable in either language. Use my native tongue in any situation requiring its use."

"Thank you," June answered. She hid her surprise when instead of sitting behind the large mahogany desk he led her to the long tan leather sofa, where he joined her at the opposite end. When she'd first met him she hadn't detected a true French accent. Since meeting Laraine she suspected that he too, though a Frenchman, had spent quite a few years in the States. She also suspected that he was of mixed heritage. Unlike his personal assistant his tan skin and dark eyes leaned more toward African than European descent. As if reading her mind, Ivon confirmed her suspicions.

"You are wondering how all this is possible, I know,"

Ivon said. "I was born in France, of a Nigerian and French father who for years has conducted business in the United States, and a Frenchwoman. My mother's family, the Chambourds, were bankers and my father started Raleigh Enterprises many years before I was born." He waved a long, slender hand with buffed fingernails. "We will dispense with talk of boring matters today." He raised a brow. "Unless there was something in the financial package you received that doesn't sit well?"

"Oh no," June answered. "The offer is quite generous, thank you." How could it be anything else? When she'd received all the details of her employment the salary was more than Caleb had first mentioned. Yes, everything was quite in order! Her heart sank. How or when could she tell this man that he had to start a new search for an assistant?

"Good." Ivon crossed his knees and ran his fingers over the razor-sharp crease in his light gray pant leg. "Then we shall spend the day talking of my country and the companies and I will try to answer any questions you might have. I want you to be comfortable and knowledgeable when you meet your employees." He gave her a pointed look. "I won't repeat the things that my assistant has told you. Although you will be spending the bulk of this stay with her, you and I will go over the mundane details here in my study. Everything you need to know is here and at your disposal, so please don't hesitate to examine the files as you see fit." He indicated a wall where four tall mahogany file cabinets stood side by side.

"Then I am to work in here?" June asked.

"Yes, of course," Ivon said with understanding. "The office is only for those visitors foolish enough to want to conduct emergency business in my home." He shrugged and his eyes twinkled. "But they never stay long and never return, preferring to meet with the store managers."

June smiled. For all his cool facade he had a wry sense

of humor. "I see." Then in a serious tone, she said, "I want to thank you again for this opportunity, but I am curious about one thing." She paused when the housekeeper appeared and set down a tray laden with coffee and biscuits.

He filled their cups. After they'd both savored the hot brew and tasted flaky croissants, he said, "Please, continue. What piques your curiosity?"

June inhaled and exhaled. "Why me?" she said, frankly. "Why did you place your trust in a complete stranger?" She splayed a hand. "You've read my résumé. I have no corporate experience."

Ivon fixed his stare on June, who waited expectantly. "You have people skills. You're intelligent, quick-witted, alert, and personable. You invite confidences." He shrugged. "I saw that before we'd conversed for a half hour." He refilled their cups. After a moment he said, "I won't deny that the hours are long and there is little time for a social life. The month that we will spend away is a time of work but also is a time for relaxing. I think you will be fascinated by what you will see." He paused. "But of course if at some point in time you find that the work is not at all suitable for what you desire, and somewhat unfulfilling, please, you will not offend me if you decide not to return in September."

A smile touched June's lips and she could only manage a nod. He was offering her an out and she remained mute!

Ivon stood and closed the distance between them. He took her hand and pulled her up. "You have spirit." He clasped both her hands in his. "Welcome to Paris, June."

Later, after lunch and close to dinner, June said good night to Ivon, who left to dress for an evening engagement. He'd spent the balance of the morning and the afternoon showing June the types of merchandise he carried in each of the stores. Tomorrow, he promised, he would spend the day with her touring the city. After that she would be in his assistant's hands.

June didn't mind dining alone again. It gave her time to put her wardrobe together in preparation for making the rounds with Laraine. When she thought of the woman June realized that whenever he referred to her, Ivon had never used her name. It was always his "assistant." "Strange Frenchman," she muttered.

At midnight, she was in bed, her head filled with the excitement of the tour she would be taking with Ivon. June couldn't help feeling anxious. Would there come an opportunity to graciously refuse his job? Giddiness made her giggle. She'd never be able to hold her mouth right to form the proper words. *Coward!* Yes, I am, she told her inner voice.

She'd enjoyed every bit of today even when Ivon's voice grew sharp when he was explaining certain peculiarities of the shops. He had continued nonstop after lunch and she'd never once thought of resting, but secretly thought of Caleb's reference to him as a taskmaster. The same chemistry that had sparked between them when they'd first met at her party was still present. No wonder he hadn't beat around the bush, June thought. After four assistants in as many years, the man knew what he wanted in nothing flat.

When Ivon had again remarked about her easy manner and practical way of assessing a situation, she'd felt a surge of esteem. He admired and respected her intelligence and had the confidence to say so, unlike so many other male types.

The soft peal of the telephone bell interrupted her thoughts.

"Hello?" She frowned at the lateness of the hour.

"It's Matt, June." He hesitated. "Did I wake you?"

A second passed before she spoke. "Matt? N—no," she said, finding it hard to adjust to hearing his voice. Her mind had been in the clouds and now she was forced to think about a painful reality. "I am in bed though. It was a long day." She hesitated. "Has something happened?"

Swallowing a biting retort, Matt said evenly, "Must there be a reason other than I want to hear your voice?"

Oh no! What is he doing to me? Please, please don't mess with my head now, Matt. The silent plea was lost in a swirl of emotion. Could just the sound of his voice play havoc with her?

"No, of course not," June said, getting control of herself. "I—I just didn't expect to hear from you."

Matt listened to what she didn't say. He remembered her "good-bye." "You mean so soon or not again?" he said softly.

"So soon."

"I see." Seconds passed before he added, "I called to say I was way off base, June. I'm sorry for those asinine things I said."

June waited anxiously for his explanation but he said no more. Her hopes dwindled. "It'd been a long day and we both were exhausted," she said.

"Don't make excuses for me." His voice was gruff. "Do you accept my apology?"

"Accepted."

Matt was filled with anguish. *She's slipping away from me. After one day she's decided to return in September.* He could sense it in every word she said and those that she left unspoken. He could feel it almost as surely as if she were standing beside him. "June?"

"I'm here."

"Are you coming back home?"

"Of course I am. What kind of question is that?" *But to what, Matt?*

"You know what I mean." Matt heard the soft sigh and his chest deflated. Before she answered, he said, "When did you decide?"

"Decide?" June said.

"To return to Paris. To work for Raleigh for . . . two

years, was it?'' Her silence was consent and Matt felt numb.
''Then you've given me my answer,'' he said dryly.

June closed her eyes and when she opened them took a
deep breath. ''Matt, we have to talk.'' She breathed deeply.
''Last night, your insinuations, your lack of trust. It's as if
you don't even know the woman you want to marry . . . that
you were comparing me to Carlotta and . . .'' Her voice
trailed away. She was making such a mess of what she
wanted to say she'd rendered him speechless.

Matt couldn't believe what he'd heard. His body stiffened.
''What are you saying, June?'' His voice was almost deadly.
''Not know you? Christ! You're telling me that I don't know
the woman I want in my bed or who I want to spend my
life with?'' He swore softly. ''That you're another Carlotta?
Then what in hell was that display we put on twenty-four
hours ago? Babies in a sandbox who don't know which end
is up? I love *you*, dammit!''

''If that was how you really felt, then how could you
even think those horrible things?'' June blurted. ''What else
was I supposed to think other than you equating me with
your treacherous ex-wife?'' June felt miserable. This wasn't
at all how she was going to approach him. How'd she let
this happen? His voice cut through her like a whip.

''You believe that I was thinking of Carlotta?''

''You didn't give me much chance to think anything
else.'' She sighed. ''I didn't want to discuss this long distance, Matt. There was something I wanted to tell you, but
it doesn't matter now. I guess it can keep.''

Matt found it difficult to speak and his voice was barely
a whisper. ''What else is there to discuss?''

A tiny sigh escaped but June was silent. Nothing she said
would make things right.

''June,'' Matt said wearily. ''I know that I love you and
want you to be my wife. But it's obvious your immediate
plans don't include a husband.'' He paused. ''There's some-

thing I'm not picking up on here. Whatever is going on in your head happened between the time you left my bed and landed in Paris in . . . Raleigh's house.'' He felt hollow. ''I can only guess that what you wanted to tell me concerns two things. You and Paris.'' He waited, inviting her to confide in him. Finally, a soft laugh erupted. ''I see she's made a fool of me again.''

''Carlotta?'' His bitterness made June flinch.

Matt smiled and wearily rubbed his temples. ''You'll figure it out, sweetheart. Good-bye, June.''

She was all over his house. Haunting memories of her laugh, her scent, her teasing when she played the seductress. Everywhere! His study, which was his refuge, was now a place that was filled with her essence. Here he would always be reminded of what he had just lost, and the raw pain of it was twisting his insides. Matt left the study and made his way up the stairs.

In his bedroom he emitted a sharp laugh when he sat on the bed. He inhaled. ''There's no escaping you, June Saxon,'' he murmured.

Four days in Paris with Laraine St. John was all the time June needed to give validity to her initial suspicions. There was a great mystery connecting the lives of Laraine and Ivon. To be certain, she observed her employer closely, which was hard to do since she barely saw him. Except for the day when he'd escorted her about she'd only seen him at the dinner hour after which they always retired to his study where they discussed her day. On that day he'd escorted her to the Eiffel Tower and Notre Dame, the two places one had to visit before leaving Paris. He remarked that when a person became a resident, those visits were left to the tourists, and he didn't want her to spend the next couple of years working in Paris and never get to see the inside of either.

Such as New Yorkers never seeing inside the Empire State Building, he'd said. When he'd taken her to the beautiful gardens, the Jardin des Tuileries, she'd experienced a moment of sadness when she thought of Matt. During their walking tour she couldn't avoid the lovers who were everywhere. Ivon said as old hat as it was it was the perfect place for sweethearts. June didn't miss the change in his voice and they abruptly left.

On the sixth day and after she'd quietly observed, June knew the secret behind Laraine's sad eyes and the veiled softness in Ivon's when he mentioned her name. The two were hopelessly in love!

With that realization came a solution to her dilemma, but how in the world was she going to pull it off? In four short days she would be going home and Ivon was still ignorant of the fact that she was not returning. Guilt pangs had been hitting her in the gut more frequently as she found every excuse in the book not to reveal her plans to her employer. Her deception had to stop and soon, because it was trapping her, just like one lie falling on top of another until they all imploded inside of her. The funny thing was that she hadn't lied about a thing. It was her secret that she hadn't confessed to that made her deceitful.

It was early Saturday morning and June was waiting outside the front door for Laraine, who had the weekend off. She had accepted her invitation to take a drive to the country. The two women, who'd been together constantly, had dropped their reserve days before. Each day June watched thin layers of Laraine's sophisticated veneer strip away revealing a warm and pleasant woman who was naturally reserved. It was today that June was going to take the chance to put her plan into action. Time was running out.

"Bonjour, June," Laraine said as she pulled into the driveway. The sun was hot and the top was down on the bright red Fiat convertible.

"Bonjour," June called. "Hold on a second, I left my sweater on the chair inside. Be right back." Her garment in hand, she nearly bumped into Ivon, who had appeared at the door. "Oh, excuse me. Guess I'm really anxious to finally get a chance to see your countryside. It's a gorgeous day," she said excitedly. "Are you sure you won't change your mind and come with us?" Laraine had joined them for dinner last night and while they were making their plans, she had invited him, but he'd declined.

Ivon looked at June with a keen eye. "No. You go and enjoy yourself." His stare was penetrating. "Tonight, when you return, come to my study before you turn in, June."

June's heart quickened. "Is there an emergency?"

"Emergency?" He appeared to ponder the question. "No. I think it's time we talked about certain things." They stepped outside. "Enjoy your day. I think you'll find our countryside quite charming." He dismissed her and stared at Laraine. *"Bonjour."*

"Bonjour, Ivon."

June looked from one to the other as a split second passed in silence.

Ivon nodded. In French he said, "Please give my regards." Without another word he turned and went inside.

They drove for ten minutes before June spoke. "We're visiting someone in particular?"

"Yes."

"Who?"

"My mother." She caught June's expression. "Surprised?"

"Yes, I am. I just assumed that you were alone."

Laraine kept her eyes on the road. "There's just me, my mother, and her sister." She hesitated. "I had an older sister. She's . . . dead."

"I'm sorry," June murmured.

"It was a long time ago."

June held her questions. She sensed the other woman's sudden reluctance to offer more information about her family. After forty minutes, she watched Laraine turn into a drive that was almost secluded. She looked astonished when Laraine parked.

"Another surprise?" They had stopped in front of a building proclaiming to be The Hotel Josephine. But to June it looked more like a charming chalet that housed a large family.

"My mother's home," Laraine said. "She is the hotelier."

"What?" If June never believed in fairy tales she did now because she was living in one. Her own. "You've got to be kidding!"

Laraine laughed at the expression on June's face. "I don't understand. You are so funny at times. What is so surprising?"

"Oh, nothing at all. Just a little on-the-job training," June said.

"What?"

June shook her head and smiled as she opened the door. "Come, let's go meet your mother, my friend."

It was after lunch and June and Laraine were sitting in the room reserved for Laraine whenever she visited. The charming French country decor was similar to the rest of the twelve guest rooms of the house. June had seen at least two other of the empty rooms and had marveled at the different themes in each. She'd never thought to dress a room and name it in keeping with the decor, and her mind raced with the possibilities for her own business. Laraine's room was called Les Enfant and was decorated with many porcelain antique dolls. Some sat on the mantel, while others were in their own tiny chairs, and another, the largest, lay on the bed decked out in an ecru lace dress with pale blue ribbons cascading from the bodice. Both women had kicked off their shoes and sat comfortably, June on the cushioned window seat and Laraine propped up on the bed.

"This is lovely, Laraine. Have you always lived here?" June asked.

Laraine's eyes clouded. "No. We grew up on the Left Bank." She waved a hand. "Living twenty miles from the city was too much travel for my father, who worked for the metro. My mother was a baker's assistant."

June smiled. "That accounts for the sinfully delicious dessert I devoured."

"She loves to bake, even after . . . well, she's always loved the kitchen."

"You mean after the accident?" June said in a soft voice.

"Yes." She stared at June. "You guessed?"

"Somehow I didn't think it was a debilitating illness that put your mother in a wheelchair." She lifted a shoulder. "The way she talks and the agility she has in getting about didn't strike me that she was ill." The break in Laraine's voice and the brightness of her eyes alerted June. The accident that had put Josephine St. John in the wheelchair was most certainly connected to Laraine and Ivon.

"You are as astute as I thought you to be from the beginning," Laraine said.

Risking a rebuff June asked in a soft voice, "Was it long ago?"

"Thirteen years this month," Laraine said.

"Care to talk about it?"

The brightness had turned to shining tears just behind Laraine's thick lashes. June wasn't surprised when a tear rolled down the woman's cheek. She turned to look out the window at the riotous color below and vaguely wondered if Parisians planted flower gardens in every patch of green available. A few guests lingered in the cool garden with tall glasses of cold beverages. She turned when Laraine spoke.

"My mother named this hotel for my sister Josephine,

not herself as people think," Laraine said in a low voice.
"She was nine years older than me. I always thought she
was the most beautiful woman I'd ever seen. Her red hair
was the color of a sparkling garnet and her green eyes shown
like emeralds."

Like yours, thought June. *Does this woman think that
she's not beautiful?*

Laraine stirred, drawing her knees up and hugging them
tightly. "She and Ivon were lovers and were planning their
marriage." She closed her eyes against the memory and
when she opened them said, "I think I loved Ivon from the
first moment I saw him when I was a little girl. Our families
were acquainted through the friendship of my mother and
Ivon's aunt, who were children together. My mother fell in
love with an ordinary working-class man while a wealthy
man swept her friend off her feet." She brushed her cheek.
"The summer I was nineteen I came home from California
all grown up and worldly. I'd lost my virginity. I was a
woman!" She smiled.

"Was that when you fell in love with Ivon?"

"Not right away. You see, I was feeling pretty, sought
after by handsome young men, having the time of my life.
Besides, Ivon and my sister were engaged. He was twelve
years older than me and taken. *Dieu!*" she breathed softly.
"He looked at me as Josephine's baby sister! On the night
of the engagement party, all that changed in an instant."

"How?" June spoke as softly as Laraine.

"He stopped seeing me as a child," Laraine said. "I
know the exact second it happened. I was dancing with a
lothario who was all hands when I looked across the room.
Ivon was staring at me with an expression I'd never seen
before. I was mesmerized and my feet got locked up with
my partner's and we nearly fell. But I couldn't break that
stare." She shivered with the memory.

"What happened?"

"Later, purely by chance, we met on the patio. We didn't speak, but moving as puppets we were drawn into each other's arms." Laraine smiled. "We didn't even kiss at first, just embraced. When he kissed me it was the sweetest thing I'd ever known. Then, and for years afterward." The dreamy look was replaced by sadness. "My sister Josephine found us there. She went into a tirade, calling us vile names, saying she hated us. I think her hatred was directed at me more than Ivon. Finally, with tears blinding her, she ran away. By that time the party had stopped and the guests were watching and listening in horror. My mother followed Josephine." The tears started falling. "I can still hear the thud and the screech of tires as my sister sped away. She never even knew that when she backed out of the space she hit my mother, who was running between the cars trying to get to her. Later, they found Josephine in the twisted metal of the car. Some say that she deliberately drove into the tree."

"Oh my God," June whispered.

Laraine's shoulders shook as she cried again for all that she'd lost. June was saddened and felt compassion for the two lovers.

"Ivon's family insisted on taking care of us," Laraine said. "With bitterness my mother accepted their generosity. She opened this hotel and the rest of my college education was taken care of."

"How did you come to be in Ivon's employ?"

"My mother. She wouldn't let Ivon stop paying for what she called his folly. So when I graduated, I was assured of a well-paying job."

"But later, after so many years, didn't you and Ivon express your love?"

"Never," Laraine answered. "I think he was devastated at what happened. When he hired me we spoke of the tragedy only once and never again. He apologized for losing his control and in the end ruining my family. Now we exist as two people who work together."

"Unhappily," June said.

"Yes," Laraine said softly. She smiled at June. "You saw even that," she stated firmly.

"I noticed," June agreed. "You never fell in love again? Or Ivon?"

Laraine shook her head. "The men were meaningless to me. Occasionally I date, but it's so boring and superficial. Ivon?" She shrugged. "I suppose it's the same with him. He's never married."

"Is it your mother?"

Laraine looked inquisitive.

"I mean does your mother still hate Ivon?"

"No, I think she's forgiven him though she is so reserved whenever they meet by chance. She's forgiven me too." She closed her eyes briefly. "I think she realizes that love is so strange and that neither of us planned that night. It just happened."

"When are you and Ivon going to end your silence?" June was surprised to see that her question brought on fresh tears. "Laraine?"

"I don't know." Her voice was just above a murmur. "June, I'm drying up inside. I want to love him, to fall asleep in his arms. I want to have his babies. It's getting too hard to live like this, seeing him day after day. Sometimes I think the only relief from this pain is when he goes away. Then it's just the wait until he returns and it starts all over again."

June listened with tears in her eyes. How could two people do this to each other for so many years? she thought. They were in love! Suddenly she went cold. She and Matt were on the verge of becoming just like Laraine and Ivon, and all because of a foolish misunderstanding about a turn of events. Matt had jumped to an irrational conclusion and she had taken umbrage and doubted her love for him. Not know each other? What rubbish, she thought. If they'd had years together they couldn't be more in love than they were now.

"I'm sorry?" June looked questioningly at Laraine, who had spoken.

"It is that way with you too?"

"I don't understand." June was puzzled.

"With the man that you love," Laraine said with a raised brow. "He is taken?"

"No," June answered slowly.

"But you ran away from him to live in Paris. Why?" Laraine was curious.

Ran away! Was that what she did? "When I accepted the job from Ivon I thought it was what I needed at the time," June answered.

"Now?"

"I know now what I need."

Laraine nodded. "I thought there was something." Her look was as direct as her frankness. "When will you tell Ivon that you will not return?"

June thought about Ivon's parting words to her earlier. "I think he already knows," she said. "Tonight, probably."

It was after nine o'clock when Laraine dropped June off at the house. She didn't come inside but whispered, "Good luck. You will call me tomorrow?"

June said, "Yes, in the morning. Maybe we can meet?"

"I'd like that."

"Are you sure you don't want to see Ivon tonight?" June asked. Laraine had confided that she would break her silence to him, but would wait for the right time. June had warned her about the dangers in that. Laraine declined the offer to come inside and waved good night.

Ivon met June in the hall. "Did you enjoy the ride to the countryside?"

"Very much," June said. "Hotel Josephine is charming. I loved everything about it and the cuisine especially! Madame Josephine is an excellent baker."

"Yes, she is," Ivon, said. Instead of leading her to the study, Ivon walked to the living room where he invited June to sit. When he offered her a drink, he poured red Bordeaux for them both, then sat across from her on a flower-patterned love seat.

He studied her. "Your eyes sparkle. Not since Long Island have I seen such effervescence. Is it the country that affects you so or something else that excites you?"

June held his gaze. She could see that there was no rancor in his look. Rather an acceptance of what he wanted her to admit. "You know, don't you?"

The tiny smile traveled to his eyes. "That you are no longer interested in becoming an employee of Raleigh Enterprises?" He tilted his head. "I didn't suspect that something was amiss that morning we met. My curiosity became aroused the next morning at breakfast. When you were reticent in making any admission I believed I was mistaken. The tour of the gardens confirmed my suspicions."

"Even then?" June was curious. "How did you guess?"

"Your expression as you pretended not to notice the ardent displays of affection." A shadow darkened his eyes briefly. "Leaving your lover was hard, was it not? You were willing to give him up for a career?"

June didn't deny what he'd so astutely guessed. "I had a decision to make," she said slowly. "Before the plane landed, I'd made it but was unable to tell you. I can imagine the trouble my work permit cost you. I felt like a traitor and didn't want to disappoint you."

"What of your career?"

"I will have a career when I return," June said. "My

own business.'' The words on her tongue made her feel proud and suddenly her blood boiled from excitement. She wanted to go home!

Ivon was thoughtful. "I see. Then I know it will be a success. I have every confidence in you.''

"Thank you, Ivon.'' A boulder had been lifted from her shoulders and she felt as light as a will-o'-the-wisp, and fearful of floating to the ceiling. What an insightful man he was, June thought. Ivon wished her happiness, yet he smothered his own. Emboldened by what she'd learned today and Ivon's frankness, she decided to broach the touchy subject.

"May I speak frankly?'' she asked.

Ivon looked amused. "But I thought we were,'' he said.

"About me,'' June said. "Not about you and ... Laraine.'' She breathed deeply. He stared at her with the darkest expression she'd ever seen and she wondered if she'd made a terrible mistake. She'd shocked him into silence. June stood. "I'm sorry. Please forgive me. I didn't mean to invade your privacy.''

Ivon stood and walked to the credenza filled with bottles. He fixed a whiskey and soda and poured another glass of Bordeaux. He handed June the glass of wine, then gestured. "Please, sit.''

The dark look on Ivon's face was replaced with one of sadness. June had seen the look many times when she'd caught him staring at Laraine.

"How much has she told you?'' Ivon asked after sipping his drink.

"Everything, I think. And that she loves you.''

"As I her.''

"You will never tell her?''

A wry smile touched his lips. "You have no doubt that I have been nothing but a pigheaded male over this.'' His voice turned weary. "My dear June, I have thought of doing nothing else for the last few weeks. I have sensed the time has come before I lose her forever.'' He heard June's soft sigh. ''It was you who made me see what a fool I was.''

''Me?'' She was astonished.

Ivon smiled. ''The gardens. You'd left a lover behind to pursue a career and when I looked at your face I knew that no career was worth living a life without love.'' He gestured to the air. ''I've been doing that for thirteen years. It will end, thanks to you.''

June was ecstatic and filled with emotion. She held back the tears.

Ivon cleared his throat. ''You're free to go home as soon as you like, June. I wouldn't wait a day longer.'' His dark eyes glittered like onyx.

''Oh, Ivon,'' June murmured. ''Thank you.''

Chapter Thirteen

Oyster Bay, New York

Matt was outside with Andre and Diane watching the clearing of the rubble left from the burned-out cottage. The stench of smoke was slow to leave the air and until it dissipated would be a constant reminder of the hate-filled act of an angry man. All three were silent as each thought of what had been lost. The Heaths' home, although it hadn't been their own, was gone along with mementos of their life together. Matt was grateful that they'd survived. But rebuilding what they'd had would take some doing.

He turned his attention to the kennels where the charred rubbish from the one destroyed building had already been removed. Days ago he'd met with the contractors, and plans for the new building had been drawn. Construction was to begin in a few weeks. Until the building was completed, Matt had delayed delivery of pups that were ready to travel from Africa.

"Stupid jerk!" Diane muttered. She had her arms folded across her chest and her eyes snapped angrily. "Hope he gets the book."

Andre snorted in agreement. "That remains to be seen," he said in disgust. "Different kind of justice for different kind of folks." He looked at Matt. "Hear any more?"

"Not since last week," Matt answered. "I think justice will be done in this case unless the judge is deaf, dumb, and blind. The kid sealed his father's fate when he blurted out the truth." He shook his head. "The man's got to be crazy. Taking the kid with him to the hardware store where he bought the kerosene and making him sit in the car while he did his dirt was nuts. What's going through that boy's mind now, knowing that his father is a criminal, God only knows."

"Crying shame," Diane agreed. "That scared little boy is going to be an anger-filled man, directing it at the wrong folks."

Matt shrugged. "Yeah, well, let's hope it doesn't lead to the death of anybody." He turned away. "Come on inside. We have some things to discuss."

At the kitchen table, Matt tossed a brochure on the table. "The Realtor dropped this off yesterday. I want your opinion. If it's not what you want, be frank and we can do something else." Diane picked up the glossy leaflet depicting a condo apartment. "You know that . . . ah . . . June will be coming home in a few days. You guys haven't talked about making other arrangements, so this is an option."

Andre leaned over and examined the leaflet with his wife. He sat back and eyed Matt. "I think me and Diane had something a little more affordable in mind. Like renting an apartment," he said.

Meeting Andre's stare, Matt said, "As I said, it's only an option."

Diane saw male stubbornness at work and turned their

attention to her when she said, "These units are great. I have a friend who bought there a few months ago." She laid the flyer down. "That's something we'll have to take time to plan on, Matt, but thanks for looking out. You've been a great friend to us." She smiled and her eyes twinkled. "What I'd really like is to stay right where I am. I fell in love with that old house the first night we slept there. Thinking about going elsewhere is too painful to consider." She chuckled. "Even Andre got as comfortable as a contented dog who's found a warm barn to live in."

Andre shifted in his chair and made a gruff sound but he nodded in agreement with his wife's assessment.

"We still have a couple of days, Matt. June said to stay as long as we liked until we found something. She's not kicking us right out." Diane caught her husband's eye. "Andre said if that's okay with me he doesn't mind. He thinks June is the genuine article and I can't agree more. She doesn't talk through her hat."

More than a week ago his brother had used almost the same words in describing her, Matt thought. Andre was the last person he'd thought would have agreed to such an arrangement. Living there in her absence was one thing, but when she returned? He and his wife couldn't stay under *his* roof but thought nothing of living with a woman they'd known for less than a month. Then why had he believed the worst of her?

"Matt?" Diane looked at the man who'd seemed to drift. She had no doubt where his mind was. "June called me."

"Called you?" Why did he feel put out? "When?"

"Two days ago. She reminded me of what she'd said and didn't want to find us gone when she walked in the door. As big as the place is there's plenty of room." She chuckled. "Said that the kitchen would welcome the hustle and bustle of two women fussing around."

A small smile touched Matt's lips. She would say something like that. He sat back in his chair. "Then I guess we can put this on the shelf for a while?" He indicated the leaflet and then frowned. "For how long?"

Andre shrugged. "Buying anything is out right now. As soon as I get a good schedule going between the part-timers and me, then I can take the time to go look at some places with Diane. You're still favoring that foot and shouldn't be on your feet as much as you are now. So we'll just take it slow for a time."

"Okay," Matt said. "Just let me know if I can help with anything." He knew his meaning was clear from the look he exchanged with Andre.

"Will do," Andre said. He stood up. "I told Doc I'd pick up Kagi today so I'd better get over there before that mutt dies of heart failure. He thinks he's been abandoned."

Diane stood and walked to the door with her husband. "You'd better not let Kagi hear you call him a mutt," she said. "He thinks he's as human as you and me." She waved at Matt. "See you later. Want anything special for dinner tonight?"

"*Anything* you make will be just fine!" he said, with emphasis. He couldn't help grinning at Diane's deep laugh as she went outside. For almost a week his stomach had endured the temporary housekeeper's efforts. She knew her way around with the vacuum but the kitchen was foreign country to her. He'd been glad when Diane assumed her duties yesterday cooking a Sunday meal that had made a pig of him.

Matt left the kitchen and walked slowly to the study, where he lay down on the chaise longue. It was only after one in the afternoon but he felt a little tired. Maybe Andre was right about putting aside the wheelchair too soon. The last thing he needed was to prevent the healing of his foot. Standing by watching others work was not his nature and the sooner he was able to pull his own weight, the better he'd feel. He closed his eyes. He knew what would make him feel better and it wasn't work.

What he did need was to hear June's voice. He needed to hear her tell him that she loved him as he still loved and wanted her. He didn't want to hear that he'd lost her to that other woman: Paris. The glitz and glamour of that city had colored Carlotta's eyes leading her to work her magic to snare a wealthy man. In just one day, had June fallen under the spell? Beguiled by Ivon Raleigh? His eyes flew open at the image of that man embracing her. How could he resist? She was irresistible!

"Stop it, man," he muttered. "You ought to take your lumps and deal with it. You were the one who messed up!" Matt crossed the room and a minute later sat down behind his desk sipping the cognac he'd poured. He'd been a fool to let that last conversation stand between them like a stone wall. But too much time had passed and the longer he waited the more it seemed futile to try to make amends. He didn't know how to tell her that he'd feared losing her from the time she got on that plane. That when she returned it would be to tell him that she couldn't marry him. He'd thought he'd been so cool and magnanimous in his behavior, assured that their love would come shining through. He'd fooled himself and now he had to face the consequences of her not being in his life. He frowned. At least not as his lover or wife. They would once again become adversaries as in the beginning of their relationship.

Since the fire, and the loss of the Heaths' home, an idea had nagged at Matt until he could no longer ignore the rumblings in his head. Diane and Andre's admission that they felt at home confirmed what he'd been thinking. He'd make another offer for June's house. The Heaths could make it their home, and whenever necessary his customers would board there as he'd initially planned.

Matt finished the cognac, then pulled a scratch pad from

the desk and started to jot down his ideas. There were many things to take into consideration including replacing Diane as his housekeeper and Andre's assistant. At two-thirty, surprised at the swift passing of time, he pushed away from the desk, pleased with what he'd accomplished. As with many another project in the past that had begun with a small idea, he couldn't wait to see it come to fruition. He took his notes to the sofa and rested his head on the plump cushions where he studied his plan.

At five o' clock, he opened his eyes and inhaled. He hadn't been dreaming. Diane had obviously returned and had his kitchen smelling divine. He followed his nose.

"Hah, thought that'd wake you," she said with a big grin when he appeared in the kitchen. "How do you feel?"

"Starved," Matt answered, ignoring the rumble in his stomach. He lifted the frying pan lid. "Liver and onions. Humph. I'm more than ready. Let me wash up. You and Andre joining me tonight?"

"No. We're having leftovers. He always tells me my pork roasts on the first day ain't got nothing on the second. Likes it even better."

Matt grinned and walked to the bathroom when he stopped. "Where's Kagi? Doc didn't release him?" He'd expected to hear his pet whining furiously to be let loose.

"Outside saying hello to his pals," Diane said. "Andre has him on a leash because that animal insists on jumping around on that cast like he's got four good paws." She eyed Matt's foot. "Just like somebody else I know around here. Go on and wash up now and come eat while it's still sizzling."

Hours after the Heaths left, Matt was restless. He'd had enough sleep and there was nothing of interest on TV. Visiting his brother was out of the question because he'd only get sour looks from Toi and George. Neither of them acted as if they had any sense when he'd told them he hadn't heard from June. George had given him that disgusted look again and Toi had just sighed and rolled her eyes. It was already tomorrow morning in Paris and he wondered what she was doing. Was she looking forward to leaving in only two more days? Somehow he doubted that and he scowled darkly.

Matt pushed the sight, sound, and smell of June out of his mind and went to get Kagi. He hadn't walked on the beach since his accident and he needed the peace, foot or no foot. At ten-thirty, his bandaged foot encased in a surgical boot, and with Kagi held firmly on his leash, Matt walked carefully on the deserted beach. But where he sought to escape his restless thoughts of her, the beach was a constant reminder of what he'd so foolishly thrown away.

June's plane landed at JFK airport at eleven o'clock Monday morning. She felt like Dorothy coming home to Kansas, but this was New York! She was grinning from ear to ear when she spied Caleb, who was waving and grinning as broadly as she was. She blew him a kiss and sighed, ''There's no place like home.''

After an hour of accident-stalled traffic on the Grand Central Parkway they traveled easily on the Northern State Parkway where traffic was normal.

''Good to see you, Junie Bug,'' Caleb said, then smiled. ''I know now what it'd be like if you went back in September. I missed you.'' He stole a quick look at her face. After her teary greeting they'd talked about superficial stuff but nothing that was close to her heart. When she called him from Paris she'd told him why she was coming home, but didn't elaborate on the misunderstanding she'd had with Matt. ''What are you going to say to him?''

June didn't play coy. ''I don't know. Guess I'll wait and see. Right now I want to sleep for hours. After that, I'll have a clear head." Her brow wrinkled. "I'm just worried about Diane and Andre," she said. "I don't want them to feel they have to pack up and leave tonight. I really like them, Caleb. They're good people and deserve a break. I wish there was something more I could do."

Caleb smiled. "I think you've done a lot. Don't beat yourself up. They'll be fine. Takes time to sort your life out after such a trauma."

"I guess so," she said. "You know what? Suppose I crash for a few hours at your place? When they get back home from work tonight and find me there they might freak out and I don't want them to be uncomfortable. I'm sorry now I didn't call them yesterday."

"No, you're not," Caleb said. "You didn't want Matt to know, before you got it together."

June smiled. "I always told Beverly that you were the smartest big brother she ever had." She watched the familiar scene whiz by. They passed posh Muttontown and East Norwich and soon they reached Oyster Bay. Historic Oyster Bay was how she planned to advertise, June thought. Tourism abounded in the town especially during the summer months when droves of people visited Sagamore Hill, the Victorian home of Theodore Roosevelt, and national historic site. There were scads of museums, including one depicting the life of the Native American in Nassau County, and many parks with fascinating nature trails. There was more than enough for a body to do than just sit on the deck and eat breakfast. The smell of the ocean was in the air and June leaned back and closed her eyes. She was home.

Caleb carried June's bags inside and stashed them by the back door. June was already on the phone with Beverly, and hearing her squeal he could only imagine his sister was in her office making identical noises. He walked from the room, leaving June to talk to her friend in private. Turning on his computer in his study, he reflected on the two women.

There's something to be said about tight friendships, he thought. *They certainly can be sustaining through tough trials.* He could attest to that. After he'd been dumped he'd had his sister and June and his own longtime buddy to help him through those rough days. He frowned. The very fact that June hadn't talked much about Matt was clear indication that she was still crazy about the guy. And if that man did anything to hurt her, he was going to have trouble on his hands from this six-foot, two-hundred-pound, pissed-off brother.

At ten o'clock June looked out Caleb's back window. Both the Heaths' cars were there and the house was dark except for the upstairs bedroom. Earlier she'd decided to stay at Caleb's overnight and in the morning after the Heaths went to work she'd go home. A phone call to Diane while she was at Matt's would be the easiest way to let them know she was back. She'd slept the day away and had eaten the pork chops and veggies Caleb had fixed for their dinner. Now she was sitting in the living room drinking a glass of red wine.

"No wonder you're still awake," Caleb said, joining her on the sofa. "You were knocked out, poor baby." Stretching, he yawned theatrically. "Well, don't expect me to stay up half the night with you. I worked all day and I'm going to bed."

"Ugh, it's disgusting," June said. "I'm wide-awake. It's your fault. You should have gotten me up at a decent hour."

"Oh, spare me from the ungrateful," Caleb groaned. Seriously he said, "You know what we talked about earlier? Well, I've thought it over and yes, you can hire me. It's a good plan."

"You will?" June's eyes sparkled as she let out a breath. "Then I'm going to have the best financial adviser in the business," she said excitedly. She smiled ruefully. "If I'd had good sense I would have hired you before but—"

He stopped her. "That's negative thinking. Don't rehash old mistakes. Gets you nowhere but disgusted."

"Okay. Forgotten. Beverly told me the same thing." She chuckled softly as she remembered her friend's excited response to her news. Already she had ideas for decorating the rooms and had even come up with some whimsical names. June giggled at one such, "Widow's Walk," in keeping with a nautical theme. "I don't think so!" June told her. "Would you stay in such a room? Reminds me of ghosts and haunts. I'm aiming for peace and serenity." They'd both hung up excited at the new venture.

Caleb stood up. "Look, why don't you take a walk? Guaranteed, you'll be crying for sleep after half an hour."

"I bet I will too," June said. "Join me?"

"Only to the road; then I'm crashing."

June linked arms with Caleb as they walked slowly toward the beach. He helped her on with her sweater, then bent and kissed her forehead. She watched him saunter away and he turned and waved before going inside the back door.

Matt was sitting on the sand with Kagi at his feet, snoozing. It was no surprise that he'd found himself parked in the spot where he first ran into June on her birthday. His thoughts were full of the events that'd happened since that night, uppermost, their falling in love.

The sliver of light that appeared when Caleb's back door opened caught his attention and he watched as a woman and a man walked outside. Matt wasn't surprised that the man had started dating again. June had told him about the broken engagement and he was glad that the brother wasn't drowning in sorrow. *Yeah, just like you.* He shrugged off the taunt.

When Matt saw Caleb kiss the woman, and she turned to watch the road before crossing, he stiffened. "June?" As if a lightning bolt had struck him, Matt was frozen where he sat. He felt as if he were being transported through the portal in a TV *Star-Gate* episode and met by weird taunting creatures. It was seconds before he was able to move and shake his head ridding himself of the vision. But the woman who was walking toward him was no vision. It was June, the woman he loved. He nearly choked. *Loved?*

Kagi lifted his head and looked around at his master. As if he could feel the tension in the man, he made a low sound in his throat, which was his closest thing to a growl. An approaching figure caught his attention and he stood up. Suddenly, he stood and clumsily bounded away.

Frightened at the sudden movement toward her, June stopped. She'd thought she was alone. She stared. "Kagi?" The small dog yodeled his pleasure at seeing her. June bent and hugged him. "Oh, boy, your foot," she said, feeling the cast. "You must be doing okay, though." She laughed as he lapped her face. "Where is—"

"Your master?" Matt finished for her. "Right here and apparently not doing as good as he is," he said softly. He was standing, leaning heavily on his cane. The sight of her brought mixed emotions and he was finding it hard to breathe. "He's a lucky dog. So is he." He jerked his head toward Caleb's house. "You're getting kisses from everybody these days. What happened? Raleigh's didn't stand up to Lancaster's? Is he your reason for rushing back?"

"Matt?" June couldn't believe the filth that spewed from his mouth. She could only stare at the man whom she wanted to share the rest of her life with, including all the joys and pain that were bound to be. But they would be together and that's all that mattered. At least that was what she'd dreamed on her long flight home.

Now, speechless, she wanted to cover her ears and close her eyes against the anger that twisted his handsome face. She took a deep breath. "You're so wrong, Matt," she breathed. "Wrong a week ago and way off the mark with what you think you saw just now." She backed up. "Sometimes," she said in a low voice, "things are best left unsaid until you get a clear picture. Words are hurtful and can't be recalled. I'll remember yours until the day I die because it's the way you've always seen me.'' She held his gaze. ''Everything happens for a reason. Maybe one day I'll be the most enlightened woman on earth. Good-bye, Matt.'' She turned and walked away.

June didn't let the tears fall until she closed Caleb's door and stumbled up the stairs to the guest room. Ten minutes later she was in the bathroom downing her pills and wondering when the throbbing in her head would end.

The next morning, June waited until the Heaths left for work before going home. All she wanted was a few hours alone without going through the motions of a happy charade. If she felt like kicking something or cursing herself out loud she wanted to do just that without an audience. Besides, she was certain that the bad feelings inside of her would show on her face and scare the poor Heaths into leaving posthaste, never to return. Thankful that she awoke headache free, she needed the energy to face up to how her life had changed so quickly with just a few hate-filled words.

There was no doubt that her plans would go forward but she'd be making them in a more reflective mood than with the elation that had exhilarated her in Paris.

Last night Caleb had heard her come in and later the muffled cries. In the morning he'd confronted her and she told him about meeting Matt and what he thought he saw. For peace's sake she didn't quote him verbatim. Caleb swore and called the man a fool.

After showering, and donning T-shirt and shorts, she wished she could go braless. She grimaced. That was one thing she had to get used to, dressing with the understanding that she was not living alone. Not only because of the Heaths but also when she opened up for business. That was one of the sacrifices and concessions that business people had to make when deferring to the customer, she thought.

At nine-thirty it was already seventy-nine degrees with the high promising to hit near ninety. What she wanted to do was laze the day away on the porch and catch the slightest breeze that came her way, but she'd promised to be ready when Caleb came over. He said there was no sense in dreaming and waiting, and the sooner she saw in black and white what she needed to do, the better her planning would be. There were myriad items to address like liability insurance, business permits, all must-dos that were unglamorous but necessary. Before he started his own workday, he'd promised to help her draw up a rough ''things to do'' list and work out some preliminary figures, primary being a start-up amount.

Later, at three o'clock, June was sitting on the porch. Caleb had been very businesslike and thorough and not once had he mentioned Matt, for which fact she had been grateful. After Caleb left, she'd gone to the supermarket, did laundry, and after lunch cleaned up after herself. Diane had kept a spotless house and June was intimidated at leaving her lunch dishes in the sink. She chuckled at the thought of the two of them getting used to each other's habits and didn't foresee them coming to blows over a thing.

Before she left for the store she'd called Matt's house, and was relieved that Diane had answered. They spoke briefly and Diane said there wasn't anything she needed and thanked June for offering to cook the chicken she'd left defrosting in the fridge.

While making the chicken marsala and rice, June had thought more than once about the conversation she'd had with Diane. The one thing she remembered was the lack of surprise in her voice and she wondered if Matt had already broken the news to the Heaths. She frowned. She'd wanted to do that. There was no way of knowing if he'd been sensitive in telling of her unscheduled arrival or if he'd let his anger get in the way, giving off bad vibes to them.

Matt was at the kennels before Diane and Andre arrived at eight o'clock in the morning. His tired eyes and evil mood told the tale of the restless night he'd spent. Kagi was a smart animal and he knew to lie quietly in his room after his master grunted a greeting. After making a lousy pot of coffee and burning an English muffin, Matt left the kitchen, turning his nose up at the mess he'd made, and hoped that this inauspicious beginning was not an omen of foul things to come.

The look exchanged between Andre and Diane after an hour of working with Matt was pure puzzlement. Both exhaled when he left after listening to Andre's suggestion about a modification in the new building. Matt decided to call the builder while the idea was still fresh in his mind.

Diane followed an hour later and while she was upstairs changing the linen, Matt appeared in the doorway. She noted the scowl was missing but it had been replaced with the same sad expression he'd worn for months after his fiasco of a marriage. It didn't take a course in relationships to guess that somehow, this time, June was behind the look.

"I know you like to leave before Andre but would you mind staying?" Matt said. "I think it's time to talk about your housing situation. With June returning unexpectedly I know you two have been thinking about things." He looked puzzled at the look Diane was giving him, and then suddenly his eyes darkened. "She's asked you to leave?"

Diane dropped the sheets on the bed and, hands on hips, said, "What are you talking about?"

"June," Matt said impatiently, wondering if there was a full moon. "Last night, did she ask you and Andre to leave?"

"The only June I know is in Paris, not due back here for another day, and unless I'm going crazy no one's asked us to leave anywhere!'' She stared at Matt, wondering if missing that woman was making his imagination work overtime.

Taking the weight off his foot, Matt leaned against the doorjamb, and rubbed his temples. "Diane," he said, "last night I took Kagi for a walk on the beach. I saw June. She came from Caleb's house and walked on the beach. We . . . spoke and . . . then I left."

"Then that makes you a member of an exclusive club because the last time me and Andre saw June was nearly ten days ago."

Matt couldn't believe his ears. Why were they ringing? He shook his head because Diane wasn't making any sense. "You didn't see June last night? Or this morning?" His voice sounded foreign and he cleared his throat. "*She never came home?*"

God, not again! Diane wanted to be anywhere in the world but where she stood right now. Except for her husband in his worst alcoholic days, she'd never seen a man crumple before her eyes, and it wrenched her heart. June had come home and obviously had spent the night with Caleb after Matt thought she was on her way home.

"Andre and I left pretty early," she said, quietly. "June may have been sleeping."

But not in her own bed. Matt's head throbbed. He'd been right! He listened to Diane's words and looked into her eyes and knew she didn't believe what she was saying. He nodded, turned, and walked slowly downstairs.

Diane clutched her chest and plopped down on the bed. "Lord, Lord," she whispered. "Grab hold of that man. *I'm* asking, Lord." Later, after June's unexpected call, Diane went to look for her husband. They had to talk.

June was in her sitting room when Diane came home. From the look on her face, June knew that the older woman was upset. Matt had done what she'd feared. It would be no surprise to her to learn that the Heaths were leaving.

"Diane," June said, standing and crossing the room to hug her. "Good to see you."

"You too," Diane said, returning the hug. "You look great."

They sat, and a short silence ensued. Both women had things to say but neither knew how to approach a subject that was private and painful to one and none of the other's business.

June sighed. "Things have a way of getting messed up, don't they?" she said softly. Somehow, she knew that their relationship had changed but she couldn't understand why.

"June, I don't know why you returned early. I *think* I know why you chose to crash at Caleb's, but that's not important right now. Whatever happened on the beach is yours and Matt's business," Diane said. She stared intently at June. "But when he left you, Matt was under the impression that you were going to be sleeping in your own bed last night."

"He knows that I didn't?" June's chest constricted.

"When he asked, I told him that we didn't see you last night, or this morning."

"I see." But she didn't, not really. June looked at Diane and said, "What are your plans? I know you have something to tell me."

Diane's eyes softened. The voice matched the lusterless eyes and her heart went out to the woman who looked as if her whole world just plummeted like a fallen star.

"Andre and I decided that under the circumstances it would be best for us to move on soon."

"How soon?"

"By the weekend," Diane said.

"That's soon."

"We'll be okay." Her look was direct. "I hope you will be too, June."

After Diane left the room, June sat as if she'd been mum-

mified. The only thing that still made her feel alive was the
fire in her brain that was being fueled by harsh reality. Matt
thought less of her this morning than he had the night before.
He actually believed that she'd left him to sleep with Caleb.
Diane didn't have to say it but June knew that was exactly
what Matt had portrayed to her and Andre. What they must
think of her! June didn't blame the couple for wanting to
get far away from a house where there would be nothing
but underlying chaos. She'd want to run for her life too!

That evening when the house was quiet, Matt hated the
silence that was forcing him to think. All day, he'd had to
keep a lid on his anger, to act like a normal man with normal
problems to handle during the course of a workday. Which
animal was sick, which one was ready to meet a prospective
owner, which one would begin to show signs of the inherent
disease that had killed Bron.

Neither of the Heaths had spoken further about the conversation they'd had while having lunch in the kitchen. Matt
had spoken frankly about their situation and it was Andre
who had provided the solution. He'd left them alone in the
study while they made some phone calls. Before they left
the house, they'd made temporary arrangements to live with
Andre's cousin, an elderly woman who lived in Hicksville,
a twenty-minute drive away. She'd offered to share her home
with them when she first heard of the fire but Andre had
refused. Because she was his father's first cousin, Andre
didn't want to meet with his father whenever he chose to
visit.

Matt was edgy and wanted to talk to someone but held
back because he feared venting his anger to George, who
was his closest confidante, would make him more incensed
if George censured him.

But how could he help what he was feeling? In her way,
June was as dishonest as his mother had ever been. His
mother had lied to herself and kept up a front to keep a

husband, and June just lied. *Why?* That question burned in his mind. What had she to gain by admitting her love for him yet rushing home to be with Caleb? Whatever was nagging at his brain had given him a raging headache.

In the living room where he sat drinking beer, he went over every detail that he could possibly remember about their conversations in Paris. That was where it'd all started. Before that, they were two people who were madly in love and he'd bet his life on that. No, he thought, it started on her first day in Paris. Matt closed his eyes and tuned out everything except June's voice when he'd first heard it the morning she'd called. From her accusatory tone to the soft "*I love you, baby. I miss you so much.*" He squirmed now just as he had then, and with great effort he forced himself to sift through every shred of that conversation. When he reached the discussion about Raleigh House, he frowned. She'd said that it wouldn't be necessary to apartment hunt in September, because . . . Matt opened his eyes. He'd interrupted her. *Why* wouldn't it be necessary to find her own quarters? What had she been about to say? That she wasn't going back?

Matt slid off the sofa and went to get another beer. He stayed in the kitchen, his feet wrapped around the rungs of the wooden chair while he racked his brain. Was it then that she'd decided to come home? Not to him but to Lancaster? Matt got up and walked to the study where lingering memories chased him back to the living room.

Their second conversation was now playing over in Matt's mind. There was nothing there that gave him a clue until she'd said, "*There was something I wanted to tell you, but it doesn't matter now. I guess it can keep.*"

"Something you wanted to tell me, June?" Matt murmured. His lips twisted in a knowing grimace when he realized he'd solved the mystery. She wanted to tell him face-to-face that she wanted Lancaster, not him! He couldn't stop the roiling in his stomach that turned into a cyclone spiraling through his body and escaping through his mouth in a raucous yell.

The only sound in the house after Matt's scream was Kagi's whine that was as soft as a baby's cry. After a while it faded and Matt heard his breathing return to normal.

If not for his aching need to be near her in some fashion by walking on the beach, he'd never have caught her in her deception. There was no need for her explanations or discussion of any kind because the scene he'd stumbled on had told him all he needed to know. His presence at the wrong time had offered her the perfect out. Matt's guilt over judging her wrongly over a possible misunderstanding fled. He'd *seen* it all!

Chapter Fourteen

The Heaths had needed only one day to move. By Friday night they were gone and the house was as still as a deserted beach cabin in the winter. On Saturday, after cleaning up, June was taking a few moments of quiet time in her sitting room. She picked up the newly typed sheets that Caleb had brought over. The rough drafts of the plans they'd made the other night could not be found and she surmised that they'd gotten thrown out somehow. Caleb had joked that if that was any way to run a business, maybe she'd better hire a caretaker. She'd chased him home so she could concentrate on adding to and embellishing some of their ideas.

Diane and Andre were surprised at the reception they'd received from Andre's cousin, who had appeared genuinely pleased to have them, and had overextended herself by preparing a welcoming feast. Relief surged through Diane at seeing her husband's rare smile. She had good feelings about their move and was content to let Andre visit while she began to unpack their boxes. In the bedroom, she dumped the contents of a box Andre had packed, shaking her head at the hodgepodge of stuff. Shirts and papers all in one box! A sheaf of papers scattered to the floor and she bent to pick them up. The unfamiliar writing gave her pause to study the pages. With a stifled cry she sat down on the bed to read. It only took a moment to see and understand what she held in her hand, and the realization was like drawing heavy drapes back from a long-hidden window and letting the sun shine in. How lives can be ruined from misconceptions and missed signals was all too swift and dangerously easy, she thought.

Diane stood and went to the door. She called Andre and he came quickly up the stairs.

"What's the matter?" he asked, staring at her ashen face and then the papers she clutched. She held them out to him and he followed her into the bedroom where they both sat on the bed.

Without a word, Andre read. When he finished, he looked at his wife.

"That's why she cut her trip short," Diane said. "She was coming home to start this." She tapped the pages. "Her own business."

"Meant to surprise him, I guess," Andre said dryly.

"Somehow she never got to tell him."

Andre stood and walked to the door. "The best way I know how to ruin a friendship is to butt in somebody else's affairs," he said. He gave his wife a meaningful look. "We can't do anything about this. We have to mind our own business." He left with a deep frown marring his face.

Diane knew exactly what her husband meant and he was right. But there was no way that she was going to keep this discovery to herself. One way or another Matt was going to know what he was about to lose forever.

* * *

Matt was surprised on late Saturday afternoon to see Diane walk around to the back of the house. He was in the dog run exercising Kagi, who needed to strengthen his leg. She waved and he waved back, curious to see her go inside. About ten minutes later she came back out and walked to him, grinning ruefully.

"What's up?" he said, amused at her expression.

"Now don't tell me something's wrong with your nose too," she said, wrinkling hers. "Your foot's healing mighty fine so you can walk halfway decently but the malady has affected your schnozzola."

"What'd you forget? Dirty socks under my bed?"

Diane wrinkled her nose. "Mildewed clothes. I left them in the washing machine the other day. It's a wonder Kagi didn't call your attention to them. They were already stinkin'." She shook her head. "They're washing now with some daisy-scented fabric softener. When they're finished just put them in the dryer and they'll be smelling as fresh as a spring day."

"You came all the way over here just for that? Why didn't you call? I'm not as helpless as all that, you know."

"Just wanted to see that they were done right. Gotta go. See you Monday." She hurried away thinking that white lies *were* good for something!

Matt stared after her. Kagi was sitting by his feet and he looked down at the dog and said, "Something's going on, boy. What do you think?" His pet looked up at him and gave a soft yodel. "Yeah, I thought so," Matt said.

An hour later Matt went inside and headed straight for the laundry room. After putting the clothes in the dryer, Matt left the room with the red folder that was sitting on top of it. Apparently, the reason for Diane's mysterious visit,

Matt thought. He carried it to the den where he opened it and began to read the top page. The heading blew him away.

The Bountiful
A Bed-and-Breakfast Proprietor,   June Saxon

Matt dropped the pages and stared in disbelief. Long minutes later, after the red spots in front of his eyes disappeared, he read some more of the roughly drawn ideas. How similar to his own hastily scribbled notes they were! He read with increasingly rising temperature and pounding heartbeat. When he finished, he dropped the pages and the soft flutter they made landing on the desktop was like a bell sounding off in his head. He stood and hurried from the study. His throat was parched and he drank ice-cold water to soothe the burning. He only wished that he could douse his brain similarly.

There was something I wanted to tell you, but it doesn't matter now. I guess it can keep. The words were like a train running monotonously over the same length of track. He didn't need a psychic to tell him what he already knew. There was no need to look for an apartment in September because June would be up to her neck in overseeing a fledgling business.

In the study, after looking over the well thought-out plans, Matt finally closed the folder. He closed his eyes against the tears that were welling up inside. And wished the voice in his head would stop the taunts. Aloud, he spoke the words. *"Matt Gardiner, you're a damn fool!"*

June wasn't surprised that it was nearly mid-August because the last few weeks she'd been up to her knees and elbows in paint buckets, wallpaper, and decorating books. Beverly had taken some time off and they'd spent days at a time scouring flea markets and antique stores for just the right item for each of her nautical-themed rooms.

She'd toyed with cutesy names for the business, and both Beverly and Caleb had laughed themselves into stroke city when she came up with The Bounty.

"Surefire mutiny from all on deck when you burn those fried eggs, girl," Beverly had screamed.

They all had agreed on The Bountiful, but Caleb had left the naming of the rooms to the women. June loved them all, but her favorite was the big master bedroom upstairs that had belonged to her grandparents. She called it The Tempest. The full name in the brochure that Beverly had designed was Tempest in a Teapot. A secret smile played about her mouth when she remembered that first week she'd come to live with them when she was eight. Her bedroom was next to theirs. After the first week she'd asked her Grandma Belle why her and Grandpa's bed made so much noise at night. She confessed that when no one was looking she'd felt all over the bed but couldn't find the squeaker. June couldn't understand why her grandfather had hurried from the room doubled over with laughter while her grandmother had buried her face in the cereal bowl.

June wanted that bedroom to be reserved for lovers who would make tumultuous love. The name defied the decor. It was as pretty as a teapot dressed in white and pale blue. There was lots of romantic lace on the bed and draping the windows. Pictures of storm-tossed whaling ships, yachts on serene waters, and sailboats being carried by the wind decorated the walls.

June had used her dwindling bank account to install a connecting bathroom. She'd insisted when Caleb had cautioned her to go slow with the ready cash, because she couldn't imagine honeymooners racing from their room to a hall bathroom! The bedroom colors were carried through with robins' egg–blue walls, white appointments with gleaming chrome fixtures, and whimsical miniature boats and wooden fishermen.

In the kitchen on a muggy Friday afternoon, June was dressed in her favorite uniform of skimpy tank top and shorts. She'd made a pitcher of lemonade to cool her hot skin, and wondered what kind of clothes she'd be wearing this time next month, preparing for her first customers. As usual her friends had come through for her. Beverly and Caleb had both gotten friends to rent rooms over the Labor Day weekend. Her eyes filled when she thought how blessed she was to have those two people in her life. The front doorbell rang, and self-consciously she checked herself. She wasn't wearing a bra but shrugged it off. Whoever it was had probably lost his way down the dead-end street.

Caleb was on his back porch chillin' with a cold beer when he saw the familiar black car pull up in front of June's house. He stared with dark eyes when Matt got out of the car and walked coolly toward the house. "What a damn nerve," he muttered. He set his bottle down on the steps and sprinted across the grass.

"Matt?" June gasped.

"Hello, June," Matt said. Before he said another word he saw Caleb coming at a fast clip and was on the porch in two hops and in his face. Matt met the angry man's stare.

"What the hell do you want here?" Caleb said, trying hard to keep his voice steady.

Matt couldn't stand the sight of June's anguish at his sudden appearance, but he wasn't leaving until he spoke with her—in private. He turned to her and said, "Excuse me," then gestured to Caleb to follow him back down the steps.

When they were away from the house, Matt said, "What I have to say to her is between the two of us."

"Like hell it is, man." Caleb stood eye to eye with the man that June was eating her heart out over. "I think you've told her enough to last her a lifetime. This time I want to hear what you have to say especially if I come into the picture again.''

Matt's jaw tightened and with an unwavering eye said, ''That was a fool talking.''

Surprise caused Caleb to back-step. He recovered quickly. ''Yes, it was,'' he said slowly, taking a long look at Matt. Understanding clicked in his head and his suspicions were immediately confirmed.

''I love her,'' Matt said.

''Yeah, it shows itself in the strangest ways.''

''I said I was a fool,'' Matt said sharply. He tapped the folder he was holding in one hand. ''I'm going to talk to June about this,'' he said. ''Later, I want you to look it over, but I want this time alone with her.''

Caleb looked thoughtfully at Matt before speaking. He knew that June wasn't in any danger from this man. At least physically. He only hoped that her heart had healed enough to listen to him objectively. He nodded and backed away. ''Be cool, man.''

Matt walked back up the steps and was glad that June had disappeared inside. He was breathing hard and he needed a second to pull it together. Before he'd made the decision to come over here with his proposition he'd promised himself that he'd back off, give her some space. But the first second Matt saw her he wanted to pull her into his arms and devour her. *God, give me strength*, he prayed.

June was just in the shadows watching the two men and wondered about the intensity of their conversation. She hadn't seen Matt in weeks and his sudden appearance unnerved her. Nothing about him had changed. Except that he was walking without a cane and she breathed a prayer that his foot had healed properly. He walked tall and straight with the confident, and almost arrogant way she'd remembered. Watching him undetected she knew that she still loved him. Would always love him. But it had to be her secret. She left and went to her bedroom where she put on a bra and a T-shirt. She knew she was going to let Matt in to hear whatever it was he had to say to her, but she didn't want to feel so naked in front of him.

The heat that leaped into his eyes had sent a shock wave of warmth through her body and stirred vivid memories of his warm mouth suckling her nipples. She had felt them hardening under his intense gaze. When he rang the doorbell she walked to the door, and opened it.

"Come in, Matt," she said, and stepped back to let him enter. He was dressed casually but for business and she knew it wasn't a social call. She led the way down the hall to the living room. "We can talk in here." She sat on the sofa and he took the big comfortable armchair, filling it just like her grandfather did in the old one. Coolly, she said, "Why are you here?"

Matt laid the folder down on the table. "That," he said and dismissed it when he met her cautious stare. "And to ask for your forgiveness." He saw her mouth tighten. "You're looking at the biggest fool you'll ever come across in your life. Everything I've said or done to hurt you should become a record in the Guinness book under my name. I let my emotions and my jealousy do the talking and I lost the respect and the love of the woman I love. The conclusions I jumped to were inexcusable." His eyes burned into hers and he gave a short snort. "On the beach, if I'd been thinking straight, I would have seen the innocence in that peck on the forehead." His lips twisted in a grimace. "But I was too incensed thinking that I was the wronged man. Any way you look at it I'm the loser because since I lost you nothing else seems to matter very much anymore."

The earth was spinning wildly around her and June wondered why she was so still. *Is he saying he still loves me? No, this can't be happening*, she thought. What of his lack of trust in her? What about the next time suspicions rose in his head?

The sudden stiffening of her body pained Matt. He'd confused and frightened her and he could see that she was mentally rejecting him. He felt deflated but understood that she'd really loved him and was protecting herself from further hurt.

"June," Matt said in a husky voice, "I'm sorry and I hope that one day you can forgive a fool." He cleared his throat. "One day, I'm hoping."

The catch in his voice speared her heart, but hers remained steady in the wake of her conflicting emotions. "You hurt me, Matt," she said. "All I want is to forget that we ever happened. Who knows? Everything that's happened occurred for a reason and maybe we were never meant to be together. It ended before great damage was done to either of us and we can both get on with our lives."

Forget that we ever happened. Matt's heart went cold. How could she believe that after what they'd shared? He straightened his shoulders. He'd promised to back off and give her some space and that's what he'd do. Only he knew that in his way he would pursue her relentlessly: to have her love again. If it took a lifetime to see the love in her eyes for him, then so be it because without that his life wouldn't be worth a wooden nickel.

Matt nodded and picked up the folder. "I respect your decision," he said in an even tone. "I had to clear the air between us before I approached you with this—and to get on with our lives."

June shuttered her eyes against his sudden aloof manner. "What is it?" she said, eyeing the pages he held in his hand.

"It's about your business. Apparently we were thinking along the same lines and I thought by working together we can get a good thing going."

"My business?" June's interest was piqued. "What do you mean?" She held up a hand. "Wait. I'll get us a cold drink. I made a pitcher of lemonade. Be right back."

Remembering the first time he'd visited her, Matt smiled. "Lemonade is a start," he said softly.

When she returned, June sat on the sofa and began to scan the pages. In seconds she grasped the plans for operating a bed-and-breakfast. Her lashes flickered. "Seems a long time ago you mentioned something like this. You want to do this now? Here?"

Matt nodded. "After the fire and what I believed were your plans to—stay in Paris, I thought a lot about making another offer for your house. The Heaths would have a home and Diane could have a business to run. They really fell in love with this old house."

"You were so certain that I would sell?"

"The offer would have been more than generous."

"I see," June said. "My returning put a damper on your plans, then."

"Yes."

"What about your original reason for wanting my place?"

"I don't see a problem with making arrangements for my customers to stay at The Bountiful." Matt held her gaze.

June shut her eyes briefly. Her plans exactly! "I was thinking along those lines," she said. Her heart cried with what they'd lost. They could be working side by side as lovers, and then as husband and wife, for surely she would have accepted his proposal. But that kind of relationship was lost to them now. If she accepted his proposition they would be strictly business partners.

"No, I can't see a problem at all," June, said. "Let's see what you have and I'll show you what I've done. Excuse me." She left to get her plans from her sitting room. When she returned, Matt had moved to the sofa and she hesitated for a second before sitting beside him. She handed him her folder. "This is it so far. A sample brochure is included."

Matt pretended not to notice her consternation when she sat beside him. If she didn't care for him, then why should it matter where he sat? Starving for any kind of sign that she still cared, he felt that he'd been given a morsel, enough to satisfy his hunger until the next time.

Both were silent as they read each other's plans and when June finished, she laid the papers down on the table. Matt had finished seconds before and he was looking at her, expressionless.

"They're similar, aren't they?" June said.

Matt nodded. "Uncannily so," he responded gravely.

"We can do this." After a moment she said, "I accept your proposal, Matt."

"What?" Matt was stunned.

"Your proposition. I accept." She gave him a curious look.

"Oh, of course." The blood had rushed to his head and he could feel it cascading warmly through his body. "I'm glad," he managed. "I'm sure it can work." He was breathing easier, glad that she hadn't picked up on her choice of words. "I'd like Caleb to look this over, give his input, if you don't mind."

"Certainly." She watched as he picked up a brochure.

"Clever. I like it." Matt picked up a calendar page showing the month of September. "I see you're starting Labor Day weekend?"

"Yes. Actually they're the real deal," she said. "I had a trial run last weekend."

"Oh?"

June smiled at the memory. "Beverly and two of her friends came and didn't give me any slack from the moment they got here. Pretended they'd never laid eyes on me before. Except on Sunday morning, Bev helped me with the breakfast. She said I passed the test though. I was the hostess supreme,'' June said proudly.

For the first time since he walked into the house, June was animated. Her eyes held the old sparkle that he loved and they flashed with excitement, and delight.

''I'm sure you were,'' Matt said and quickly turned his attention back to the calendar before he blew his game plan. He wanted to kiss her badly and the need had shown in his voice. He was sure of it because she'd given him another strange stare.

''Did you solicit these or was it through advertising?'' he asked, trying to sound businesslike again.

June gave a tiny laugh. ''My friends again. If it weren't for them . . .'' She didn't finish the thought as she stared at his face. ''Something wrong?'' she asked.

Matt was staring at two names penciled in on the Thursday before the long weekend. Ivon and Laraine. Spellbound, he remembered a conversation from weeks ago. Ivon Raleigh and his assistant were lovers? Matt looked at June with a question in his eyes.

''Ivon and Laraine married two weeks after I left,'' June said softly. ''They've been cruising around the world for the last month and will stop in New York before flying to Paris. They can't wait to see The Bountiful.''

''Married?'' Matt had the incredible feeling of being shrunk down to the size of a miniature man in a child's dollhouse.

''Yes,'' June answered somberly. ''They were madly in love but . . . circumstances kept them apart. They're together now.''

''God,'' Matt breathed. He rubbed his temples. What a colossal jerk he'd been!

''Matt?'' He looked at her and June had to stop herself from reaching out and grabbing his hands. They were clasped

tightly together as if he held himself back from hitting something.

"June, I . . ." He couldn't finish. What was there to say
to her now?

"Let's go upstairs," June said quietly. "You can see
what I've done so far and I'm open to suggestions for any
changes." She wanted to do anything to get his mind off
her revelation.

Matt stood. "Okay. But give me a minute." He walked
from the room and went outside where he breathed in the
salty air. The sky was at its bluest and he wondered if it
was the brightness that made his eyes tear. With hands
jammed in his pockets he leaned against the rail and stared
at the bay, wishing that the works inside his head would
begin to turn as smoothly and effortlessly as the engines in
the finely tuned yachts. He wondered if the racket in his
head was eternal or would remain only as long as he thought
himself a fool.

June was waiting for him in the kitchen. When he appeared
in the doorway Matt said, "I'm ready," and was grateful
that she didn't say a word. Silently, he followed her upstairs.

The decor in the smallest of the three bedrooms brought
an immediate chuckle to Matt's lips.

"You like it?" June was happy at the unusual sound that
lightened the gloomy funk he'd fallen into. Her soft laughter
joined his. "If Kagi saw this he'd claim it for his own,"
she said.

"I think you're right about that." He looked around in
amazement. "How in the world did you get that wallpaper?"
Dogs of every kind were doing something nautical, in or
around boats, sailing the boats, playing captain with jaunty
caps, and peering through antique binoculars.

"With much patience and fortitude," June said. "Beverly
pulled a tantrum when I wanted to buy another of those."
She gestured around the room at the whimsical carvings of

boats, fishermen, and dogs. The room was red, navy, and white anchored with pale gray carpet.

"I wondered what the Salty Dog room looked like," Matt said, tapping the brochure he held in his hand. He raised a brow. "I'm ready for Nothing but the Beach."

"Follow me." June stepped back and let him precede her into the room. "What do you think?"

"Do people say 'Wow' anymore?"

"Only at the risk of sounding downright corny."

"Then I'm at risk." He walked across the wool carpet that was the color of sand, and stood at the foot of the bed. The huge picture on the wall over the bed was of a wide shot of a deserted beach, except for a lone couple sitting in the shade of an umbrella. Their naturally tan skin was bronzed from the sun and the woman who was in a red bathing suit was clasping her drawn-up knees. She had a Mona Lisa smile on her face and appeared to be staring out at the ocean. The man was sitting just behind her watching her intently. He wasn't smiling.

"Isn't it beautiful?" June said.

"Yes," Matt answered. He was still looking at the picture. "Quite a conversation piece. Where'd you find it?"

"Beverly found it in an art gallery in Brooklyn. The owner said customers leave arguing about what the woman is smiling about and what the man is thinking. Does he love her or hate her?"

Matt looked at June. "Definitely not hate."

June turned away from his intense look and gestured. "I kept it fairly simple," she said. "What do you think?" She'd covered the bed in white cotton eyelet, and sheer cotton curtains hung from the windows. Red accents, in a throw cover draped over a chair, and in smaller beach scene pictures, completed the room.

"Restful," Matt said.

"That's the feel I wanted. I intend to replace the furniture with whitewashed oak but that's in the future. This dark mahogany isn't in keeping with the theme.''

''You've seen what you want?''

''Yes.''

''Then order it,'' Matt said. ''Will it get here by opening day?''

''But . ..''

He stopped her with a frown. ''But what? I thought we were in this together.'' Matt refused to let her look away. ''Aren't we?''

June nodded.

''Then can we get a delivery date in time?''

''Yes, if they have stock,'' June said.

''Good. Let's see what Tempest in the Teapot looks like. If nothing else, the names of these rooms will send the curious running to The Bountiful.''

Swallowing the lump in her throat, June walked beside Matt to the master bedroom. Somehow she didn't want to be in there with him. She stood by the door and watched as he walked inside. ''This was my grandparents' bedroom.''

She watched as he inspected the newly installed connecting bath, and walked around the room looking intently at the decor. He remained silent for a long time. Matt's back was to her and he was just staring at the bed. This was her favorite room and he hadn't said a word. ''You don't like it.''

Matt glanced briefly at the brochure, then turned to June. ''You've done an excellent job with this room. A bride couldn't want better.'' His voice was strangely quiet.

''Thank you,'' June whispered. She nearly went limp with relief. When she'd shopped for this room she had herself in mind as the bride spending blissful nights in that bed with the man she loved. She didn't realize she'd closed her eyes and when she heard his voice so close, whispering her name and his finger on her cheek, they flew open. ''Yes?''

Matt brushed her damp lashes. "Tears?" he murmured. "Why? I think you've done great work here in such a short time."

A sigh escaped. "It appeared that you liked this one the least and wanted to suggest—"

"Shh," he whispered, wiping a tear from her cheek. "I wouldn't change a thing in this room. The love in here is like a cloak." The feel of her soft skin was overpowering and as if hypnotized, Matt was drawn to her. "June," he murmured, cupping her face in his hands. His lips touched hers gently and he closed his eyes, almost shaking with the love he felt.

June's lips softened beneath his tender caress. *Matt, I do love you.* The silent cry was soul stirring. How she wanted him! She leaned into him and was shaken when she felt his arousal. She stiffened and stepped back. He was staring at her with pain-filled eyes. "We can't do this," she whispered.

Back off! Heeding the savvy of his inner voice, Matt dropped his hands from her face and stepped away. "You're right. We can't."

She didn't know whether to feel relief or deprivation when he widened the space between them. "It's all about business now," June said. "We can't go back."

Nodding in agreement, Matt said, "Caleb's waiting to hear what I've got to say. Ready for him?"

"Yes. I'll call." She slipped past Matt, very much aware of his closeness as he followed her back down the stairs. "I'll only be a minute."

"Sure," Matt answered, and left so she could use the kitchen phone in private. He walked to the living room and sat on the sofa, where he exhaled. *She loves me!* Without a doubt he knew that he was playing it right by going slow. It would take time for her wounds to heal, but he was going to do his damnedest to make her see the truth, that she still loved him. His only regret was the irretrievable time lost without loving and living their lives together, and he hoped that it wouldn't take a lifetime because he wanted to spend the rest of his days making her happy.

Matt was pleased about the sparkle returning to June's beautiful eyes, but his jaw was set with determination. The next time he saw that sparkle it would be because he'd put it there. Not The Bountiful.

Chapter Fifteen

A week before Labor Day, June and Matt were in Nothing but the Beach. She stood by excitedly exclaiming over the new furniture that had arrived that morning.

"Just consider my response as corny as before," Matt said. He was leaning against the whitewashed oak dresser looking around in admiration.

June laughed. "Okay, then I'll say it this time. Wow!"

"I think you have a flair for decorating, lady," he said, then raised a brow. "How long does one keep the same decor? Do you have to change every so often?"

"Who knows? I'm new at this, remember?" She wrinkled her nose. "I don't really want to change anything, ever. I love it just the way it is."

Matt smiled. "Things get old and have to be replaced. You have to think about redecorating sometime."

"I suppose so," June sighed. "Do you know how long it took to come up with these themes? I should start now if I'm going to have new ideas in five years!"

"We can plan together," Matt said softly.

"I'd like that." June caught the look on his face before he turned away, pretending to examine something on the dresser. Several times during the past few weeks she'd seen that same shadow and heard the sadness in his voice but they'd disappeared instantly.

Matt cleared his throat. "Thanks for calling me over. The place looks great and ready for customers, but I have to get back. I've overseas calls to make." He followed her from the room.

"Oh." June was disappointed. "Can't you stay for lunch?" She'd gotten used to him dropping by, lending a hand wherever she needed one, and sampling her different menus. He was always frank, almost brutally so, and they'd argued about some of the things she wanted to keep and he'd teased her about having one-time-only customers.

He peered into the kitchen. "I don't smell anything burning." He sniffed loudly and yelled "Ouch," when she poked him in the ribs. "Okay, I admit it smells good. What is it this time?"

"Salmon croquettes Bountiful," June said proudly, lifting the pan lid.

"More sauces?" Matt groaned. "You're going to sauce our people to death," he said, holding back a teasing laugh. "Take my word, in the morning, no one is going to care whether their salmon is a plain old pattie or all dressed up in white mush." One look at her face and he couldn't contain the laughter any longer. "All right, you got yourself another guinea pig today." He sat down. "But keep the bicarb handy."

June pinched his muscled forearm as she walked behind him to get a plate from the cabinet. "For that remark, you can suffer in silence, Mr. Gardiner." Suddenly she laughed. "That's what the customers will do, too embarrassed to toss it out in front of me."

"Oh, that tickles you, does it?" Matt said. "When the cash register is no longer tilling, then we'll see who's laughing. You're going to cook us right into the poorhouse!"

She set the plate before him and then sat to watch. "Well, what are you waiting for?" she said anxiously. He was holding his fork in the air, giving her a slant-eyed look.

"Am I in this alone?" Matt cocked one skeptical brow.

Indignant, June said, "Do you think I'd experiment on you first? I've tried them and they're delicious!"

"Hmm." Taking an interminably long time to dig in, Matt finally tasted the first bite. Then another. And another. He felt her impatience and he was tickled to death at teasing her so unbearably. They'd been the best of friends since the day they'd decided to work together and he'd seen that beautiful smile more often than not. But he'd yet to see that look that was meant only for him. The one that said she loved him.

"Matt Gardiner!" June was nearly bursting.

"I approve." He finished the last bite. "Quite good, actually."

"Would I lie?" June said, pleased that he'd cleaned the plate.

He looked around. "What else you got?" His stomach was talking to him.

"More of the same and I made some of that dressing for the mixed greens that you like." She looked a bit sheepish. "Well, nothing really makes a complete meal. I was just trying out different things and perfecting others. I made the German potato salad again and the okra soup."

"You're kidding me, right?" Matt asked with disbelief.

"If you try everything, guaranteed you'll be satisfied until dinner," June said.

"That's if my stomach doesn't revolt," he grunted. He got a gleam in his eye. "Tell you what, let's make a deal."

"What?" June looked skeptical.

"Supposing I survive all this and am still walking around tonight, would you have dinner with me?" There was no teasing in his voice and his look was serious.

"Dinner? Well, I—I don't think that would be a good idea." June sat up straight, drawing away from the table.

Matt observed her sudden discomfort and the invisible barrier she'd erected. Now was not the time to undo all he'd accomplished so far. She was still tender. "Okay, no deal," he said lightly. "Just consider me a captive taster." Pretending to give much thought to his choices, he said gravely, "Bring on the soup."

Moving hesitantly, June ladled soup in a bowl. "It's still hot," she said when she set it on the table along with biscuits and butter. Unprepared for his sudden request, she busied herself around the stove until she recovered. Ever since they'd fallen into such easy camaraderie when discussing the business, their relationship had evolved into one of friendship. They'd become lovers before their friendship had deepened, and now she realized that she liked him and knew that the feeling was mutual, but his asking for a date was unnerving.

"Come sit, June." Matt spoke quietly.

She sat across from him.

"I upset you."

"Just surprised," June answered.

"I know that came out of left field," Matt said. He shrugged. "I've enjoyed these last weeks together, helping to plan your venture, watching your excitement, especially today. I suppose I just wanted to extend the good feelings I have. Forget what I asked. It won't happen again."

June watched the familiar shadow on his face come and go. He no more wanted to keep that promise than she wanted him to, she thought. When she'd told him that they couldn't go back, she'd really believed it. After spending so much time together, laughing and arguing over silly stuff, she found herself wishing that the night would end with them falling sleepily into each other's arms. She was actually surprised one night when he got up to leave, and then remembered that he was going home to sleep in his own bed. Never had she seen any indication from him that he wanted to resume their former relationship. Not once. Until now.

Several different expressions crossed her face as Matt watched June wrestle with her thoughts. He'd obviously struck a nerve and he beat himself up mentally, ruefully thinking that he'd ruined the progress they'd made.

"Did you have a particular cuisine in mind?" June asked softly.

"What?" Startled, he searched her face. He refused to anticipate her next words.

"Dinner." She wrinkled her nose. "I don't think I want anything that comes from the sea." Then, "Have you had a real burnt steak lately?"

Matt nodded solemnly. "Yes, last Saturday when I called myself barbecuing dinner. My shepherd disowned it." He stared steadily at her. "I could use a medium rare about now."

"Me too." June gave him a tentative smile. "About six o'clock?"

"I'll be here." Matt hoped that his voice sounded cooler than the heat that was enveloping his body.

At six forty-five, Matt touched his champagne glass to June's. "To . . ." He hesitated.

". . .the best medium-rare steak we've ever eaten," June finished. She saw the relief in his eyes at intentionally lightening the mood. Since he'd picked her up he'd been unusually quiet and she could only attribute it to his wondering what was ahead for them because this dinner was out of the realm they'd established for themselves. They weren't ready for soul-searching conversation and confessions, and June aimed to keep it light. That is, if she could keep her hands to herself. Not once, but twice in the car, she'd tapped his hand for emphasis while making a point. Another time she'd poked him in the ribs when he teased her about her okra soup. A definite bomb, he'd said.

"I'll drink to that," Matt said. "We won't be disappointed, though. Guaranteed. Your taste buds will be clamoring for seconds on the marinated steak." The James Grill in Oyster Bay was a place he frequented and he was never disappointed no matter what he ordered.

During their meal, they spoke quietly of sundry things, staying far away from matters of the heart. In response to her question about his business, she noticed the furrowing of his brow.

"Bad news?" June asked.

"Could be better," Matt answered. "I won't have as many pups coming over next year." He frowned again. "I'd anticipated quite a few."

"From Africa?" June knew that he'd talked to his employee earlier.

"Yes."

"What is the problem?"

"I hope there's not a problem," Matt said with a twinkle in his eyes. "At least not a long-term one."

June looked puzzled.

"They couldn't mate and the time's past." He smiled. "Let's hope it's just something in the water or a full moon."

"Do you think that there's a medical problem?"

Matt laughed. "None other than it didn't happen." He shook his head. "Can't have much of that kind of inactivity. If they don't breed I can close up shop."

"Oh no," exclaimed June. "What could have happened?"

"Don't know." He really was at a loss for an explanation.

"What about your breeders over here?"

"So far, so good," Matt said. "We had a hundred percent cooperation from all concerned."

"Well, will that take up the slack and keep things going?" June had never even thought of the kennel losing business.

"Partially," Matt answered. "I have customers for those African pups and now they may not want to wait. There are other breeders they can go to."

"Yes, but they came to you because of your reputation, and quality of your animals," June said. "Don't you think they'd want to wait?"

Matt shrugged. "Maybe, maybe not. Guess it depends on their situation." He frowned, then in a regretful tone added, "This definitely will impact your business, June."

She hadn't thought of that. They'd calculated the out-of-town customers he had, and the number of potential Bountiful guests was gratifying. June watched Matt beat himself up and she reached over and touched his hand that was gripping the wineglass. "There's nothing you can do to control nature," she said and smiled. "It was out of your hands."

Her touch only reminded him of what he'd so foolishly thrown away with his lack of trust and he held on tightly as if never wanting to end the moment. "I know," he said. "Thanks for the boost."

Her hand still singed from his touch, so June sought relief from the chill of her own champagne glass. "Don't put a jinx on us now by thinking bad thoughts," she said. "Things'll work out. We're going to do an ad campaign and of course we're hoping for word of mouth to help a lot." She grinned. "If I know Beverly, she's already got a crew lined up for the spring."

Matt studied her.

"Don't you agree?" June asked worriedly. He'd gotten so serious.

"Yes."

"Oh, you had me scared for a second there."

"I was just thinking that you always speak unselfishly in terms of we and us when you mention the Bountiful. It's *your* business." Matt met her puzzled look. "I'm only a backer and consultant."

Seconds passed as she digested his words. "I guess I never really got over thinking that way," she said, quietly. "When I first conceived the idea, I never thought in terms of just me." She dropped her eyes briefly, and then caught his gaze. "I always saw you as being there, helping with advice and suggestions, because you'd been there and done it alone." She shrugged. "As it turned out you are here and I can't thank you enough."

"Thanks isn't what I want—or need, June." *Oh God, I'm going to blow it!* "I want you back." His voice ended in a husky whisper. "I love you."

"Oh, Matt," June whispered. She swallowed, unable to say any more.

Kicking himself for his loss of control, Matt signaled for the check. He should have known that the intimacy of dinner together would be his undoing. But he hadn't anticipated the sadness in her beautiful dark eyes to stab his heart the way it did.

They were both quiet during the fifteen-minute ride to June's home. Matt helped her out of the car and walked with her to the steps. He watched her walk slowly upstairs and then turn to watch him as she leaned against the rail. "Good night, June," he said. "Call you tomorrow?" He turned away when she nodded slowly.

"Matt, don't go." June was wearing a long black skirt covered with tiny multicolored flowers and a black, short-sleeve, V-neck top. She hadn't worn a sweater and the night air held a chill. Gathering her skirt around her legs, she sat down on the top step and hugged her arms. "Please," she said when he hesitated. "I want to talk."

He was beside her and when she shivered, he removed his jacket and wrapped it around her shoulders. They both stared out across the bay at the hundreds of twinkling lights. One lone yacht was making its way slowly to its berth in the cove just out of their view.

"It's beautiful here, isn't it?" June murmured. "How can things not work out? If *I* were a guest here, *I'd* make it my business to come back every year!"

"You're just a little bit prejudiced," Matt said, smiling at her indignation.

"I think I am," June sighed.

"Do you want to walk?" Matt asked. It was just past nine o'clock and he saw her glance at the late-night beach strollers.

"Yes, I'd like that," June said and rose. "I'll be right back." She shrugged off his jacket and handed it to him. "I'm going to get a sweater. No sense in you shivering instead of me."

When she returned, Matt looked at the blanket she thrust into his hands. Without a word she put her hand in his and they walked down the steps. He didn't even try to put any meaning to her actions. Deep in his soul he wished that this night would end in a second chance for him. If he were a fanciful man he'd have wished on the stars in the sky. He squeezed her hand as they walked.

"Toi dropped by the other day," June said casually. "She fell in love with the place."

"Yeah, she told me," Matt answered, remembering the excited call he'd received. "She said she's been spreading the word." He chuckled. "If I know my sister-in-law I can imagine what kind of favors she's been calling in. Whatever she's doing it just might pick up the slack from the loss of my customers."

June felt him tense up. "Don't worry about that now," she said.

After walking back to the beach from the dock where they'd stood and watched people party quietly on their boats, Matt spread the blanket. Expecting June to finally speak her mind about them, he waited, observing her by the light of the moon. He was reminded of the night they'd met almost in the same spot.

"I've never stopped loving you, Matt." June's voice was clear yet as soft as the gently lapping waves in the bay.

It took all the strength Matt had not to let out an audible breath. If he'd never prayed for anything in his life, he did now.

"Your words and your thoughts, in Paris and on the night I returned, hurt me so badly I couldn't breathe or even think straight." June drew up her knees and hugged them. "I thought that if I never saw you again, it wouldn't matter, I'd just get on with my life. And I did," she said thoughtfully. "I didn't have to go hither and yon to find myself. I was here all along . . . and I liked what I found." Her eyes sought Matt's. "I learned soon enough that not having you, loving you, did matter. But I steeled myself against letting you inside because I couldn't take the chance of being hurt by you again. We were no longer lovers and there was nothing that either of us had to do to trust in each other." She paused. "So I would never know whether I ever had your trust."

Matt exhaled slowly.

"The day we decided to work together on my project, I knew that you loved me." She waved a hand. "Oh, not because you'd apologized and even admitted your love; to me, the words were hollow. But I knew when—" Her voice broke. "When you lost it after learning about Ivon and Laraine. I knew then, without a doubt."

Matt wanted to catch her and hug the breath out of her

but he stayed where he was, allowing her to recover. She was deeply shaken.

June buried her face in her knees. After several minutes she lifted her eyes to his. "I do love you, Matt," she whispered. She reached for him and he was by her side instantly, holding her, rocking her in his arms. Her arms went around his waist and she squeezed him tightly.

Almost speechless, Matt could only whisper his love in June's ear and silently thank God for listening. He was vaguely aware of couples walking by but he clung to her like a lifeline. He'd landed in a safety net and he wasn't letting go.

June reached up to caress his cheek and was surprised at the dampness on her fingers. "Matt," she whispered. On her knees she wrapped her arms around his shoulders and hugged him, kissing the tears from his eyes.

"Sweet love, can you ever forgive me?" Matt murmured.

"Yes," June said. She caught his face in her hands and looked into his eyes. "Yes," she repeated and bent to kiss his mouth.

Matt covered her mouth hungrily, drawing in her tongue and savoring the sweet kiss that rocked his soul. His urgent kisses explored the rest of her face, lingering along her jaw, her lips, her eyes, and when his tongue touched the soft hollow of her throat she squirmed in his arms, flattening herself against his chest. The feel of her breasts made his pulses throb. He wanted to make love to her on the spot, and the soft breast cupped in his hand brought a raw cry rumbling from his throat. Matt got control, pulling himself back from what would be a mistake. He wanted to love her but not here; not yet.

June felt his arms slip from around her and immediately understood his withdrawal. It wasn't time. She lay down and looked up at him.

Matt traced her swollen lips with his finger. He bent and kissed them, then lay beside her. June caught his hand.

They lay side by side looking up at the moon. June smiled. A long time ago she knew that the midsummer moon would play a major part in her life. It had brought her Matt.

On the Saturday of the Labor Day weekend, June and Beverly were preparing lunch for a crowd. All week, June had been going nonstop, shopping, making sure the cleaning service hadn't missed a speck of dust, and getting a casual wardrobe together so she'd wake up in the morning knowing what she was going to wear.

Beverly glanced at the clock. "It's almost time to put these salads outside, lady," she said. "You don't want to wait too much longer past two o'clock, do you?" She patted her stomach. "*I* can't wait much longer past two!"

June nervously grabbed her special dressings from the fridge. "I'm ready."

Tickled at her friend's jitters, Beverly chuckled. "I've never seen you like this before. Lighten up. You know everyone who's coming. They're all your friends."

"I've never had an open house for my own business before, either," June snapped.

"Snippy! Snippy!" Beverly teased. "Relax, sweetie. You're doing just fine."

"I am?"

"Yes, and you look fabulous too." Her eyes roved approvingly over the sleeveless royal blue wide-legged pants outfit, complemented by white sandals and huge white dangling earrings. Beverly pinched June's cheek. "I haven't seen those roses in a month of Sundays." Her tone turned serious. "I'm glad you and Matt are working things out. How's it going?"

"Cautiously," June answered, not revealing that she and Matt had yet to make love.

Beverly frowned. "Why? I thought you were both sure. He hasn't proposed again?"

"Uh-uh. We're not there yet."

"There, where?" Beverly sputtered. "Not from what I can see," she said, rolling her eyes in exasperation. "Every time I look at the both of you I know I'm looking at two people in love." She thought for a moment, then said, "You know, you two almost remind me of the way you described Ivon and Laraine when you first met them. In love and not doing anything about it. Remember?"

June looked at her friend, surprised that she'd made that analogy. "Yes," she said slowly, "I do remember. Strange you'd think of that."

"Not really. When you look at them now, what do you see? Two people so in love and content in each other's company the world ceases to exist for them."

"They're so much in love," June said. Ivon and Laraine had arrived on Thursday and all three had been ecstatic to see one another. They hugged and kissed like old friends, and June and Laraine had tears in their eyes when they embraced. Later, they'd complimented June on The Bountiful and both had fallen in love with The Tempest room. On Friday morning June had gone about her business with a secret smile on her face. There were definitely no squeakers in the bed because she hadn't heard any complaints from either of her other guests.

"So are you and Matt," Beverly said. "Be right back." She carried the salad bowls outside.

"Here she is, *mon cherie,*" Laraine said to her husband, who held her lightly around the waist. "What are you doing, June? Come outside with us. Everyone wants to toast to your success!"

Ivon echoed his wife's command but he studied June for

several seconds before he spoke again. He kissed Laraine's forehead and said in a low voice, "Look at our friend, *mon cherie*. What do you see?"

Laraine puckered her brows as she looked from Ivon to June. "Ah," she exclaimed in a soft voice as she looked up at her husband. "You are the observant one. You've seen what I have missed."

Ivon nodded and looked at June. "Why are you not happy, my friend?" He waved a hand, dismissing the house. "It is not this because I have seen the pride you display in your business. I remember a young woman who was so happy to return home to her lover." He frowned. "It is over?"

June met Ivon's direct stare. "It was for a while," she admitted.

"And now?" Ivon persisted.

"We are working it out," she answered softly.

Laraine and Ivon exchanged solemn looks.

With one finger, Ivon lifted June's chin until her eyes met his. "Even one day apart is too long, my friend. I know." A painful memory darkened his eyes.

Laraine leaned over and kissed her friend on the cheek. "*We* know," she murmured. "Please don't wait."

June hugged her friends. "I won't," she whispered. "Thank you."

Matt and his brothers were at George's house. Although the whole Gardiner clan had been invited to June's open house, Sutherland had called an emergency meeting beforehand. The men were in George's study while their wives and children waited impatiently outside on the sundeck.

After Sutherland finished his speech, George observed his younger brother closely, wondering how Matt was going to handle the situation.

"What makes you think that a year is all you need from my life?" Matt asked his oldest brother in an even tone.

Reuben answered quietly. "Because we calculate that one year is all it'll take to get this new plant running successfully, Matt. You can step into my shoes here while I run things in North Carolina." He spread his hands. "We didn't want to call on you but we had no choice. We concluded that David wouldn't work out. You're family and we need you." He paused. "It is a fact that like all of us you have a stake in this."

Matt knew that all too well. Almost overnight his business was taking losses. He'd had to resort to his family income to meet the obligations for his new building. His voice hardened. "What's wrong with David? As far as I know, my younger brother is not working for himself with a business to keep afloat." He looked at the serious faces of his brothers. "Has anyone ever heard of a person coming out of retirement? What about our father?"

"That's a last resort and we hope it won't come to that," Sutherland answered. "David is no longer a consideration because we think he's finally found something to hold his interest. At least you're on the board and attend meetings. You know what's going on and you have the know-how of running an operation."

"Now, ain't that a joke," Matt snorted.

"Dad asked that you consider stepping in, Matt," Sutherland said. "Mabel Foods is still family owned and operated and he wants to keep it that way for now. We could have used a headhunter to find a crackerjack person but you're a Gardiner."

Reuben eyed his brother. "We're not asking you to give up your business, Matt. Every business has setbacks. You know that. We thought that while you were in a lull you would consider this. You'll be helping us as well as yourself."

Sutherland stood. "I know it's a big decision to make and no matter how you look at it your life will be changed for a while. But I'm hoping you'll say yes." He clasped his brother's shoulder. "Let us know what you decide in two weeks," he said. "There's plenty to put into play if Reuben is going to uproot his family." He patted his stomach. "Let's go eat, guys. From what I hear, Matt's lady is a cook after my own heart."

Outside, Matt watched the cars fill up with the excited kids. He saw George walking toward him and he waited by his car.

"Hey, man," George said.

Matt nodded. "You were mighty quiet in there," he said, eying his brother closely. "You're all for this?"

George nodded. "I think you'll do a dynamite job," he said simply.

"Yeah, sure." Matt tossed him a disgusted look. "Like I'm doing now with my own thing."

"You heard Reuben. Things happen. This might be a chance for you to step back and look things over with an objective eye." He shrugged. "Who knows, you might want to revamp your whole business, sell a variety of breeds, maybe concentrate more on breeding the German shepherds for a while. You have to put pen to paper and plan it out." He cocked an eye. "When you were no more than a kid you did it. Who's to say that you can't do it again?"

"I did, didn't I?" Matt agreed.

"Yep." George waved to his kids, who were yelling for him. "We can talk more about it later." He started to walk away. "But I'm hoping you'll come aboard. I think once you get your feet wet, it'll be hard to turn the reins back to Reuben."

"You think so, huh?"

George winked. "I'm willing to bet on it."

Finding a place to park at June's was a feat and Matt

found himself a block away. When he reached the house he looked approvingly at the scene. At three o'clock apparently most of the crowd had eaten and were off doing their own thing. His family was just digging in and he joined them, scanning the burdened table for some of June's latest concoctions. He chuckled when he saw her version of southern spoon bread. Actually this dish was quite good, he remembered.

"What's so funny, sir?" June asked. She slipped her arm around his waist.

Matt was startled at her outward display of affection, but he was so pleased that he turned and caught her in his arms. "Just me, sweetheart." He kissed her. "Everything going all right?"

"Yes," June murmured. "I was missing you," she said, just for his ears. She kissed his mouth, then stepped out of his arms. They were catching smirks and stares especially from his family.

Matt was warmed down to his toes. "Hmm, let's see if we can do something about that." He filled a plate and caught her hand and led her to the grassy area near the edge of the woods. When they were seated, he set his plate down and kissed her again. "I liked the sound of that," he whispered. "Now, let's see how much." He cupped her face in his hands and gently kissed her eyes, nose, and brushed her lips. "Mm, you taste like more." He caught her lips again and kissed her long and deeply. When he released her, he looked into her eyes and experienced his second shock of the day. He moved away.

"That's all you wanted?" June teased. She noticed his stunned look. "Was I that electrifying?" She laughed softly.

Matt studied her. "Yes," he said, catching his breath. When June had admitted her love for him that night on the beach, he thought he'd been given the world. But even in the days that came and went and they acted like lovers, there was something missing. He had yet to see that sparkle in her eyes that was meant only for him. The one that said she loved him. The same look she'd had when they made love on the floor in his study. He saw it now. Wondering why it suddenly appeared, Matt refused to question fate. He only knew that now he was ready to ask her again. This time there was no doubt in his mind that she would consent to be his wife.

"I love you, sweetheart."

June smiled. "I know. I love you too."

"Will you marry me, June?" He spoke calmly.

Her voice was as soft as his. "Yes, I will be your wife, Matt." She slipped her hand in his.

Matt pressed his lips against her hand. He closed his eyes briefly, then looked at her. She smiled at him, then turned her face toward the beach and the sun-splashed water. Matt followed her gaze. When Ivon and Laraine passed their view, Matt and June shared an intimate look. No words were needed and both sat silently, hand in hand.

For two days after June's grand opening party, Matt stayed away. There were many areas in his life that needed thrashing out and when he presented his problems to her he wanted some clear idea of what he was talking about. She'd agreed to marry a man who bred dogs, not some corporate suit. Hell, he didn't even own a closet full of office threads like his brothers.

It was late in the afternoon when he arrived at her place now empty of guests. The cleaning service had come and gone and the extra chairs and tables had been picked up. June was outside in her garden, discarding the damaged flowers that had gotten trampled by the kids. He caught her hand and led her to the porch. "I need to tell you something," he said quietly. They talked for a long time.

* * *

Matt was sitting on the porch. It was dusk and he wondered what June was doing after disappearing over ten minutes ago. He got up and went inside.

"June?" he called.

"Up here," she answered.

On the landing, he said, "Where?"

"In The Tempest."

"What's up?" Matt asked looking around curiously.

"Just putting fresh flowers in here," she said and stepped back to scrutinize the bright splash of color on the dresser.

Matt smiled. "Why? Expecting more guests so soon?"

"You might say that," June said with a mysterious smile. She turned the bedspread back and the lavender scent drifted in the air. "Mm, I'm pre-t-t-y positive that there will be some action in here, mighty soon."

"Oh?"

June walked to him and wound her arms around his waist. She rested her head on his chest and closed her eyes briefly, then lifted her head to look into his eyes. "Matt, you're not really going to take two weeks to make your decision, are you?"

Matt hugged her. He ran his fingers through her short curls and bent to kiss the tiny silvery spot on her temple. She smelled as clean and fresh as the flowers she'd picked. "No."

June kissed him, then sighed. "I'm glad." Her hands were caressing the hard muscles in his back. He'd been tense since the long talk they'd had and she knew what he was going to do even before he told her. "It's going to be one interesting year," she murmured against his chest.

Matt understood. He tilted her chin until he met her eyes. "You don't mind?" His voice was husky. "It's a different world than the one I promised you, love."

June was tugging the shirt from his pants. When it was loose, she slipped her hand underneath and made a tiny sound of pleasure when she touched his hot skin. He smelled delicious and she never wanted to leave the warmth and safety of his arms.

"June?" Matt's voice was a ragged gasp as she suckled his nipples. "Answer me," he groaned. His erection was pressed against her and he muffled the yell in his throat against her hair. He wanted to love her where they stood.

"It's a world that we'll share together, Matt," June murmured when she looked into his eyes. "That's all that matters."

When he saw that look, Matt melted against her. Lord, he loved this woman and he hoped that one day she would know how much. Her soft laugh was infectious and he smiled with her. "What?"

June's eyes twinkled. "Remember the story I told you when I named this room?"

"I remember."

"Well," she said in her sexiest drawl, "I couldn't wait for everyone to leave so I could experience the magic in this room." She gave him a saucy look as she fondled his erection. "I've been dying to see if you can make it live up to its name."

Matt groaned and caught her hands. "Is that right?" he rasped, as he hurried her to the bed. "Watch me, sweetheart."

And she did.

Epilogue

Two years later

On Christmas Eve, three months after he proposed, June married Matt in a quiet ceremony at the hundred-year-old Hood AME Zion church in Oyster Bay. Later, after a small reception hosted by George and Toi in their home, June and Matt slipped from the gathering. They spent their wedding night in The Tempest and on Christmas Day flew to Paris for a two-week honeymoon. Every so often June teased her husband about doing righteous justice to the room's name each and every time they'd made love there.

It was the night of the midsummer moon and June's birthday and they were sitting on the beach in their favorite spot. Kagi was laying half in June's lap, annoyed at the obstruction in his way.

"Silly dog," Matt muttered. "I don't know what he's going to do when he can't get his snoot in your lap in three more months." He patted June's stomach. "Everything all right in there?"

June laughed. "For the twentieth time today, yes, Daddy, everything's just fine. Baby girl Gardiner should arrive in three months, right on schedule." She snuggled in his arms. "Just in time for Labor Day and The Bountiful's second anniversary. Quite appropriate don't you think?"

"Can't deny that," Matt said and then squeezed her shoulders. "As long as you don't saddle our kid with a name in keeping with the occasion." They both noticed the figures coming from Caleb's house at the same time. "That's pretty serious, I think."

June watched Caleb and his date drive off. She knew that he'd fallen hard and hoped that he wouldn't let his past painful rejection get in the way of loving the new woman in his life. But she wondered if his sister would beat him to the altar. After years of working for the same man, Beverly had fallen in love with her boss. She'd confessed to June that she had no idea of how to act like a mother to a rebellious eight-year-old stepdaughter.

"Ready to go, sweetheart?" Matt felt her shiver.

"In a minute," June said. "It's still so peaceful here. Diane told me she's gotten into the habit of coming here after everyone is quiet for the night." She looked affectionately at the big house. "I'm glad the bed-and-breakfast is a success. Not just for what it meant to me, but for Diane. She and Andre really love it, Matt."

The Heaths had been living in the house since June and Matt married and just recently, when June found it harder to navigate, she'd given Diane full run of the place.

When Matt had moved into Reuben's VP spot at Mabel foods, he had turned over the major portion of running the kennels to Andre. Now months later, Andre was happily and proudly operating his own kennels in nearby Hempstead with most of Matt's breeders, but his stock was varied with many other breeds.

"Are you having any regrets, love?" June asked her husband.

Matt knew what she was asking. Six months ago he'd sold his stock and all but one building where he kept one purebred Basenji and two shepherds that he occasionally mated. What was once his livelihood was now his hobby.

Just as George had prophesized, Matt fit in to his brother's position smoothly, bringing his own brand of expertise to the marketing division of the company. When Reuben called to say that his family loved North Carolina and so did he, Matt was secretly relieved. He liked his work and wanted to stay in the job.

"No regrets, sweetheart," Matt said and helped June to her feet. He looked up at the moon. "Your day's almost gone," he said. He kissed her. "Happy birthday, sweets."

June looked up at the sky and smiled. Two years ago on such a night as this, she'd had an omen that a dog and a man would play important roles in her life. And it became true.

"Hmm," she said, "about our baby girl's name . . . what do you think about Moon? After all it did bring us together."

"I dare you," Matt growled and propelled his wife from the beach.

But June had another thought that she didn't share. Summer was a downright appropriate name for their little girl!

Dear Reader:

I've had the idea of writing a summer romance for quite some time, but it never came about 'til now. I envisioned a couple that would meet on a beach, fall in love, and live happily ever after. A real "sweet" romance is how I think of June and Matt's story. I hope you enjoy them along with the rest of the Gardiners, the Lancasters, and the Raleighs.

Many readers have asked about my references to bed-and-breakfasts at one point or another in some of my novels, namely NIGHT SECRETS, JUST ONE KISS, and now MIDSUMMER MOON. As some of you are aware, I have a fascination for unusual occupations, big old houses, and the people inhabitating them. So I've outlined a future story that will have its *beginnings* in a B&B, instead of *happening* on it! Many interesting characters will be passing through.

Look for my next release scheduled for 2002. It's tentatively titled RHYTHMS OF LOVE and is suspenseful. It takes place in New York and involves the relationship between a dancer who is on the verge of ending her career and the musician who loves her.

To all of you who have written such wonderful letters to me about my past stories, please accept my heartfelt thanks. I'm ever grateful for your support and hope to continue to give you the stories you want to read. For a reply, please include a self-addressed, stamped envelope.

Thanks for sharing,

Doris Johnson
P.O. Box 130370
Springfield Gardens, NY 11413
E-mail: Bessdj@aol.com

ABOUT THE AUTHOR

Doris Johnson lives in Queens, New York, with her husband. She is a multipublished author. During her travels, she's always looking for that one snippet of conversation, that interesting face, or that unusual occupation that will fire her imagination to eventually create a fascinating story. She enjoys antiquing and collecting gemstones.